SHEILA ROBERTS

A LITTLE
Christmas Spirit

mira™

Recycling programs
for this product may
not exist in your area.

ISBN-13: 978-0-7783-1214-7

A Little Christmas Spirit

This edition published by arrangement with Harlequin Books S.A.

For questions and comments about the quality of this book, please contact us at CustomerService@Harlequin.com.

Mira
22 Adelaide St. West, 40th Floor
Toronto, Ontario M5H 4E3, Canada
BookClubbish.com

Printed in U.S.A.

For Sammy, with love.

A LITTLE
Christmas Spirit

1

IT WAS THE SIXTH CALL IN TWO DAYS, ALL FROM the same person. Wouldn't you think, if a man didn't answer his phone the first five times, that the pest would get the message and quit bugging him?

But no, and now Stanley Mann was irritated enough to pick up and say a gruff "Hello." Translation: Why are you bugging me?

"It's about time you answered," said his sister-in-law, Amy. "I was beginning to wonder if you were okay."

Of course, he wasn't okay. He hadn't been okay since Carol had died.

"I'm fine. Thanks for checking."

The words didn't come out with any sense of warmth or appreciation for her concern to encourage conversation, but

Amy soldiered on. "Stan, we all want you to come down for Thanksgiving. You haven't seen the family in ages."

Not since the memorial service, and he hadn't really missed them. He liked his brother-in-law well enough, but his wife's younger sister was a ding-dong, her daughters were drama queens and their husbands were idiots. The younger generation were all into their selfies and their jobs and their crazy vacations where they swam with sharks. Who in their right mind swam with sharks? He had better things to do than subject himself to spending an entire day with them.

He did have enough manners left to thank Amy for the invite before turning her down.

"You really should come," she persisted.

No, he shouldn't.

"Don't you want to see the new great-niece?"

No, he didn't. "I've got plans."

"What? To hole up in the house with a turkey frozen dinner?"

"No." Not turkey. He hated turkey. It made him sleepy.

"You know Carol would want you to be with us."

He'd been with them pretty much every Thanksgiving of his married life. He'd paid his dues.

"You don't have any family of your own."

Thanks for rubbing it in. He'd lost his brother ten years earlier to a heart attack, and both his parents were gone now as well. He and Carol had never had any kids of their own.

But he was fine. He was perfectly happy in his own company.

"I'm good, Amy. Don't worry about me."

"I can't help it. You know, Carol was always afraid that if something happened to her you'd become a hermit."

Hermits were scruffy old buzzards with bad teeth and long beards who hated people. Stanley didn't hate people. He just didn't need to be around them all the time. There was a difference. And he wasn't scruffy. He brushed his teeth. And he shaved...every once in a while.

"Amy, I'm fine. Don't worry. Happy Thanksgiving, and tell Jimmy he can have my share of the turkey," Stanley said, then ended the call before she could grill him further regarding those plans he'd said he had.

They were perfectly good plans. He was going to pick up a frozen pizza and watch something on TV. That sure beat driving all the way from Fairwood, Washington, to Gresham, Oregon, to be alternately bored and irritated by his in-laws. If Amy really wanted to do something good for him, she could leave him alone.

At first everyone had. He was a man in mourning. Then came COVID-19, and he was a senior self-quarantining. Now, however, it appeared he was supposed to be ready to party on. Well, he wasn't.

Two days before Thanksgiving he made the one-mile journey to the grocery store, figuring he'd dodge the crowd. He'd figured wrong, and the store was packed with people finishing up the shopping for their holiday meal. The turkey supply in the meat freezer was running danger-ously low, and half a dozen women and a lone man crowded around it like miners at the river's edge, searching for gold, each trying to snag the best bird from the selection that re-mained. A woman rolled past him with a mini-mountain of food in her cart, a wailing toddler in the seat and two kids dragging along behind her, one of them pointing to the chips aisle and whining.

"I said no," she snapped. "We don't need chips."

Nope. That woman needed a stiff drink.

Stanley grabbed his pizza and some pumpkin ice cream and got in the checkout line.

Two men around his age stood in front of him, talking. "They're out of black olives," said the first one. "I got green instead."

The second man shook his head. "Your wife ain't gonna like that. Everyone knows you got to have black olives at Thanksgiving."

"I can't help it if there's none left on the shelves. Anyway, the only one who eats 'em is her brother, and the loser can suck it up and do without."

Yep, family togetherness. Stanley wasn't going to miss that.

He'd miss being with Carol, though. He missed her every day. Her absence was an ache that never left him, and resentment kept it ever fresh.

They'd reached what was often referred to as the *Golden Circle*, that time in life when you had enough money to travel and enjoy yourself, when your health was still good and you could carry your own luggage. They'd enjoyed traveling and had planned on doing so much more together—taking a world cruise, renting a beach house in California for a summer, even going deep-sea fishing in Mexico. Their golden years were going to be great.

Those golden years turned to brass the day she died. She didn't even die of cancer or a stroke or something he could have accepted. She was killed in a car accident. A drunk driver in a truck had done her in and walked away with nothing more than some bruises from his airbag. It wasn't right, and it wasn't fair. And Stanley didn't really have anything to be thankful about. He didn't like Thanksgiving.

There would be worse to follow. After Thanksgiving it would be *Merry Christmas!*, *Happy Hanukkah!*, *Happy Kwanzaa!*, you name it. All that *happy* would finally get tied up in a big *Happy New Year!* bow. As if buying a new calendar magically made everything better. Well, it didn't.

Stanley spent his Thanksgiving Day in lonely splendor, watching football on TV and eating his pizza. *It's not delivery. It's DiGiorno.* Worked for him. He ate two-thirds of it before deciding he should pace himself. Got to save room for dessert. Pumpkin ice cream—just as good as the traditional pie and whipped cream, and it didn't come with any irritating in-laws. Ice cream was the food of the gods. After his pizza, he pulled out a large bowl, filled it and dug in.

When they got older, Carol had turned into the ice cream police, limiting his consumption. She'd pat his belly and say, "Now, Manly Stanley, too much of that and you'll ending up looking like a big, fat snowman. Plus you'll clog your arteries, and that's not good. I don't want to risk losing you."

Ironic. He'd wound up losing her instead.

Between all the ice cream and the beer he'd been consuming with no one to police him, he was starting to look a little like Frosty the Snowman. (Before he melted.) But who cared? He got himself a second bowl of ice cream.

He topped it off with a couple of beers and a movie along with some store-bought cookies. *There you go. Happy Thanksgiving.*

For a while, anyway. Until everything got together in his stomach and began to misbehave. He shouldn't have eaten so much. Especially the pizza. He really couldn't do spicy now that he was older. Telling everyone down there that all would soon be well, he took a couple of antacids.

No one down there was listening, and all that food had its own Turkey Day football game still going in his gut when he went to bed. He tossed and turned and groaned until, finally, he fell into an uneasy sleep.

"Pepperoni and sausage?" scolded a voice in his ear. "You know better than to eat that spicy food, Stanley."

"I know, I know," he muttered. "You're right, Carol."

Carol! Stanley rolled over and saw his wife standing by the side of his bed. She was wearing the black nightie he always loved to see her in. And then out of. Her eyes were as blue as ever. How he'd missed that sweet face!

But what was she doing here?

He blinked. "Is it really you?" He thought he'd never see her again in this lifetime, but there she was. His heart turned over.

"Yes, it's really me," she said.

She looked radiant and so kissable, but that quickly changed. Suddenly, her body language wasn't very lovey-dovey. She frowned and put her hands on her hips, a sure sign she was about to let him have it.

"What were you thinking?" she demanded.

He didn't have to ask what she was referring to. He knew.

"It's Thanksgiving. I was celebrating," he said.

She frowned. "All by yourself."

"I happen to like my own company. You know that."

"There's liking your own company, and there's hiding."

"I am not hiding," he insisted.

"Yes, you are. I gave you time to mourn, time to adjust, but enough is enough. Life is short, Stanley. It's like living off your savings. Each day you take another withdrawal, and pretty soon there's nothing left. You have to spend those days wisely. You're wasting yours, dribbling away the last of your savings."

"That's fine with me," he insisted. "I hate my life."

He hated waking up to find her side of the bed empty and ached for her smile. Without her the house felt deserted. He felt deserted.

"You still like ice cream, don't you?" she argued.

Except for when he paired it with pizza.

"Stanley, you need to get out there and...live."

"What do you think I'm doing?" he grumped.

"Going through the motions, hanging in limbo."

What else could she expect? "It's not the same without you," he protested.

"Of course it's not. But you're still here, and you're here for a reason. Don't make what happened to me a double waste. Somebody snatched my life from me, and I wasn't done with it. I want you to go on living for the both of us."

"How can I do that? This isn't a life, not without you sharing it."

"It's a different kind of life, that's all."

It was a subpar, meager existence. "I miss you, Carol. I miss you sitting across from me at the breakfast table. I miss us doing things together and sitting together at night, watching TV. I miss...your touch." He finished on a sob.

"I know." She sat down on the bed next to him, and he couldn't help noticing how the blankets didn't shift under her. "But you have to start filling those empty places, Stanley."

"I don't want to," he cried. "I don't want to."

He was still muttering "I don't want to" when he woke up.

Alone. For a moment there, her presence had felt so real.

"She wasn't there at all, you dope," he muttered.

Except why was there a faint scent of peppermint in the bedroom? It made him think of the chocolate Christmas cookies she used to make with the mint-candy frosting and sprinkles on them. After a few big sniffs, he couldn't detect so much as a whiff of peppermint and shook his head in disgust. Indigestion and memory. That was all she was.

2

STANLEY FIRST SAW CAROL BARRETT AT A CAR show, eating a corn dog and checking out a 1954 Thunderbird. He was a gawky nineteen-year-old, and she was a vision in a red top and white hot pants that showed off the most gorgeous pair of tanned legs on the planet. She had full lips and blond hair that fell straight to her shoulders. She wore sunglasses so he couldn't see her eyes, but he was willing to bet they were as gorgeous as her lips.

Those lips were smiling, giving away a hint of dimples. He bet she smiled a lot.

She was with another girl and a guy. The girl's hair was almost the same blond as hers. Similar round face and slender body. Sisters? The guy was dark-haired and looked like a water heater with a head. Probably not related. A boyfriend, then? *Say it ain't so.*

Stanley's friend Walt elbowed him. "Check that out."

From the expression on Walt's face, Stanley knew he wasn't talking about the Thunderbird. Cars were cool. Who didn't love cars, especially muscle cars? But girls beat cars by a mile. And this woman beat cars by about a million.

Was she stuck-up? In Stanley's experience most cute girls were. They didn't bother with average guys. They went for the class president or the captain of the football team or valedictorian.

Stanley had been neither. He'd done okay in high school, especially in shop. And math. But history? It was all about memorizing dates. Who did what and when. He hadn't cared. And English? He hadn't been interested in reading most of those books his teachers assigned. *Lord of the Flies* had been pretty okay, but he'd much preferred novels by Ian Fleming and Dean Koontz to those other long-winded books full of flowery words his teachers had wanted him to try to digest. Anyway, reading was for camping trips, when you read in the tent by flashlight. As for grammar, what did he care about diagramming sentences, about verbs and adverbs and adjectives?

Except now. Adjectives. How to describe this girl? *Eye-popping, heart-stopping*. Then another adjective came to mind: *unattainable*.

He knew that word because for him it had applied to just about every girl he'd liked all through high school. He'd never mastered the easy charm so many other guys seemed to have. Walt was always giving him pointers on what to say to girls. Good stuff, but the words usually got stuck at the back of Stanley's mouth. He was much more comfort-able hanging out with his pals, working on cars or shooting some hoops, or racing on the viaduct on a Friday night than trying to impress a girl.

This girl was different. He already wanted to impress her in the worst kind of way.

"Man, oh, man, wouldn't you like to have that girl riding shotgun with you?" Walt said.

Like to? No, he had to.

She looked his way and shared that smile with him. It was a friendly one. It said *Come on, take a chance.* Maybe she wasn't so stuck-up. Maybe there was hope.

"I'm gonna go talk to her," Stanley said.

"Whoa, man, slow down. You know you're not that good with women, and that one's not just a woman, she's a goddess."

Yes, a mere mortal working as a gopher at a construction company was not even close to her league. Suddenly, like a gift from Cupid, a quote popped into his mind. Something from a poem he'd had to read in English class. *...a man's reach should exceed his grasp, or what's a heaven for?* He'd never understood that poem before, wasn't sure he fully understood it now, but one thing he was sure of. It was a sign.

"I know, but I've gotta meet her."

"I'd better go with you so you don't mess this up," Walt said.

She was way out of Walt's league, too. Walt was short and no better-looking than Stanley. At least he had the gift of gab and a reputation for being able to charm the ladies. If they could get close enough for him to use it.

Stanley was medium height, still filling out. He had brownish hair and an okay face—nice brown eyes (or so his mother always said)—but he was no Steve McQueen or Clint Eastwood. He was never going to get this girl. What was he thinking?

That he wanted her more than air. He tried to put on a cool, casual front to hide his terror.

Once they got close enough he let Walt start things out. "Hey, there," Walt said with a big grin to the goddess. "That your dream car?"

"It's pretty cool," she said and smiled at Stanley.

"It's okay," said the other guy, stepping into the conversation. "I got a Chevy."

Walt nodded. "Yeah? What model?"

His friend was distracting the competition. Here was Stanley's chance. "Hi," he said. "I'm Stanley."

The goddess's smile widened. "I'm Carol. This is my sister, Amy. That's her boyfriend, Jimmy."

She wasn't taken. Was it truly possible? *Ask.* The words turned into cement and lodged in his mouth.

He cleared his throat. "You into cars?" *You dumb shit. Of course she's into cars. Otherwise she wouldn't be here.* He started to sweat, and it had nothing to do with the July heat.

"I think they're fun to look at. I like cute little sports cars, and I love red ones." She moved a little away from the others, took a nibble of her corn dog. Stanley followed her like a hungry puppy. "One of my friends at Lincoln— that's where I went to school—had a red Mustang. It was so cool. I think she was rich." Carol finished with a shrug. "I'll probably never have one."

If he had the money, he'd have promised right then and there to buy her one. "'Stangs are cool," he said. "I've got a red car. A GTO. That thing can move." Yes, when it came to cars, he could talk up a storm. But this wasn't getting to the heart of the matter.

"I bet it can." She took another bite of her corn dog, waiting for him to say something else.

"You still in school?" he asked. Another dumb question. *Went to school. That means she's done.* So far he was not making a good impression.

"I graduated this year. How about you?"

"Last year."

"Where'd you go?"

"Queen Anne."

"Queen Anne High School, on the hilltop," she began to sing, and he chuckled.

"You went to Lincoln, and you know our fight song."

"I went out with a guy from Queen Anne a couple of times. I always thought your school song was catchy."

She had to be going out with somebody. She was too perfect not to have a boyfriend. He couldn't stand the suspense any longer. "Are you with someone now?"

"My sister and her boyfriend," she said, her smile teasing.

He frowned. "You know what I mean."

"I'm not with anyone right now. It's just as well, I suppose. I don't want to get distracted. I'm going to U-Dub this fall."

The University of Washington. A college girl. Yep, totally out of his league. He'd have had better success trying to reach the moon in a paper airplane than getting this girl to go out with him. So much for poetry.

"Guess that counts me out," he mumbled.

She cocked her head. "You sure give up easy."

"Look, I'm not going to college. I did okay in school,

but another four years, that's not for me. I don't want to sit in a classroom and then end up sitting in an office all day. I like to build things. I like to work on cars. And I like to be outside, hiking or fishing in a stream. I'm no football hero," he added. "I wasn't even that good at track. I bowl."

Good grief. When did he catch diarrhea of the mouth? He could feel his cheeks burning, and he clamped his lips shut.

She smiled. "I can't bowl very well, but I think it's fun."

He blinked in surprise. "You do?"

"Sure. And I like to hike."

"Really?"

"I also happen to like classrooms," she said, raising an eyebrow. "I want to be teacher."

"Yep, you're a brain," he said. It was hopeless.

"Everybody's a brain, Stanley. There are all kinds of ways to be smart." She paused, smiled again. "Did I mention that I like to ride in fast cars?"

Was that a hint? Did he dare ask her out? "Umm."

"And I could use some pointers when it comes to bowling."

That was definitely a hint. He hoped.

"Would you like to go bowling?" he ventured.

Her smile lit him up inside. "I would."

She fished in her purse and pulled out a pen. Then she took his hand. He felt the zing all the way up his arm and clear into his chest. She clicked the pen, turned his hand palm up and wrote her phone number on it. Wow. He swallowed hard.

"Call me," she said.

Her sister and the boyfriend had moved on. Walt had

let them go and was pretending to look under the T-Bird's open hood. Stanley and Carol were in the middle of a crowd of old guys, teenagers and kids running every which way, but all those people seemed to disappear, leaving just the two of them. They could have been Adam and Eve.

He could barely think, barely speak, but he managed to say, "I will."

"I'll see you around," she said, then turned and ran off to catch up with her sister, her hair swaying as she went.

Wow again.

Walt came around the car and stood next to him, watching the vision run off. "So?"

Stanley held up his hand, showing off the number.

"Lucky dog," Walt said teasingly. "I should have cut you out."

"Don't even think about it," Stanley said and was only half kidding.

"Hey, she's all yours, buddy. If you can manage not to blow it."

"I can," Stanley said, determined.

Stanley called her that very night. A girl's voice answered.

"Uh, Carol?"

"No, this is Amy. Is this that guy she met?" She sounded completely unimpressed.

"Yeah."

"She told me about you."

Yes, she was unimpressed. He could tell by her tone of voice. Stanley had no idea what to say to that, so he said nothing.

"Carol," she called. "It's him."

A moment later Carol was on the phone. "Him who?" she teased.

"Him who wants to take you bowling. Will you come?"

"Sure. Why not? I'm busy tonight. How about next Friday?"

"Great." He had a date with Carol. He wanted to throw back his head and howl with delight, but he managed to contain himself enough to set a time and get her address. Then he hung up the phone and let out a whoop.

"Did you win a million bucks?" teased his brother Curtis, who was walking through the front hall on his way upstairs.

"Better. Got a date."

"Huh. No kidding. Don't blow it."

Yep, nothing like a little brotherly encouragement. "I won't," Stanley said and hoped he was right.

Stanley finally got to see Carol's eyes when he picked her up on Friday night. They were as blue as a cloudless sky. Those crazy platform shoes she was wearing made her look even more like a model, but he could tell that once she exchanged them for bowling shoes she'd be just the right height to kiss.

If he could ever get up the nerve.

"You have your own bowling ball?" she asked as they walked into Sunset Bowl in the Ballard neighborhood. "You must be really good."

He was. "I'm not bad," he said modestly.

"Hey, Stan," the man working the shoe-rental counter greeted him. "How's it goin'?"

"Good," Stanley replied, trying not to grin so much that he looked like a dope.

So far he didn't think he'd blown it. He hoped he was doing okay with Carol. Lucky for him, she was easy to talk to, and she carried most of the conversation for him.

"I like your car," she'd said as he opened the door for her.

From there it was on to talk of the church youth-group bowling party she'd been to earlier in the year. "I love parties," she'd said.

Stanley wasn't exactly a party animal. He had his close friends, and they hung out, worked on their cars, played Ping-Pong at Walt's house and, of course, went bowling. He'd been to some bigger parties, always in somebody's basement. There was often dancing, which made him feel self-conscious, noisy talk and teasing, where he never seemed to be able to come up with a cool thing to say, or a game of Twister that could get awkward when you had to bend over a girl in an effort to put your hand on a certain colored circle. He did better with just one or two people.

"How about you?" she'd asked.

"I guess parties are okay," he'd managed. "But I'd rather do things with just a couple of people." *Maybe even just with you.*

"But you do go to parties, don't you?" she persisted.

"Oh, sure." He hadn't wanted her to think he was a social reject. Still, he'd been glad when they arrived at the bowling alley and left that subject behind.

After getting her shoes and getting set up on a lane, it was time to find a ball. "I can never find a ball I like. They're all so heavy," she said, picking one up and frowning.

He found a lighter one. "Here, try this twelve-pounder," he said, handing it to her.

She took it and wrinkled her nose. "It still weighs a ton."

"I bet you can handle it," he said.

"I'm sure going to try."

And try she did. She couldn't get the ball to go straight down the lane, but he had to give her credit for enthusiasm. After rolling gutter balls her first two times, she jumped up and down, squealed and clapped like she'd gotten a strike when she'd actually knocked over three pins.

"I've got potential, don't I?" she crowed.

"Oh, yeah," he agreed. Everybody had potential. He came and stood next to her. "Just try and keep your arm straight when you throw the ball. Follow through. Like you're on the pitcher's mound." He demonstrated, and she nodded.

"Follow through," she repeated. She tried again, and her arm went crooked, and off the ball skittered, edging toward the gutter. Which it hit right before the pins.

"Better luck next time," he said and rolled a strike.

"You make that look so easy," she told him, and he puffed up like a rooster.

"Here, let me help you," he offered as she got ready to take her turn. He pointed to the line of dots on the floor in front of them. "See all these spots? If you use them to line up, you'll have a better chance of the ball going where you want it."

"Really? Where should I stand?"

It was the perfect excuse to make contact. He took her arms, stood behind her and gently moved her to a spot he thought would help. Suddenly he wished they weren't in a bowling alley. He wished they were somewhere quiet, maybe by a mountain stream or on a moonlit beach.

"So here?" she asked, yanking his thoughts back to the game.

"Uh, yeah. That's great. Now, remember, keep your arm straight. Four steps up, and then let the ball go."

"Four steps up, and let the ball go," she repeated.

"Start swinging the ball back as you approach."

He stepped back and watched her, trying to stay objective as he observed her form, and not fully succeeding.

She managed to take down four pins and on her next throw got two more down. "See? Potential," she said happily.

"Yep," he agreed. "Potential." But he wasn't just thinking about bowling. Did they have potential?

He longed to kiss her when they stood on her front porch saying good-night, but he didn't want her to think he was a wolf.

"I had fun, Stanley," she said. "You're the sweetest guy I've met in a long time."

Her words wrapped around him like a hug. It was almost as good as a kiss. Almost.

"Will you go out with me again?" he asked.

"I will. Call me," she said as she walked inside.

Call me. Best words in the English language. He practically floated back to his car.

Their next date was to a movie. Sitting there in the dark theater, he longed to hold her hand, but he couldn't get up the nerve. Instead, he kept his hands busy digging into the popcorn.

After the movie it was off to Zesto's for a burger and

shake. "How did they ever get that car up there?" she wondered, looking at the 1957 Chevy on the roof of the hamburger joint.

"I don't know," he said, "but I think it's cool."

"Yes, it is," she agreed. She moved her straw around to suck up the last of her chocolate shake.

He watched her, wishing he could kiss those pretty lips. What was she doing out with the likes of him?

"I bet you were a cheerleader in high school," he said.

"How'd you guess?"

He shrugged. "You're...bubbly. Were you on the honor roll?"

"I was."

"I wasn't."

"I told you before, there are lots of ways to be smart, Stanley."

"Hey, I never flunked any classes," he quickly clarified.

"I'm sure you didn't."

"It's just that some subjects didn't interest me."

"What does interest you?"

He shrugged. "I like math. I like putting things together. Working with my hands." *I like you.*

By their third date he actually felt comfortable talking with her. Words were coming out more easily instead of stubbornly lodging at the back of his mouth and having to be yanked out.

Once more they found themselves fueling up on burgers and shakes, and he was able to find the nerve to ask, "So how come you're not with anyone? I can't believe you don't have a boyfriend."

"I did."

"I bet he was a football star."

Even though the boyfriend was no longer in the picture, Stanley couldn't help feeling a little jealous. He should have gone out for football. Girls loved football players. Except Stanley had never liked the idea of getting tackled and crushed. *No guts, no glory*, as the saying went. So now here he was, perfectly intact but with nothing to brag about.

Carol made a face. "He was a selfish jerk. Everywhere we went, everything we did, it was all about him and what he wanted. Not that I minded doing things he wanted to do," she hurried on, "but after a while I began to wonder why he never asked me what movie I'd like to see or where I'd like to go eat, why he never asked me what I thought about anything. He did all the talking, and I did all the listening. After a while it didn't feel like we were together. I was just…"

"Fuzzy dice," Stanley supplied, looking at the ones dangling from his rearview mirror.

She smiled at the metaphor, gave them a flick with her finger. "Exactly. He didn't really care about me. I was just decoration, something to make him look cool."

Stanley nodded, taking that in. The ex-boyfriend was obviously a dope who didn't know what he'd had.

"You know, Stanley, I'm not looking for someone who's a hotshot or Mr. Cool. I'm looking for someone who's kind, someone who wants to have fun together. Most important, I'm also looking for someone who thinks about more than himself, someone who wants to be a team. Are you that kind of guy?"

"I am," Stanley said, determined to be.

"Good," she said with a nod. "I'm glad to hear it."

After that conversation he didn't dare try to kiss her. He didn't want to come across as a selfish jerk, out to get what he could as soon as he could.

But he didn't have to. When he brought her home she closed the distance between them there on the front porch.

"Stanley, you really are sweet," she said and kissed him.

It wasn't a long kiss, but it was a perfect one. Her perfume, her soft lips, that beautiful body up close to his was a heady mixture, and for a moment there he was sure he'd died and gone to heaven.

She pulled away and smiled at him.

"Wow," he breathed.

Her smile got bigger. "Yeah, wow. You know what made that so special just now?"

"You."

She chuckled and shook her head. "Knowing that you really care about me."

"I do." *I want to spend the rest of my life with you.*

He didn't say it, but he knew. And he hoped she felt the same, because as far as he was concerned the kiss said it all. They would be together for the rest of their lives.

3

LEXIE BELL AWOKE ON BLACK FRIDAY BEFORE HER six-year-old son and went downstairs to the kitchen, where she pulled out the leftover pumpkin pie she'd brought home from the so-called Orphans Thanksgiving dinner she'd attended.

She didn't know very many people in the town of Fair-wood yet, and she'd appreciated the invite from one of the older teachers at Fairwood Elementary who had wanted to make sure everyone, especially a newcomer like Lexie, had a place to go. She'd met some nice people at that party, and it gave her hope that she'd find her tribe and be able to settle into her new town as well as she was settling into her new job. She'd already made one good friend, Shan-non, another single teacher at school, and she was looking forward to making more.

As for settling into the job, that had been easy. What was not to like about being a kindergarten teacher? She enjoyed working with children, especially the little ones. She looked forward to going to work every day and seeing all those smiling, innocent faces, looking up at her, eager to learn.

And she was always eager to teach. She loved children, would have liked to have more than one herself. But so far one was all that was in the cards. She'd just discovered she was pregnant when her fiancé confessed that he'd been cheating. She'd ended things right then and there, and there had gone the plans for the big destination wedding they'd been saving for, not to mention the big, happy family she'd dreamed of having.

"That's what comes of putting the cart before the horse," her grandma had said.

Thankfully, she'd only said it once. The last thing Lexie wanted Brock hearing about was horses and carts and how foolish his mother had been and what a loser the man she'd fallen for had turned out to be. She supposed there would come a time when she'd have to address that but not yet.

The cheater had signed over his parental rights and moved to San Diego, so it had always been just Lexie and Brock. A sweeter, more precocious boy you would never find, and while she may have made a mistake in the man she picked, she didn't regret the child she'd gotten out of the deal.

She wished her grandma was still alive so she could see what a great kid Brock was. She hoped Granny would be proud of how Lexie was raising her son. She felt she was doing okay. They both were.

She cut the big slice of pie in two, leaving the slightly smaller half for Brock, then squirted a pile of canned whipped cream on top of her piece. Nourishment for the quest that lay ahead: shopping Black Friday specials online for the perfect presents for her aunt and uncle and cousins back in California, and her mom and, of course, Brock.

She loved holiday sales. They were the only time she could actually afford all the expensive gifts that were usually out of reach for a single mom on a teacher's salary. She settled on the couch with her pie on the coffee table and her laptop in her lap, started some Taylor Swift playing, cracked her knuckles, limbering up. Then she brought her computer to life. Let the adventure begin.

She'd already purchased a plane ticket for her mom so she could fly up from sunny California and join them for the holidays, but Lexie wanted something to put under the tree as well.

What to get? Perfume? No. Mom would say "Your father's gone. What's the point?"

It was what she said about everything, from getting her nails done to whipping up the gourmet meals she used to love cooking. For years Lexie had gotten her a can of tennis balls as a stocking stuffer because Mom loved to play tennis, but that wasn't an option. She'd stopped playing. She'd also given up her book club, claiming that since Daddy's death, it was hard to concentrate on the words on the page, so there was no point in getting her a book. Something for the house? Her mother had enough stuff.

Chocolate! Even the most miserable of women could be helped by chocolate. Lexie knew that from experience.

She ordered a box of Godiva truffles.

She found a deal on body butter and ordered some for

the cousins, then started the search for the perfect present for her aunt.

"I'm awake, Mommy."

She looked up to see her son entering the living room, looking adorable in his superhero pj's. His brown curls (a gift from the father fail) were tousled, and he rubbed his eyes (brown, also from the father fail) as he joined her on the couch, snuggling up next to her.

"What are you doing?" he asked.

"I'm checking out the sales. I have to get my holiday shopping done."

"And we have to see Santa," Brock reminded her.

"Don't worry. We have plenty of time to see Santa," she assured him.

"Does he know I want a puppy?"

"I think he does, but I think he also knows that Mommy said no puppy yet. You have to wait until you're older."

Brock's lips dipped downward. "I just want a puppy."

"You'll get one eventually, but not this Christmas. Start thinking about something else to ask Santa for."

The lower lip jutted out.

"Oh, my, what a sad, pitiful mouth," she teased. She leaned over and picked up her pie from the coffee table. "I think it needs something to make it happy," she said, forking off a bite.

Brock squirmed in delight and opened his mouth.

"There. Did that make your mouth happier?" she asked once it was in.

He nodded, chewed and swallowed. "My mouth wants some more."

"It's a good thing I have a piece saved for you in the refrigerator, then. Want to go get it?"

He nodded again, this time even more eagerly, and followed her to the kitchen.

Not the most nutritious breakfast in the world, she thought as she dished it up. But not the worst, either. After all, it did have pumpkin and eggs. Anyway, it was Thanksgiving weekend. Everyone deserved to party a little on a holiday weekend.

She'd hoped to find some people to party with right here in her cul-de-sac when she'd first moved in. She'd fallen in love with the house, with its simple lines and big front porch, and had assumed that there'd be another family living in one of the neighboring houses.

But she hadn't found a family when she moved in. Instead, she'd found workaholics who were rarely around and a divorcing couple whose quarrels she'd heard clear over on her front porch. They'd soon moved out and taken their sulky teenager with them, leaving the house standing empty. The Sold sign now posted in the front yard gave her hope, but it was about her only hope. The little old lady who occupied the house two doors down didn't come out much, and there was a reclusive older couple next door.

At least she assumed it was a couple. So far she'd only seen the husband, and he wasn't inclined to chat.

Once, she'd caught sight of him driving toward his house when she was outside, raking the leaves from the big maple tree in her front yard—a hefty man with thinning gray hair and bushy eyebrows. She'd given him a friendly wave and a smile, and he'd nodded and managed to lift his fingers off the steering wheel, then he'd turned into his garage, and it had swallowed him up. She'd seen him one other time and gotten the same half-hearted acknowledgment. She'd taken over some cookies once when she'd thought she caught sight of someone in their dining-room window, but the only welcome she'd gotten had been from a couple of garden gnomes sitting on the front porch. When no one had answered the door, she'd wound up leaving them on the doorstep.

Did he have a wife? If he did, she had to be bedridden or as reclusive as him. It was like living next door to Boo Radley.

Well, she'd find her peeps. She was working that direction with Mrs. Davidson of the Orphans Thanksgiving dinner and Shannon, who was also nearing the big three-oh and who taught fourth grade. Her social life would sort itself out. Maybe, if she was lucky, her love life would also.

She settled Brock at the kitchen counter with his pie, promising him a trip to town for hamburgers for lunch—let the fun continue—then returned to her computer. There was a lot of Black Friday left, and she had shopping to do.

Stanley sat down at his computer to check the stock market and then his email. Not many emails came for him anymore. Still, out of habit, he checked. The inbox was filled with Black Friday offers. Fifty percent off this. Get that now before it's gone. BOGO. Enter this coupon code.

He deleted them all. No need for shopping bargains when he wasn't going to shop. That had been Carol's department, not his. She'd spent a fortune on her sister's family and all her girlfriends, buying stuff that would probably end up in a garage sale or a landfill.

"It's a way to show people you care," she'd tell him.

She had a point there. He still fondly remembered the year she'd gotten him a slick, new bowling ball. She'd wrapped it and put it inside a huge packing crate with a bow on it so he couldn't guess what it was.

"Do you like it?" she'd asked when he took it out of its box.

He had and, more than the gift itself, he'd liked that loving expression on her face.

Even though he never bought gifts for anyone else, he'd always gotten something nice for her: bubble bath, chocolates, jewelry. One year he'd bought season tickets to the local theater because the season included several musicals. Carol loved musicals. (Stopping in the middle of what you're doing to sing a song never made sense to him. But then, he'd been an electrician, not a poet, so what did he know?)

There was no one he needed to lavish presents on now, no one he needed to show that he cared. "Waste of time and money," he muttered. *No holiday shopping this year. Or ever. No presents for anyone. Did you hear that, Carol?*

People shouldn't waste so much time buying crap. When you weren't wandering in and out of stores, you had more time for other things.

Stanley gave his nose a scratch. Other things. Like checking the stock market, doing your sudoku puzzle... He scratched his nose again. Watching TV. Yeah, he had a busy life.

But don't forget keeping the house maintained, emptying the garbage.

Shaking his fist at heaven.

How he'd looked forward to retiring and enjoying himself, spending more time with Carol, doing things together! There was no together. Only the solitary doing of routine.

He sighed and turned off the computer. It was almost

time for lunch. A slice of toast with some peanut butter. A glass of milk. A couple of cookies. Hardly gourmet fare, but who cared? He'd never been much of a cook. He wasn't going to start now.

After his busy day of sudoku and TV, he made dinner. This time a ham sandwich. No more spicy food before bed. He topped his meal off with some more ice cream and called it good.

Now, what to watch on TV tonight? He flipped it on and checked his options. Hulu, Netflix, Amazon, Home Movies.

Home Movies! He didn't have a Home Movies option, and he'd never seen that old-fashioned movie-projector icon before. He blinked and leaned forward, squinting at the TV screen. There were his options. Hulu, Netflix, Amazon.

Okay, take a deep breath. That was just a weird…something.

He went to Netflix and opted for one of his favorite police series. There you go. Cops called to a murder scene, people standing behind the yellow tape, gawking. There, toward the back of the crowd was… He let out a yelp and pushed back against his recliner. It was Carol, middle-aged and with that short haircut he'd told her he liked even though he hadn't. She waved at him.

Oh, man. What was wrong with him? He took a deep breath, leaned forward and stared at the screen. She was gone. He kept looking for her throughout the rest of the show, but she never returned.

Both frustrated and unnerved, he shut off the TV and opted for a book. That would do him just fine.

He read until he was sleepy, then went to bed, torn between hoping Carol would make another appearance and dreading another scold. Being nagged from beyond the grave was unsettling.

She did return late that night, and where her first visit had been unsettling, this one was downright scary. She wasn't cute like she'd been the night before. The nightie was gone, and she was in jeans and a red sweater, topping off the outfit with a Santa hat.

That part was okay, but the face under the Santa hat was a different story. Her pretty blue eyes had been replaced with what looked like red-hot coals. *Aaah!*

He bolted upright, his heart pounding. "Carol?" he whimpered, pulling the covers up to his chin like a shield.

Some shield. What he needed to do was dive under the bed.

"Don't be silly. I'd find you there," she said, reading his mind. "I wanted to watch home movies, Stanley. Obviously, you didn't get the message. I don't think you're taking me seriously."

"I am," he whispered, averting his gaze.

Averting didn't work. She whooshed right in his face, forcing him back against the headboard. "I heard what you said about not shopping."

He squeezed his eyes shut tightly. "That was your thing, not mine." Arguing. He was arguing with a ghost. What was he thinking?

"All right, I'll give you that. But you're going to have to find some way to get involved with life. Take an interest. There are people all around who need you."

"Nobody needs me," he grumbled. Not anymore, not with her gone.

"That's not true. There are always people who need you. Open your eyes, and you'll see them."

He didn't want to open his eyes. He might see her.

"If you'd watched those movies like I wanted, you'd have realized how good life is when you're out there doing things."

He'd gotten all their home movies digitized, and they'd barely made a dent in watching them before she was gone.

"There's no point, because I was doing things with you. Life's not good now, and watching them will just piss me off."

"Stanley, stop feeling so sorry for yourself. Start looking out and focusing on others instead of in and only on yourself. It's the season of peace on earth, goodwill toward men. Get out there and show some goodwill. And, while you're at it, decorate this place. It's so...un-Christmassy."

Decorate? "Oh, come on, that was your thing, too," he protested, eyes still squeezed shut.

"Not hanging lights. That was always your job."

"There's no reason to hang the lights. You're not here to appreciate them."

"I'm here now."

He cracked one eye open, only to see those fiery eyes boring into him. Yes, she was.

"I know," he said, "and, no offense, but you don't look so good, babe," he added and shut that eyelid back down.

"It's because I'm not happy. You're killing me, Manly Stanley."

It would probably come across as callous to point out that she was already dead.

"You'd better start taking me seriously."

"I always took you seriously."

"Then, get with the program. I'm going to haunt you till you do."

"Please, no. Don't do that," he begged. "I can't handle seeing you like this." Those glowing eyes really were creepy.

"Then, I suggest you start thinking about making me happy."

"I will, I will," he promised.

"Good. I'll be watching," she said and left in a swirl of cold wind.

Stanley's eyes popped open, and he saw his covers had fallen off. No wonder he'd felt a breeze. It was his subconscious telling him he was cold, that was all. Like those times he'd dream he was looking for a bathroom and would wake up to realize he needed to take a whiz.

But why was he seeing Carol? Why was she choosing now, of all times, to haunt his subconscious?

Because she'd loved Christmas, of course. That was it. That was all.

He could swear he smelled peppermint again. Was there such a thing as olfactory hallucination? That had to be what he was suffering from. Had to be.

He abandoned the idea of trying to go back to sleep. It was four thirty in the morning. He'd conked out around eleven. Five and a half hours was enough. Anyway, he'd rather walk around gritty-eyed than take a chance on meeting Burning-Coals Carol again.

He showered, he shaved. He got dressed. Proof that he was, indeed, taking an interest in life.

"That ought to make her happy," he muttered.

Make her happy. He'd have liked nothing better. If she was still alive. But she wasn't. And he was laying off the ice cream. Ice cream was the culprit.

Or else he was going insane.

No, that couldn't be. Surely if he was going to lose his mind he'd have done so long before this. Of course, it was never too late to go around the bend.

He drank his morning coffee and ate a bowl of cereal. Then he watched the morning news and went online and checked the stock market. His stocks were still holding strong. All was well. Not that his stocks mattered much, these days. He had what he needed to live on stashed away in a retirement account that was intended for two, and no one to leave any money to. Still, it was good to have something to check.

Come ten o'clock, he fetched his coat and hat and gloves and went to the garage. Time to take the SUV to the shop and have snow tires put on. There was no snow in the forecast yet, maybe wouldn't be any at all this winter, but Stanley liked to be prepared.

Stanley also liked to be organized, which was why he always kept the garage immaculate—a sheet of cardboard under the SUV to catch oil drips, his tools neatly hung on a pegboard or stored under his workbench, bins of seasonal decorations that he'd hauled in every year for Carol that belonged on the shelves.

But now one was sitting in the middle of the floor, tipped sideways.

On the floor! What the heck?

4

"LET'S PUT UP CHRISTMAS LIGHTS," CAROL SAID AS they drove home from her parents' late Thanksgiving Day. "Lots of lights with lots of colors."

Stanley sighed inwardly. After eight years of marriage he knew what *let's* meant in a case like this. It meant she had an idea for a project, and he'd be the one doing it.

He also knew how much hassle this would involve. "Do we really need Christmas lights?"

"Yes. Last year our house was the only naked one on the block, and that was just plain sad. The house will look so pretty trimmed with all those colors. Anyway, Christmas lights are to the holidays what frosting is to a cookie. They make something special even better."

He shot a look over at her. "So if I put up lights, does that mean you'll bake those frosted cookies?"

"I will," she promised. "It'll be your reward."

"Okay, deal," he said.

The next day they went shopping for lights. Carol gathered enough to light up the whole street. Plus a string of red plastic letters that spelled out *Season's Greetings*.

"We can hang it across the outside of the living-room window," she said.

Yep, the infamous *we* again.

"Think we might have gotten carried away?" he suggested. *Think I'll be done hanging these before January first?*

"Well, maybe a little," she said. "But better to have too many than not enough. Anyway, we don't have to do only the house. We can do the bushes, too."

It was going to be a Christmas-light marathon.

He got busy outside, and she got busy inside, making cookies. As Stanley was working, Edgar Gimble from next door came by to offer sage advice.

"Better make sure they're nice and secure. Got a windstorm predicted for later this week."

"I will," Stanley assured him. He was an electrician. He knew all about lights.

It took forever plus an eternity to hang the things and another millennium to decorate the bushes and put up the *Season's Greetings* sign, but at last he was done. First ones on the block to have their decorations up that year. He grinned smugly as he put away the ladder.

The house smelled like sugar and vanilla, and Carol was frosting cookies shaped like trees when he came into the kitchen. Their dog Goober, the mutt they'd rescued from the pound, lay nearby, his head on his paws, watching mournfully, knowing he wouldn't get so much as a crumb.

Stanley gave him a dog treat, then snagged a cookie frosted with green frosting and sprinkles. Someone had to sample them.

"This is good," he said. "Thanks for making these."

She danced over and kissed him. "You deserve a reward after all your hard work. And maybe I do, too," she said with a flirty grin. "Think I might get a reward tonight?"

"I think you might," he said, grinning right back.

As soon as it was dark she insisted on turning on the lights and going outside and admiring them. She'd been right, as usual. The lights did make their house look special.

"It's so pretty," she said with a sigh. "It makes my heart happy."

Then, it was worth every moment he'd spent out there freezing his ass off. "I'm glad," he said.

A cold wind was stirring, and she shivered.

"Come on, let's get back in before you freeze," he said, wrapping his arms around her.

"Good idea," she said, squeezing him back. "Let's get inside and warm up."

"It's nice to be inside and cozy," she said later, as they snuggled together.

"It is," he agreed.

Actually, it was more than nice. Being with Carol like this filled him with contentment.

The contentment wasn't quite so deep when he heard her on the phone with her sister the next morning.

"I think that's a great idea," she said.

Uh-oh. What kind of great idea were they talking about?

"I'll check with Stanley. I'm sure he won't mind."

Whatever those two were concocting, he bet he would.

"What won't I mind?" he asked after she hung up the phone.

"Having a little party to kick off the holidays," she said airily.

"A little party," he repeated. He knew Carol and Amy's idea of a little party did not and never would match his. "Define *little*."

"Just the families. Well, and the Gimbles. They're such good neighbors."

That meant both sets of parents, his brother, Amy and her husband and two bratty kids, and probably all the grandparents. Plus Carol would be bound to slip in an extra neighbor or two.

He groaned. "It'll be a zoo."

"Zoos are always fun. You never know what you're going to see."

"I know what I'll see at this one. Your Grandpa Howard will doctor his punch with gin when nobody's looking and get snockered. Amy's girls will break God knows what, and your mom will bring something nobody wants to eat but we'll all have to. Where did you ever learn to cook? Not from her."

"You have a very bad attitude, Manly Stanley. Now, can I tell you what will really happen?"

He leaned against the door frame. "Sure. Go ahead."

"Grandma Bartlett will make that pound cake you love, and I'll make those frosted brownies. You'll gorge yourself, and then you and Curtis and Jimmy and my dad will set up the Ping-Pong table in the garage, and we won't see any of you after that."

"You sure won't," he assured her. Her sister and the girls

were enough to make any man want to hide. Some kind of drama was a given anytime they were around.

"Then, it's settled?"

"It looks that way," he grumped.

They'd wind up doing this sooner or later, so there was no point in postponing the inevitable.

"You know you'll have a good time. You always do once these things get going."

"I guess," he said, reluctant to admit that there was a measure of truth in what she said. "When is this big bash supposed to happen?"

"Next Saturday. We'll kick the month off with a bang."

"That's what I'm afraid of," he muttered.

As he'd predicted, Carol did sneak in some extra names to the guest list, but since they were a couple of buddies from his bowling league and their wives, he could hardly complain. The week before she went into party-prep mode, cleaning and baking, and the whole house smelled like a bakery. Stanley was put in charge of vacuuming and pulling down the punch bowl from the top cupboard where she kept it and borrowing folding chairs for extra seating from his parents. There were many evening phone conversations with her sister as they came up with games to play and debated over what kind of punch to serve.

Reluctant as he was to have to entertain a crowd of people in his house, Stanley tried to look on the bright side. He would be with friends and family (some of whom were irritating, but oh, well). He didn't have to worry about impressing anyone. And he would for sure be setting up the Ping-Pong table. There would be lots of good food and lots of smiles, especially on his wife's face. And seeing her happy was what mattered most.

The afternoon before the party, a windstorm swept into town, blowing over garbage cans and making tall fir trees sway.

"It's crazy out there," Stanley said when he came in the door from work. "I wouldn't be surprised if we lose power."

"Don't say that. I don't want to cancel our party," Carol said.

"You might have to. Plus I heard on the radio that they're expecting snow." If it snowed, their party size would definitely shrink. People in the Pacific Northwest could handle days of rain on end, but let one snowflake fall and everyone panicked. Their families, all presently located in Seattle, wouldn't so much as poke their noses outdoors, let alone drive twenty-five miles to Fairwood.

Stanley almost smiled. No crowd; small gathering; more cookies for the few who made it: it worked for him.

Carol made a face. "It better not snow until after the party."

They were just sitting down to dinner when the power went out.

"Oh, no," she moaned.

"I'll get the candles and the flashlight," he said.

"What if it doesn't come on before tomorrow?" she fretted.

"More cookies for me," he said jokingly.

Carol was not amused.

But by early Saturday afternoon whatever power line had been taken out had been fixed. The lights were on, the fridge was humming, and the party was a go.

Amy and her family were the first to arrive, her girls excited and dashing through the front door, winding up Goober and making him bark. She carried a bag filled with wrapped boxes for the white-elephant game the sisters had planned and a large foil-covered plate.

"We're here," she announced. "Let the games begin." Then she turned to Stanley. "What's with the *Season's eetings?*"

"Season's eetings?" he repeated, confused.

"Look at your window," she said. "Good job, Stanley."

He stepped outside and saw the string of letters he'd hung across the living-room window were dangling perilously. The *G* and *R* had dropped from *Greetings*. Yep, *Season's eetings*. It looked stupid. He frowned.

"Leave it up," Amy said as he went to fetch the ladder to take down the ruined decoration. "It's funny."

Yeah, anything for a laugh. Some people could laugh at themselves, he supposed, but he had his pride. The sign was coming down.

The sign turned out to be…a sign.

Goober got excited chasing Amy's girls around, and his wagging tail sent several plates of seven-layer dip and chips flying from the living-room coffee table onto the carpet. Mrs. Gimble leaned too near the candles on the dining table when reaching for a piece of pound cake and came close to setting her hair on fire. One of the girls tried to feed Goober a brownie, causing total panic.

Stanley and his fellow Ping-Pongers escaped to the garage for a brief respite. Stanley was good at table tennis, and he and Jimmy were well-matched. It was nice not having to worry about anything but that little white ball bouncing back and forth across the table. But eventually they had to rejoin the chaos of the party.

The capper came later when everyone assembled in the living room to play the Bartlett family's favorite white-elephant game and steal presents back and forth. Grandpa Howard, as Stanley had predicted, had spiked his punch and gotten tipsy. They were halfway through the gift game when he laughed so hard that he lost his balance and fell into the tree, knocking it over and trampling several of the remaining presents still under it. No harm was done to most of the ornaments, but the same couldn't be said for Amy's carefully coiffed hair when the top boughs landed on her, making her shriek.

Both her husband and Stanley had rushed to try and stop it toppling but failed. Jimmy tramped two more presents in the process. One of them, obviously an inflated whoopee cushion, made a noisy protest that sounded like a fart. That about summed up the situation.

"Oh, my gosh, I have sap in my hair," Amy cried, frantically trying to undo the damage and sending fir needles flying.

What comes around goes around. *Leave it there, it's funny*, Stanley thought, remembering her comment about the *Season's Greetings* letters. But he was smart enough to keep his mouth shut.

"Well, will you look at that," said Grandpa Howard with a grin and a hiccup.

"You should have secured that better," Amy informed Stanley, frowning at him.

"Or else secure Grandpa," he retorted.

The tree was righted and the mess cleaned up, and the

game went on. Stanley held his breath, hoping they could get through the rest of the evening without any more disasters. They did. After some major hair repair Amy's sense of humor revived.

Finally, all the food was consumed and the punch bowl drained, the fun and games were over, and the children were exhausted. Someone looked out the window and discovered it had started snowing, and that put a period to the party. Coats were hastily donned, empty serving platters and white-elephant presents gathered, and the guests departed. Stanley breathed a sigh of relief as the last car pulled away from the curb.

"That was fun," Carol said happily.

"Is that what you call it?"

She shook her head at him. "You know you had a good time."

"Yeah, putting the tree back together was a really good time."

"Everyone helped. And that's what it's all about."

"Putting messes back together?" he responded, determined to be obtuse.

"Being together. We need each other. It's important to stay connected."

He wouldn't have minded disconnecting from some members of her family.

"And really, no harm done with the tree."

Stanley thought of Amy, sputtering and buried under boughs of fir, and snickered. Then sobered. "Harm could have been done if I hadn't seen Mellie trying to feed chocolate to Goober. He'd have been one sick pup."

"But we caught her, and now she knows."

Stanley just shook his head. "What a night. Your family is something else."

She smiled. "Yes, they are, and I love them. And I love you," she added, hugging him. "Thanks for helping me get the season off to a wonderful start."

"Anything for you," he said and kissed the top of her head. "I'm glad you had a good time. That's what matters most to me."

"You are a good sport," she said. "Let's enjoy a quick walk in the snow. I bet our lights look beautiful."

They did, indeed. Some of their neighbors had decorated their houses that day and with the snow and the gaily lit homes, it felt a little like being inside a snow globe. As he and Carol stood on the sidewalk, bundled in their winter coats, taking it all in, their arms around each other, he couldn't help but think what a perfect moment it was.

I am one lucky man, he thought. "I wish you could bottle times like right now," he said.

"I guess in a way we do," she mused. "That's what memories are. Let's make sure we bottle up a whole bunch."

Of course, after that year, hanging Christmas lights became a tradition. Much as Stanley hated being out in the cold messing around with them, he always enjoyed seeing how nice the house looked once they were up. Even more, it made him happy to know that he was making Carol happy.

5

STANLEY'S HEART RATE WENT FROM A STROLL TO an uneasy trot as he walked around the front of his vehicle and saw the overturned red bin. Its lid was off, and the carefully wound Christmas lights were escaping.

The trot went to a gallop. How could that bin have fallen? It had been securely stowed on the shelf for nearly three years, right above the one containing the tree ornaments and the one with the nativity set, the Santa teapot Carol had found at a garage sale one year ("Look, Stanley, it's Fitz and Floyd!"), and the ceramic gingerbread house that had been her mother's, along with the myriad scented candles she'd loved to scatter around on every possible surface.

Maybe there'd been an earthquake in the night that he

hadn't felt. He could easily believe that. He'd been preoc-
cupied with other things.

Carol.

He frowned. This was not some supernatural message.
There was a logical explanation for it. He wished he knew
what it was.

He decided to stick with the earthquake theory. It was,
after all, the Pacific Northwest, and once in a while they
did get a shaking. Hadn't had an earthquake in years. Not
even a tremor. It was time. So that was it.

He put the lights back in the bin, set it on the shelf, got
in his car and drove to the tire shop.

When he came home he aimed the remote at the garage
door.

As it creaked its way up he saw the bin was back on the
garage floor again. Once more the lid was off, and the
lights were spilling out.

Okay, he was cracking up.

"You're not cracking up," whispered a voice as he got
out of the car.

He whirled around, looking for the source. No one was
there. A gust of wind swept into the garage, playing with
his pant legs. Wind in the trees. That was what he'd heard.

"I won't stop till you get with it."

The voice again. He shivered in spite of the fact that
he was wearing a warm, wool coat and the red scarf she'd
knitted for him several Christmases ago.

Okay, he'd put up the lights. To honor Carol's memory,
not because he thought she'd tipped that box over. He was
not being haunted. He didn't believe in ghosts. Anyway,

this was Christmas not Halloween. There were not ghosts at Christmas.

Unless you counted the ones that visited Ebenezer Scrooge. An invisible, icy finger tickled its way up his spine, making him shiver harder.

"I *am* finally cracking up," he told himself.

He wished he could talk to someone about what was happening to him, but there was no one. Without Carol to nudge him into what she called his *nice clothes*, he'd stopped going to church. All those concerned faces and big noses anxious to poke into his business, not to mention a predatory widow or two, laying out casseroles like bear traps. No, thanks. He and God could hang out here at home just fine.

He'd given up on his bowling league, too. He'd gone once, a few months after losing her, but it hadn't been fun, and he'd dropped out.

At first his buddies had called to see how he was doing, leaving him voice mails encouraging him to come back. "Come on, Strike King, we need you."

"Hey, Hambone, where are you?"

Who cared how many strikes you bowled? He never called any of the guys back, and after a while they gave up.

Which had been fine with him. He'd never needed a lot of people around to make him happy. All he'd needed was Carol.

The day he lost her it was as if he'd gotten sawed in half. He still was only half of what he'd been when he'd had her, and that wasn't going to change. He could dream about her all he liked, but she wasn't coming back. Life was gray, and it would stay that way no matter how many Christmas lights he put up. Still, to appease…whatever, he'd do it. After lunch.

After lunch, though, he needed a nap. He settled in his recliner. He'd just shut his eyes for a few minutes. Just a few…

"You haven't hung those lights yet," Carol whispered in his ear.

He brushed her away like a pesky fly. "I'll get to it. I'm trying to rest."

"You've had three years to rest. You need to get off your rear, Stanley. I'm losing patience. Stanley! Will you please look at me when I'm talking to you?"

He didn't want to, not after what he'd seen the night before. He took a leery peek, raising one eyelid, then shut it again quickly. The scary, red eyes were still there. What was she doing hanging around here? Shouldn't she be off in heaven, where she belonged?

"I will be soon enough," she said.

"There you go, reading my mind again," he complained. She'd always been good at that. Irritatingly good, as a matter of fact, often finishing his sentences before he even could. That had bugged him, even when what she said had been exactly what he was going to say.

What had bugged her was how he didn't always pay attention when she was talking to him. But honestly, a man couldn't pay attention to everything.

"Stanley!"

"What?" He jerked awake, looking around. Of course, there was no one in the living room but him. Sunlight was filtering in through the sheers at the window, beaming on the fake brown-leather couch they'd picked out together, spreading over the coffee table where she used to set her coffee mug when she was reading.

"*Staaanley.*" He heard his name, soft as a whisper.

"Okay, okay," he said and pushed up from his chair.

This was how they'd often operated. He'd promise to do something and then put it on hold, and she'd keep after him until he did it. He liked to do things on his own time-table. Why couldn't she understand that?

"Because certain things never get on your timetable," she'd once explained. "You say you'll do something just to shut me up."

"I do not," he'd argued. But, truthfully, sometimes he did. He wished she was still there to keep after him.

"*I am here.*"

Being nagged by his flesh-and-blood wife was one thing. Being nagged by...this red-eyed apparition was quite another and not something he wanted to encourage. But there was only one way to make it stop. He fetched the lights and the ladder and got to work.

Lexie liked to spend Thanksgiving weekend setting out her decorations. It always put her in a holiday mood. Plus it was fun for Brock, who enjoyed helping. As he was getting older she was allowing him to handle more of her treasures.

She started some holiday music streaming and hauled in the box with their decorations, Brock bouncing along beside her.

"I get to help," he reminded her.

"Yes, you do," she said.

She opened the cardboard box, and it was like opening a treasure chest of memories. There was the faux mistletoe she'd bought when she and he-who-would-not-be-named first got together. She'd kept it even after they'd split, thinking she'd make good use of it again. She hung it every year as a kind of positive affirmation. Someday she would find someone wonderful.

So far no one worth kissing under that mistletoe had come along, though. Being a kindergarten teacher didn't exactly throw a lot of single men her way. But you never knew. And you couldn't decorate for the holidays and not hang mistletoe.

One by one, she unwrapped and handed over the vintage wax candles shaped like choirboys and angels that had been her grandma's. Brock lined them up along the coffee table, which he proclaimed to be the perfect place for them. Of course it was. That way he could play with them on a regular basis.

He set the snow globe she'd handcrafted from a jelly jar several Christmases ago right in the middle of the coffee table. It had turned out quite well for a first attempt, if she did say so herself.

Next she let him put the green, pine-scented soy candle in the guest bathroom. She wouldn't light it unless she had company, but even unlit it provided a lovely, fresh fragrance.

As he did that she pulled the ceramic Christmas tree her mother had made back when she was first married out of its box. It had miniature lights on it and cast a gentle glow once it was plugged it in. She set it on the kitchen counter near an electrical outlet.

"There," she said, plugging it in so Brock could see.

"Our guests will be able to enjoy it from the living room and the kitchen."

"When are we going to get a big tree?" he asked.

"Closer to Christmas. We're going to get a real, live tree, and we don't want to put it up too early and have it dry out."

Her family had always had an artificial tree. Now that she was in Washington, she wanted a real one for Christmas.

She let Brock settle her cloth elf on the back of the sofa, but her Santa collection she would set out herself. She had china ones and ceramic ones, antique collectibles and newer whimsical ones. They'd look cute on the mantel.

She'd never before had a fireplace and had been thrilled when the Realtor assured her that the insert in this one worked great. She was looking forward to hanging their Christmas stockings from the mantel, enjoying cozy fires and drinking hot chocolate.

There. The house looked so festive. All she had left to do was to set out her Santas, string the garland along the mantel and find a spot to hang the mistletoe. Maybe from that beam that hung between the kitchen and the living area, so accessible from all directions. Then the place would be all dressed up and ready for Christmas.

Funny, she'd never considered owning a house. It had always seemed like such a big step. But when she'd come up here it somehow felt like the thing to do. "A house is a good investment," her dad used to say.

Yes, it was. Buying this one was also a testament to her confidence in her future, that her new job was secure and this life she was starting wasn't simply temporary. No more substitute teaching, no more part-time day-care jobs. She was a real teacher now.

Brock, being six and full of energy, had no desire to sit and watch her string a garland along the mantel. "Can I go play?"

"*May I go play?*" she corrected.

"May I go play?"

"Yes, for a little while. Let's get you bundled up." The famous Pacific Northwest drizzle had stayed away so far, but the sky was gray, and it was still nippy outside.

Once she had him in his red parka and his red knit cap and mittens, she started for the back door to usher him out into the back yard.

"I want to play in the front yard," he said.

The back yard was fenced, a big patch of lawn, sur-rounded by flower beds full of shrubs and flowers and beauty bark. It was great for games of Mother, May I? and bocce ball and two-person tag with Mom. But Brock was in love with the front yard. It offered both the potential for a rare neighbor-sighting as well as that big maple tree with a thick trunk and twisted boughs low enough to reach. He loved scrambling around in it when she was working out there, weeding the flower beds or raking leaves.

Still, the front yard wasn't fenced, and though they were in a cul-de-sac, she didn't like the idea of Brock being out there without her. Any crazy person passing by could grab her little boy and abscond with him.

"No, I think the back yard, Brockie," she said.

"I want to climb the tree," he protested.

It would be hard for a kidnapper to pull her boy out of a tree, she supposed. And on a cold, gray day, how many kidnappers were wandering their quiet suburban neighborhood? It wasn't like Brock had asked to cross the street. Still...

"Please," he begged, both hands steepled in little-boy prayer.

Lexie caved. "All right," she said, doing an about-face. She'd keep an eye on him from the window while she finished up. "Stay in the yard," she commanded as she opened the front door for him. "And don't climb too high in that tree. No more than three boughs up, remember?"

"I remember," he said and dashed across the porch and down the steps.

She watched as he hurled himself across the lawn to the tree, grabbed a thick bough and started clambering up his own personal jungle gym. He got his feet anchored in the Y between those bottom branches and stood there, surveying his domain.

A rather lonely domain. So far, he hadn't quite found his feet socially, and she hadn't managed to score any playdates for him, but she planned to change all that in the New Year. Little boys, like their mamas, needed friends.

She went to the kitchen and made herself some tea and poured it into the Best Teacher Ever mug her aunt had given her when she got her job. "Because you will be," she'd said.

Then she returned to the living room to decorate the mantel and keep a watchful eye out the living-room window.

The maple tree was bare. No leaves. No little boy. He wasn't in the yard, either.

Lexie's heart stopped, and the blood drained from her face. She dropped her mug and raced for the front door.

Stanley was at the top of the ladder, stringing multicolored lights along the roofline when a new voice invaded the silence. "What are you doing?" it asked.

It sure wasn't Carol. She knew exactly what he was doing.

He looked over his shoulder and saw a little boy looking up at him. He had a round face and brown eyes and a stray brown curl stuck out from under the red knit cap on his head. He was stuffed inside a bulky parka and had red mittens on his hands.

"Where'd you come from?" Stanley asked. It would be nice if the kid said "Far away," but a feeling of foreboding told Stanley that wasn't the answer he was going to get.

The kid pointed to the tan two-story Craftsman next door. "There."

The friendly neighbor who tried to flag him down whenever he drove by, who'd used cookies like a Trojan horse in an attempt to gain access inside his house. Of course it would be her kid.

Stanley grunted and got back to work. "You should go home."

"There's nobody to play with."

Not Stanley's problem. "Go play with your mom."

"She's putting up Santas. I don't get to touch them."

"I'm busy here." Stanley said it brusquely, hoping his tone would shoo the boy away.

Little kids obviously didn't understand the subtlety of brusqueness.

"You're hanging Christmas lights. I like Christmas lights."

"Yeah, a lot of people do." Including Carol.

"I'm going to ask my mommy if we can have Christmas lights," the boy volunteered.

"Good idea. Go do that."

The kid didn't go. "My name's Brock. What's yours?"

"Stanley."

"That's a nice name."

Oh, brother. Stanley shook his head, climbed down the ladder, moved it and went back up to secure more lights.

"Do you have kids?"

"No."

"How come? Don't you like kids?"

"I can take 'em or leave 'em."

"I'm a kid."

"Thanks for sharing."

At that moment the boy's mother appeared on their front porch, calling him, her voice frantic.

The kid waved at her and called, "I'm over here, Mommy."

Bugging the neighbors.

"You come home this minute!" she called.

Stanley knew what that tone of voice meant. He'd heard it enough when his own mother had gotten after him. It said *You're in deep shit.*

"I gotta go now. Bye!"

Yeah, bye. Good riddance.

Kids were pests.

6

"I WANT TO HAVE AT LEAST THREE CHILDREN," CAROL said one summer evening when they were strolling the beach at Golden Gardens. They'd been together for a year and were talking more and more of a future together.

Stanley wasn't into kids all that much, but he knew he'd be fine with any kid who was part Carol.

"You'll be teaching them once you get your degree," he'd said. "Maybe after working with them you'll change your mind about wanting any."

"Oh, no. I love children. Don't you?"

His cousin Belinda had just had a baby. Holding it had terrified him. "Don't know much about them."

"Nobody does when they first start out. You learn as you go."

"You'll already be an expert," he said. He'd depend on her to help him figure out the whole parenting thing.

There were more conversations as things continued to get serious between them, and one of them had been with her dad, who summoned him into the living room one evening for a chat.

The family did all their true living in the family room. The living room had cream-colored carpet and fancy furniture and was reserved for important company. And important conversations.

An important conversation with Mr. Bartlett. Stanley began to sweat. Mr. Bartlett had been an army lieutenant during World War II. He'd gone to school on the GI Bill and gotten a teaching degree. Teachers didn't earn much at all back in the fifties, but he'd kept with it and finally become a high-school principal. He was a deacon at his church and a member of the local Lions Club. A cultured, educated man, a mover and shaker. He was everything Stanley wasn't, everything Stanley would probably never be. Stanley stood four inches taller than him, but as they settled in the living room, Mr. Bartlett on the cream-colored sofa and Stanley on the edge of a matching chair, he felt about three feet tall.

"You and my daughter appear to be very fond of each other," Mr. Bartlett began.

"I love her," Stanley blurted.

Oh, boy. That was going to go over like a lead balloon. Every sweat gland in his body went into production, and he felt like his whole face was going up in flames.

Mr. Bartlett nodded solemnly. "Of course you do. What's not to love?"

Did that mean he had the old man's approval? Or...? Stanley's shirt collar was suddenly way too tight.

"Carol is a very special young woman."

"She's the best," Stanley agreed. "I know I don't deserve her." But he wanted her, anyway. Needed her. Couldn't imagine his life without her.

"So what are you going to do to deserve her?"

"Work hard?"

"At what?"

What? What? Stanley frantically searched his mind for the right answer.

Mr. Bartlett didn't wait for it. "You need a skill, Stanley. Something you can depend on." Here he looked meaningfully at Stanley. "Have you thought of going to college?"

"No, sir." Boy, did that make him sound unworthy. He needed to rethink his future.

Mr. Bartlett frowned. "Well, you need to do something more than working as an unskilled laborer. Find out what it takes to move up the ladder or pick a new skill to learn. You can't drift along through life without a purpose, not if you're serious about having a future with my daughter," he added, lowering his brows.

"Yes, sir."

"Carol wants to be a teacher, and she'll be a wonderful one. She's got plans. Goals. She's going places. Where are you going, young man?"

To school. Stanley enrolled in an electrical technology certification program the very next day.

Both families celebrated their accomplishments, but when Carol finally got her teaching degree, her family did so with twice as much fanfare: a big garden party with family and friends, cake, balloons, speeches and plenty of congratulatory cards, most of them filled with money.

Stanley had made his best effort, getting her a card and a book he'd found on child psychology.

"Thought it might come in handy on the job," he said when she opened it.

"That was a very clever gift, Stanley," her mother approved. "Now that you've got your teaching credentials, you can start thinking about other things," she said to Carol and smiled encouragingly at him.

Yes, other things. It was time to propose. But it had to be special. Romantic. Stanley had no idea how to be romantic.

"Give her a long-stemmed red rose," his pal Walt advised. "Women love that. And take her someplace really nice for dinner. With a view."

Dinner and a rose. He could do that. He made reservations at the Windjammer on Shilshole Bay Marina, requesting a window table so they could enjoy the view of the boats. He made a seven-thirty reservation so they'd still be there to catch the summer sunset. That would be romantic. He picked up the rose after work and put it in the trunk so she wouldn't see it. Then he went home and showered and shaved and got dressed in his stylin' flared slacks and sports jacket.

"So this is it," Curtis said, checking out the look.

"Yep."

"She's great," his brother said in approval. "Wish I could find one just like her."

"You're not looking that hard," Stanley pointed out.

"You're right. I'm not ready to settle down."

Stanley was. He could hardly wait to start living with Carol. That was when his life would really begin.

She looked picture-perfect, all dressed up for the big night out he'd promised her in a white granny dress printed with little pink roses. It made him think of wedding dresses. He hoped she'd say yes.

Of course she would. They were in love. He was still nervous.

They got to the restaurant, and he hurried around to the trunk to get the rose. He'd hide it inside his jacket then present it to her when their dessert came and pop the question. Carol had already hopped out of her side, and she came around the car just in time to see him staring aghast at the wilted red thing.

"What's this?" she asked.

"Nothing," he said and started to shut the trunk.

She stopped him. "It looks like something to me." She reached inside and picked it up. It bent its head in shame. "Oh, Stanley," she said softly. "Was this for me?"

"It looked a lot better in the flower shop," he said miserably. "So much for the romantic gesture."

"Dinner at a nice restaurant, a romantic gesture... Hmm," she mused and cocked her head at him.

"I was going to ask you to marry me." Oh, good grief. Just what every woman dreamed about: a proposal in a parking lot with a dead rose.

"Oh, Stanley," she cried and threw her arms around him, apparently unbothered by their surroundings. "You know I will."

"Really?"

"Of course really."

"Wow." Carol Bartlett, the sweetest, most beautiful girl

in the world had just said yes. He grabbed her and twirled her around, both of them laughing for joy.

"Everything's turning out beautifully," she said later as they sat at their table, the wilted rose lying next to her plate.

"Yes, it is," he agreed. It didn't get better than this.

But it did get better. He survived the big church wedding and managed to come up with enough groomsmen to match the six bridesmaids she had. Her cousin, who fancied herself a singer, sang Paul Stookey's "Wedding Song." She didn't murder it, only maimed it severely. Stanley didn't care. All he cared about was seeing Carol in that wedding dress, smiling at him, just as eager to begin their life together as he was.

The reception was in the church basement—punch, nuts and mints, and a three-tiered wedding cake. He didn't care about any of it. All he wanted to do was get to the motel where they were going to have their wedding night.

That, it turned out, was well worth waiting for.

They honeymooned in Victoria, barely leaving the room except to take a romantic, evening carriage ride and do some souvenir shopping. When they returned they moved to the town of Fairwood, north of Seattle, where her first teaching job was waiting. Stanley found employment as well, and they rented an apartment which they furnished with furniture their parents had given them and a few garage-sale bargains. Life was perfect.

After two years they decided it was time to start a family, and Carol began to talk about buying a house.

"It should have at least three bedrooms," she said. "One for us and two for two kids."

"You said you wanted three," he reminded her.

"Two can share a bedroom until we can afford a bigger house."

He laughed. "You aren't even pregnant yet, and we're already talking about doubling kids up in a room and looking for bigger houses."

"You have to plan ahead," she said, that trademark smile beaming at him.

Planning ahead. Kids. The idea of parenthood made him nervous. It was a big responsibility.

"You'll make a wonderful father," Carol assured him when he expressed doubts.

He supposed he'd cross the fatherhood bridge when he came to it. Meanwhile, they bought that three-bedroom house on a cul-de-sac in a nice neighborhood. The woman next door befriended Carol instantly, and the couple across the street who were about their age became friends. Everything was going according to plan, and they were having a lot of fun working on making a baby.

But where were the results? Disappointment became a monthly occurrence, and the pressure to produce began to leech some of the fun out of the procreation process. After three years of failure and enough tears to form a lake, they consulted a specialist. That consultation turned out to be the seal of doom.

"It's all right," Stanley said as they drove home, Carol crying next to him in the front seat. He reached over and laid a hand on her leg. "We still have each other."

That wasn't the comfort he'd hoped it would be. She continued to cry.

Once they got home, he settled with her on the couch, his arms around her, as she sobbed against his shoulder.

"I'm sorry, babe," he kept saying. *Sorry* was small comfort for such a huge disappointment. He'd never felt so helpless in his whole life.

The next few weeks felt robotic. They ate breakfast together, they went to work, they came home. She graded papers, he grilled burgers. She talked on the phone with her sister and her mom. They watched TV. They even went bowling a couple of times, but Carol's smiles were weak, and she didn't care what spot she stood on.

"I don't think I was meant to be a bowler," she finally said, and he knew that was one activity they wouldn't be doing together anymore.

There was another activity they weren't doing very much anymore. Carol was always conveniently asleep by the time he came to bed, even if it was only five minutes after her. Or she didn't feel up for it. One time they made love, and he felt so connected, as if they were finally healing...until he saw her tears.

"What's the point?" she said miserably.

"The point is we love each other," he said.

"I do love you, Stanley, you know I do. I'm just so unhappy."

How long was she going to be unhappy? Would he ever hear her laugh again? If only he could think of some way to bring back those genuine smiles and her love of life.

"What about adopting?" she suggested one evening as they waited for the pizza they'd ordered to be delivered.

"Adopting?" he repeated. "Somebody else's kid? I don't know."

"It wouldn't be someone else's. Once you bring a baby home, it's yours."

She had a valid point. But it was still a big leap for him mentally.

"Well…" he said, stalling.

"We have a lot of love to give."

Yeah, to each other.

She was looking at him so hopefully. How could he say no? What kind of selfish jerk would that make him? *Selfish jerk.* He suddenly remembered when she told him about the boyfriend she'd broken up with. He didn't want to be that man. He wasn't that man.

"All right," he said. "Let's go for it."

It was like he'd turned on the sun. The old Carol came back, so bubbly and happy, so energetic and full of plans. Yes, this could work. She was right. They had a lot of love to give.

After a long search, everything started coming together. They met the birth mother. She gave them a thumbs-up as parents for her baby. They painted the nursery and got a crib and changing table and clothes. Stanley sold his GTO, and they bought a station wagon. They were ready.

The baby came. It was a boy. They called all the family and shared the news.

Then the birth mother changed her mind. She decided to keep the child.

The crib in the nursery mocked them, and there were more tears.

"That's not the only baby in the world," Stanley said that evening as they sat at the kitchen table, their dinner untouched. "We can start again."

He'd hoped to lift her spirits, but he failed.

She shook her head. "I'm done. I can't go through this kind of disappointment another time." She sighed heavily. "I think it's a sign to quit. Maybe we're not supposed to have children."

Maybe they weren't. He was fine with it being just the two of them. But was she?

"Are you okay with that?" he asked.

"I guess I'll have to be, unless a miracle happens and I get pregnant."

"You never know," he said and tried to smile encouragingly. She didn't reflect it back to him. "And don't forget, you already have a whole classroom of kids."

"They're not ours," she snapped.

Carol never snapped, and he blinked in surprise. He wasn't sure what to say next.

He thought a moment, then tried again, hoping to help her look on the bright side. "They're yours every day when you have them in class. That's kind of important, isn't it?"

She bit her lip and looked down at her hands. "I suppose so."

"And Amy's got two daughters now. She'll share."

The look on Carol's face told him what she thought of sharing.

"You'll be their favorite aunt."

"I'll be their only aunt."

"Guaranteed favorite, then. And we still have each other." If he said it enough, maybe it would be enough.

She nodded. "Yes, we do," she said, but she didn't sound all that enthusiastic.

"We can still have a good life."

"You're right, we can."

Just not the one she'd dreamed about.

He never said anything, but he mourned their loss nearly

as deeply as she did. Not so much because of the baby. Even though he'd gotten excited over the prospect, it had never seemed real to him. What had been real was his wife's misery and the knowledge that, while he could comfort her, there was nothing he could do to make up for what they'd lost.

Like she'd said, it was probably a sign. Kids were not supposed to be a part of their life together.

Carol managed to make the best of things. She stayed heavily involved with her nieces, and over the years she kept in touch with many of her students as well.

She and Stanley went hiking, attended church potlucks, watched as friends and family had children. Sometimes he wondered what his life would have been like if he'd had a son to hang out with or a daughter to walk down the aisle. What it would have been like to sit proudly at a kid's high-school graduation or hold a grandbaby in his arms.

But he didn't bother with wondering for long. What was the point? Anyway, Carol had been enough for him. And they'd had a couple of dogs along the way. Carol called them their fur babies. Unlike kids, dogs never gave you any lip, never had you up late at night worried because they'd missed their curfew. Never fell in with the wrong crowd or did drugs. They'd dodged a lot of heartache. And that wasn't such a bad thing, was it?

7

STANLEY FINISHED HANGING THE LIGHTS AND SET the outdoor socket timer. Then he put away the ladder, set the empty bin back on the shelf and went inside where it was warm.

Okay, he thought. He'd done his Christmas chore. The house was decorated, and he'd proved he had Christmas spirit. Now, maybe he could enjoy some peace and quiet.

He'd just gotten a beer out of the fridge when the quiet was shattered. Not by Carol. This time some neighborhood mutt was on his front step, making a ruckus. Good grief. Couldn't a man get a quiet moment to himself?

"Shut up!" he hollered and plopped in his recliner, his remote in hand.

The stupid thing refused to shut up. It kept barking.

And barking, and barking. After half an hour Stanley had had all he could take.

Okay, no more Mr. Nice Guy. He unreclined himself and marched to the front door and threw it open to give Fido the boot.

Before he could say "Scram," the dirty thing rushed past him and into the front hall.

"Hey!" Stanley protested.

Arf! the dog replied happily, prancing around him, tail wagging.

It wasn't a big dog, didn't even come up to his knees. With its pointed ears and doggy snub nose and those bright eyes, it looked like a West Highland terrier, the same breed Carol had been wanting to get before she died. Only this one was so dirty its fur was gray instead of white.

Dirty as the animal was, Carol would have pronounced it adorable. But that was Carol. She'd loved kids and dogs. After their German shepherd, Max, died, Stanley had been done. Carol had lobbied for getting another and really wanted a Westie, but he'd kept resisting. You got too attached to pets, and then they croaked.

His attitude hadn't changed.

"You don't belong here," he informed the intruder. "Out."

The dog sat on its haunches, tail sweeping the carpet, and cocked its head at him as if to ask *What is your problem?* It was a girl. That explained the stubbornness.

"Out!" he commanded more firmly. To make sure she got the message, he moved a foot to her rear and gave her a nudge toward the open door.

The dog let him push her only so far before dodging to the side, backing up and barking, tail wagging.

"This is not a game," he informed the beast.

He'd have grabbed her by the collar and hauled her out the door, but there was no collar, not even a flea collar. What kind of irresponsible loser didn't even get his dog a flea collar?

Maybe the dog had been treated and didn't need a flea collar. Maybe she'd slipped her regular collar and gotten away. Maybe she was chipped. Yes, that was it.

There was one way to find out. "Okay, Dog, we're going to take a ride."

He shut the front door and started for the garage. His visitor trotted along happily after him, probably thinking they were on their way to the kitchen for food. Nope, they were on their way to the garage door. And the SUV. And the vet.

"We're going to find out who owns you," he said to the animal. "I can tell you right now, that's not me, and you're not staying."

The dog was happy enough to hop into the car and sit its muddy butt on the front seat. "You smell," Stanley informed her.

She didn't care. She sat there with her tongue lolling, looking at him like they were buddies. He shook his head and pressed the garage-door opener.

The dog should have been in a pet carrier, but Stanley didn't have a carrier, had no need for one because he had no need for a pet.

He hadn't seen Dr. Graham in several years, but the receptionist remembered him. "Max's daddy, right?"

"That's right." He'd always thought it was stupid to refer

to oneself as an animal's parent, but Carol had thought it was great fun.

The receptionist leaned on her counter and smiled at the dog resting happily in Stanley's arms, getting his coat all dirty. "I see you have a new baby."

"She's not mine. I found her. I want Doc Graham to see if she's chipped."

"One would hope," said the receptionist, taking in the dog's lack of collar. "Doctor's giving O'Malley an exam right now, but after that he can fit you in. Just take a seat."

So Stanley took a seat, the dog still in his lap. She was so happy to be there, she offered a public show of affection.

"None of that," he said, moving his face out of range and putting up a hand. "You use that tongue to lick your butt."

The dog whined, her feelings hurt.

"It's okay. You're a good dog," he said and patted her head.

Which, of course, made her want to lick him again.

He was still trying to keep out of range of the scruffy dog's tongue when a woman left with an Irish Setter in tow. It was a beautiful animal with a silky coat. The woman gave Stanley a polite smile, then took in the condition of the dog in his lap, and her smile changed to a disapproving frown.

"I found her," Stanley said and then felt stupid. He didn't have to explain himself to strangers.

The woman wasn't interested, anyway. She and the beautiful O'Malley kept walking.

The receptionist showed Stanley and the dog to an exam room, and he set the animal on the stainless-steel exam table. She seemed perfectly content to sit there. No antsy squirming, no whining. This dog had probably never been to a vet, never had shots. Never had a chip put in. Stanley frowned.

He was still frowning when Dr. Graham entered the room. He was still a young man, not yet out of his forties. No paunch. Happily married. Stanley remembered he had a couple of kids. Life was still good for Doc Graham.

The vet greeted him like an old friend. "Stan, it's been a long time. How are you?"

"I'm okay," Stanley lied, then got right to the point. "I found this dog. I want you to see if she's chipped."

"Sure," said Dr. Graham. "How's Carol?"

"She's dead."

The doctor's easy expression turned to embarrassment. "I'm sorry. I didn't know."

Stanley frowned. He'd put an announcement in the obituaries.

But, then, who liked to read the obituaries? And why would someone Doc's age even bother? Stanley sure never had.

"Just tell me who owns this mutt."

"Sure thing. Where'd you find her?"

"On my doorstep."

Dr. Graham checked. "Nope, not chipped."

"Great. And she didn't have a collar."

"She might have slipped it." The vet shook his head. "Hard to imagine anyone not wanting this little cutie."

"I don't suppose you'd like her," Stanley ventured.

The doc shook his head. "I already have two rescues. My wife said that's enough. I guess you can take her to the animal shelter, ask if anyone's been looking for her."

Stanley did. No one had been looking for the dog. And

seeing all the mutts in cages, he knew he couldn't leave her there.

"You have to belong to someone," he said as he started up the car. "We'll make some posters."

The dog whined.

"Hey, it's the best I can do."

And if nobody responded to those, well, that was it. The dog would have to go to the shelter.

"I can't keep you. I'm done with dogs," he explained as they pulled into the supermarket parking lot.

But he wasn't so heartless that he was going to make this one starve. They made a quick stop at the store where he purchased a double-bowl dog dish and a flea collar. And a regular collar. And a chew toy.

Okay, enough was enough.

Back at the house he filled the dish with food and water and then watched as his houseguest tucked in, vacuuming up everything as if she hadn't eaten in days. Maybe she hadn't. She obviously hadn't been bathed.

"Okay, you are getting a bath," he informed her. "I'm not having you stink up the whole house."

So upstairs they went to the guest bathroom where he filled the tub with warm water, then lowered the animal in. She stood patiently, shivering and looking miserable while he soaped and rinsed her, then drenched him by shaking off the water.

"Thanks, I needed that," he grumbled.

She wagged her tail, then showed her gratitude by trying to lick his face yet again as he toweled her off.

"None of that, now. We're not going to go getting attached."

The dog cleaned up well. With her coat white once more she looked good enough to enter a dog show.

"There," he said. "That's what you're supposed to look like. Okay, now, time to get your picture taken."

Getting the dog to sit still for a picture was a challenge. She obviously didn't know the command to sit. But she was smart, and it didn't take too many times of saying *Sit* and pushing her rump down, followed by praise and pets, for her to catch on. She was a natural model and sat observing him at work with his cell-phone camera, head cocked.

"Who do you belong to?" he wondered. "They must be going crazy looking for you." He certainly couldn't imagine a family moving away and abandoning the animal.

And yet people pulled that crap all the time. Pets and kids. You shouldn't have one if you weren't willing to invest the time.

He loaded the picture onto his computer. It didn't take long to make a poster, and it didn't take more than a few minutes to put some up around the neighborhood. *Did You Lose Me?* it asked. His phone number was under the dog's picture. He figured he'd get a call by the next day at the latest.

Meanwhile, though, the dog made herself at home after they got back to the house, settling in at his feet as he looked for a good movie to watch. Later, he let her out in the back yard, where she proved she was housebroken.

Good. She could sleep inside. He set out a folded blanket for her in a corner of the kitchen and gave her the chew toy he'd bought to keep her happy.

She didn't stay happy for long. He'd only gotten halfway upstairs when she appeared, ready to follow him to bed.

"Oh, no. Back down you go."

Back down they both went and into the kitchen again, where Stanley settled her on the blanket with her toy and a firm "Stay."

Of course, this wasn't a command she'd learned, either. He was just climbing into bed when she padded into the bedroom and sat by the foot of the bed, looking up at him. Waiting for an invitation.

Oh, for crying out loud. "You have a bed," he reminded her as he got out of his. "Come on, back into the kitchen with you."

She trotted after him, and he settled her yet again, this time with a piece of beef jerky.

Which she ate in a gulp and then was ready to go back to the bedroom with him.

He turned, held out a hand and said, "No."

She looked at him as if he was speaking a foreign language.

"Yeah, I'll bet, whoever owned you, you didn't hear that word from them very often."

You had to show a pet who the big dog was. He took her by her new collar and led her back to the blanket, said, "Sit" and shoved her rump down. Held up his hand and once more said, "Stay."

She looked at him and thumped her tail. *Yes, sir.*

"Okay, lie down," he said and extended her front paws out in front of her. "There you go. Good dog."

She wasn't interested in being good. It took several more tries and some whining to get her to stay put. Finally, it looked like she had the idea, and he trudged off to bed.

He wasn't alone for long. He'd just turned off the light when she jumped up on the bed and curled up against his leg.

"Okay, fine. It's probably only for one night. You may as well enjoy your visit."

He was drifting off to sleep when a voice whispered, "Name her Bonnie."

Oh, boy. There went his imagination again. Well, he wasn't listening to it. There would be no dog-naming. You named a dog, and it was yours.

"I'm calling you Dog," he informed his houseguest the next morning as he poured food in her dish. "You probably already have a name, anyway. There's no point in getting you confused."

Hopefully, someone would call, and then he and Dog could both get on with their lives.

"Can we have Christmas lights like next door?" Brock asked as Lexie made his lunch.

"May we have Christmas lights?" Lexie corrected. Okay, really, who talked like that these days? Still, good grammar was important, and she was, after all, a teacher.

"May we have Christmas lights?"

Lexie flipped over his grilled cheese sandwich and contemplated. Those lights had lured her little boy right out of the yard. She'd brought him in and set him in a kitchen chair for six minutes (match the time to the age) and forced him to contemplate his disobedience.

Lights had been his downfall. Would it be good parenting to put some up? Even though she taught little children and had a college degree that proclaimed her an expert in early-childhood development, she often felt totally adrift when it came to parenting her own child. Parenting was such a huge responsibility. What if she screwed it up?

"Our house would look pretty with Christmas lights," Brock continued.

Yes, it would. So should she acquiesce, or shouldn't she? She had disciplined him, and they'd had a talk about how important it was not to go wandering off and scaring Mommy.

Brock had agreed that it wasn't good to scare Mommy. He'd learned his lesson. No more wandering off.

She did enjoy holiday lights, especially the ones that dangled like icicles. When her father was alive, he'd put them up every year. Those lights had turned their modest tract home into something magical and had brought a warm glow to a dark night. How could she not do the same for her child?

But she'd never put up Christmas lights before, and she had no idea how to go about it. Still, how hard could it be? She was sure she'd find a tutorial on YouTube or wikiHow.

"Stanley has lights," Brock pointed out.

Yes, Stanley, the next-door neighbor, Brock's new best friend. He'd come home with a wealth of information about the man. Stanley, it appeared, could take kids or leave them.

"But he likes me," Brock had concluded after sharing.

"How do you know that?" she'd asked.

"'Cuz he talked to me."

Well, there you had it. And it was more than she could say.

Brock was looking at her eagerly. It was their first Christmas in their new house. Their very own house. They needed to make it special.

"All right," she said, setting his plate in front of him.

"We'll go to the hardware store after lunch. How does that sound?"

"That sounds good," he said with a grin and dug into his sandwich.

She sliced half an apple for him and added the slices to his plate, then ate the other half herself.

"An apple a day keeps the doctor away," her grandma used to tell her when she was growing up. She eventually did a little research on the health benefits of apples and learned that apples did, in fact, provide not only fiber but vitamin C, antioxidants and potassium. Ever since then, she'd become an apple-a-day girl, and Granny had approved.

Actually, Granny had approved of almost everything Lexie did. She was a good student and had graduated from college with honors. The only dumb thing she'd done was plan a future with the wrong man. Maybe someday she'd get a chance to do that right.

Although she had no idea where she'd find a new prospect. Not at work. Most of the teachers at school were women. There were two men on staff, but one was middle-aged and married, and the other was gay. No single dads had come across her path, though several rom-coms had convinced her they would. Lexie had a theory about that. Men didn't tend to get discontent in their marriages until their children were older than kindergarten. The novelty hadn't yet worn off.

Oh, listen to her. What a cynic she'd become.

But she wasn't a cynic, not really. She'd hung her mistletoe, and she still had hope. Maybe she'd try online dating again. Every man out there wasn't still living with his parents or fresh out of a relationship and bitter. Right?

After lunch she and Brock got in her well-seasoned Chevy Volt and drove to Family Sam's Hardware Store. According to Lexie's new friend Shannon, Family Sam had been divorced three times and wasn't on speaking terms with two of his offspring. But what could you do? It would be poor marketing, indeed, to change his store name to something more accurate. Grumpy Old Guy Supplies? Divorced with Drill Bits?

The temperature had dropped to freezing overnight and hadn't warmed up much since. Sidewalks and roads were still slippery. The car slid a little as Lexie backed it out of the driveway.

Maybe this was not a good idea. She didn't have snow tires yet.

But there was Brock, squirming in anticipation in his seat and asking if they could get lights just like the ones Stanley had.

"I like those pretty colors," he informed her.

"Then, that's what we'll get," she said and kept the car backing down the driveway. She'd go slowly. They'd be fine.

Everyone in town seemed to be taking advantage of a rain-free Sunday afternoon on this holiday weekend to dress up their houses, and Lexie and Brock passed several homes where people bundled in coats and scarves and gloves were busy stringing lights. Many yards had inflatable snowmen and Santas and reindeer laid out, waiting to get blown up come dark.

This was Lexie's favorite time of year. She loved the atmosphere of celebration and happiness, loved the sights and the sounds, the Christmas pageants and winter concerts, the gatherings, the hopefulness of it all. If only it could be Christmas all year long, how much happier people would be!

The hardware store was a beehive of activity, with men in jeans and jackets and boots in the lighting and plumbing aisles or poking around among the nuts and bolts, and couples checking out various displays of decorations.

One couple was looking at artificial trees, and Lexie felt a twinge of wistfulness. That had been her when she'd first got engaged, standing with Mistake Man, choosing their first tree together. Oh, the visions she'd had of a growing family gathered around it, opening presents!

If only she hadn't wanted that big, expensive, blow-out wedding and waited so long. They'd have gotten married and...then divorced. Things hadn't worked out with a diamond on her finger. It was foolish to think a band of gold would have made any difference.

"Can we get a tree?" Brock asked.

"*May we get a tree?*" she corrected.

"May we get a tree?"

"We're going to get one, but remember, we're getting a real tree this year," she said. "That's why we're waiting."

"I like that one," he said, pointing to the tree the couple was checking out.

"I do, too, but you'll like a real one even more," she assured him.

Speaking of real trees, better get a tree stand while supplies lasted.

"A real tree," Brock repeated, following her down the aisle.

With the tree stand taken care of, they moved on to the

Christmas lights. The selection was already looking a little picked over. Good thing they'd come when they had.

"Miss Bell, Miss Bell!" called a childish voice.

Lexie turned to see one of her students running toward her, his parents following behind.

"Hello, Henry. How are you?" Lexie greeted him.

"I know my numbers now," the little boy informed her. "My daddy helped me."

"Very good," Lexie said.

As she greeted Henry's parents, who'd come up behind him, she heard Brock saying to the little boy "My Stanley helped me."

Helped him what? And *his* Stanley? With one short conversation he'd adopted their reclusive neighbor.

She sighed inwardly. It would be so nice for Brock to have a daddy, one that came with a grandpa. But she didn't have a magic wand she could wave and instantly produce one. They were doing fine on their own. Not every child had a daddy. Not every child had a mommy. And not every child had a grandpa. These days families came in all varieties.

It was time to have that chat, as her son was obviously hoping for the traditional kind of family, using Stanley as a stand-in.

A moment of chitchat and Henry and his mama and daddy went on their way, leaving Lexie and Brock alone with the lights.

"Brockie," she said gently, "it's a little early to be claiming Stanley for your own."

"But he likes me," Brock insisted, looking up at her with those beautiful brown eyes.

What was not to like? "I know, sweetie. But he's not related to us, and we don't know him that well."

"We could. He could be my new grandpa."

"Maybe someday you'll have a grandpa again," she said. "Meanwhile, let's be happy with just the two of us. Shall we?"

Stanley looked down at his boots, a sure sign that he wasn't inclined to think this a good idea.

"There are all kinds of families," she said.

"Like Tommy Dinkler? He has two daddies. And two grandpas," Brock added jealously.

"Yes, and you have a mommy and a grandma and Uncle Fred and Aunt Rose and Auntie Jen and Auntie Angie."

Lexie could tell he was weighing the benefits of what his old kindergarten playmate in California had against what he had, and the scales still weren't balancing.

To distract him, she said, "Let's decide what lights we want. How does that sound?"

It sounded good enough for him to forget about daddies and grandpas.

They selected multicolored lights to cover the front roofline and then got a ladder. Lexie could already envision how charming their house would look all dressed up in colored lights.

As she was daydreaming, a man with a beautifully sculpted face and an equally well-sculpted body appeared behind the counter, dressed casually in jeans and a red flannel shirt. Where had he come from? She'd been in the store a couple of times since moving to town and had never seen him before.

Those gorgeous hazel eyes of his lit up at the sight of her, and she could feel sparks fly her way across the counter.

Lexie's gaze immediately zeroed in on the naked ring finger on his left hand. Sparks and a naked finger—a strong sign that her Christmas could get merry and bright.

"Hey, there," he greeted her as she wheeled up her long cart with the ladder and lights. "Getting ready for Christmas?"

"Yep. It's my favorite holiday."

"Mine, too," he said as he scanned the bar code on the ladder. "Are you new in town? I don't think I've seen you before."

"I've been in a couple of times."

"Must have been my day off. I'd have remembered you."

Brock had been dawdling nearby, checking out a display of prelit standing reindeer. Now he called for Lexie, racing to her, nearly knocking an older man in a jacket and baseball cap off balance and making him scowl.

"Mommy! Look at the reindeer," he cried.

"Brockie, you have to watch where you're going," Lexie scolded. "Say sorry to the man."

"Sorry," Brock mumbled, looking at his feet.

"No harm done," the man said, his scowl downgrading to a frown, and moved on.

The gorgeous man with the hazel eyes looked warily at Brock, and Lexie could feel the sparks die. He finished ringing up her sale with a much less friendly smile, and there was no more talk about the holidays.

Well, then, your loss, she thought as she handed over her credit card. She was incapable of falling for any man who didn't fall for her son. Like her mom told her after her breakup, she'd gotten an education in love. That conversation was embedded in her brain.

★ ★ ★

Lexie's mother, aunt and cousins had all gathered on the back patio only hours after her fatal conversation with the man she'd thought she'd be marrying. It was a beautiful summer day, the sun sparkling off the water in the pool. The gardenias were in bloom and scenting the whole back yard. It was an idyllic setting for a meltdown.

Which Lexie was in the middle of having. "I can't believe this. I thought he loved me. We finally had all the money we needed for the wedding, and I was about to start making reservations, order the invitations, shop for my wed…wed…"

Instead of finishing the sentence she broke into fresh tears. There would be no wedding-gown shopping, no reservation-making, no ordering of invitations. No perfect beach ceremony in Hawaii. No perfect life with her perfect man. Who, it turned out, wasn't so perfect after all.

"I'm sure he did love you," Aunt Rose said in an effort to console her.

"He just found someone he loved more," added her cousin Angie.

"Oh, that was helpful," her other cousin, Jen, said, frowning at Angie.

Mom patted Lexie's arm as Aunt Rose poured more lemonade into her glass. "These things happen. He wasn't the right one. Better to find out now than later."

Lexie hadn't wanted to find out at all. She'd been perfectly happy in her ignorance.

"I thought he *was* the right one," she protested. "We had so much in common."

They both liked movies and street tacos and hanging out at the beach. Come to think of it, he'd also liked checking out the other women at the beach. Lexie looked darned good in a bikini if she did say so herself, but that never stopped his eyes from wandering. Hmm.

He'd always say it was her he loved and it meant nothing. Looking back, she realized it had actually meant something. He wasn't ready to get married.

"I always thought he was conceited," Jen said.

"And not half as smart as you," put in Angie.

Except Lexie hadn't noticed that anything was wrong, so how smart was she, really? Well smart enough to say adios. Most mistakes deserved a second chance, but not cheating.

"Darling, someone better will come along," Mom said.

"How will I recognize him?" Lexie said miserably. "Obviously, I don't know how to pick the right man."

"You will after this," her aunt assured her.

"Try to think of it as an education in love," said her mother.

This particular education was ten times more costly than her college tuition. She was paying for it with her heart.

She could still see him sitting there in their apartment living room, right next to her on the sofa. He'd taken both her hands in his and said, "Lex, I have something to tell you."

She'd wanted to say, "I have something to tell you, too." After the latest deposit she'd made in their joint savings account, they finally had enough money for their dream wedding. She'd planned to tell him that and then mention the other little surprise that neither of them had planned on just yet. But the sadness in his eyes stopped her.

"I've met someone," he'd said.

"Good riddance if he's been cheating on you," said her cousin Angie, bringing her back into the moment.

"For sure," Jen agreed.

"I know it doesn't look like it right now, but this is a blessing in disguise. You can do better. You deserve better," said her mother.

Yes, she did.

"And next time you'll know better," put in Aunt Rose. "Take your time. Be picky. You owe it to yourself and the baby."

"Now, there's something to celebrate," said Jen. "I think we should have a baby shower."

"I think we should spend that money and go to Hawaii," said Angie. "Let's all go on your honeymoon!"

"Good idea," said her aunt. "You girls go and have a good time and forget about…"

"He-who-shall-not-be-named," said Jen.

The three cousins did fly to Hawaii. They shared a room at a fancy resort, played on the beach and drank fancy drinks with little umbrellas in them—virgins for Lexie and the baby. The whole time she tried not to be jealous of the couples she saw walking the beach, holding hands. It should have been her.

It would be someday, she told herself. But she was going to hold out for someone special, who understood the meaning of commitment.

"There's someone for everyone," her mom kept telling her. "You'll find yours. And the next time it will be the right choice because you'll be wiser."

Lexie was, indeed, wiser now, and she knew better than to get taken in by a handsome face. She was looking for more than a great smile and a beautiful body. She wanted a beautiful heart.

Another store employee, a teenage boy with a crop of

pimples, carried the ladder to her car for her, Brock bouncing along next to her as if he had springs in his shoes, chant-
ing, "We got lights. We got lights."

The only thing they didn't *got* was a rope to secure the
ladder on the top of the car, which she now realized they
needed.

"I should have thought of that," she said, frowning at the
car and ladder, both of which had disappointed her.

There was nothing for it but to hurry back inside the
store to purchase some rope.

"I'll wait here," her ladder Sherpa promised.

"Thanks," she said. "Come on, Brockie. Let's go."

She took her son's hand, and they hustled back across
the parking lot. It had been salted to take care of ice and
keep customers from slipping, but there were a few dips
and dents in the asphalt.

Lexie's foot found one. Her ankle turned in a direction
no ankle was ever meant to turn and, like a puppet with its
strings cut, she went down, landing on her side. *Ow. Ow,
ow...* No, more than *ow.* Paaain. And cold, hard ground,
people (including her own son) gawking.

Oh, and look, the stars had come out early. There they
all were, dancing right in front of her eyes.

8

"MOMMY, YOU FELL!" BROCK EXCLAIMED, SQUAT-ting down next to her and looking at her with concern.

The ladder Sherpa joined them. "You okay, lady?"

She would be if she could breathe. "I...oh...my...ankle."

"We can put a SuperBob bandage on it," Brock said. "SuperBob makes everything better."

A couple who looked to be somewhere in their forties rushed up. "I'm a doctor," said the man. "Are you hurt?"

Her pride. "I'm fine," she said, gritting her teeth. She'd endured unmedicated childbirth. She could survive anything. *Deep breaths. No, pant.*

Never mind the breathing. Whimper.

A large man with salt-and-pepper hair and a scruffy beard of the same color, wearing boots, jeans and an old army jacket trotted up to them. "What happened here?" he demanded. Was this Family Sam, himself?

"She slipped," said the woman.

"We salted the parking lot. You couldn't have slipped on ice," the big man informed Lexie. Yep, Family Sam, worried about a lawsuit.

"What about the rope?" asked the pimply teenager.

"I was coming back in to get rope to tie down the ladder," Lexie explained. And never mind the rope. She needed painkillers.

"For God's sake, go get some rope," the big man growled at his employee. "Get Carl to help you tie it down. Here, let's get her up," he said to the doctor.

"Can you stand?" the doctor asked Lexie.

She bit down on her lip and nodded. She didn't have much choice. She couldn't lie there in the parking lot.

They managed to get her up on her own two (at this point, one and a half) feet.

"There, good as new," said the big man.

"Would you like me to examine it?" the doctor asked her.

No, what she wanted was to get away. This was all so embarrassing. "I'm sure it's fine."

"You might have a chip fracture," the doctor warned.

"She's fine. Aren't you?" The big man gave her a fatherly pat on the shoulder and smiled. He had a big, toothy grin. It made her think of the Big Bad Wolf. *Grandpa, what big teeth you have!*

Lexie wasn't one to make waves. "I'm sure it's nothing," she said. Except this *nothing* sure hurt.

"Yes, you're young," said the big man, as if that made her invincible.

The teenager was back, another man with him (not the handsome one with the hazel eyes). "Ah, there's your rope. Get that ladder secured, boys. On the house," the big man said to Lexie.

"Thank you," she said between gritted teeth.

"It's the least you can do, considering she slipped in your parking lot, Sam," the woman with the doctor said, frowning at the big man.

So it was indeed Family Sam himself to the rescue. Except Lexie was sure he was more concerned with avoiding an insurance claim than rescuing a hapless customer who took a spill in his parking lot.

"You really should get that x-rayed," the doctor advised her.

She was aware of Family Sam's fatherly smile fading. "If your insurance doesn't cover it, you just send the bill to us," he told Lexie and gave her another fatherly pat.

"A lot cheaper than a lawsuit," the woman taunted.

"Let me help you to your car," said Family Sam, edging Lexie away from the Good Samaritans. "You go home and put some ice on it, and it will be good as new."

She wasn't so sure. Putting any weight on her foot brought tears to her eyes and made her gasp.

By the time she got home her ankle had swollen up like a softball. The doctor was right. She needed someone to look at it.

"I'll get you a SuperBob bandage," Brock offered.

"That's very sweet of you," she said, happy to encourage her son's chivalry. But SuperBob wasn't going to cut it.

She called her friend Shannon. "Are you busy?"

"Absolutely, binging on Hallmark holiday movies," Shannon replied. "You and Brock want to come over and join me?"

"Actually, I think I need a ride to the emergency room." No way did she want to drive anymore and keep putting pressure on her poor, swollen right ankle.

"The emergency room! Oh, no! What's wrong? Is it Brock?"

"No, he's fine. It's me. I fell in Family Sam's parking lot and twisted my ankle. It's kind of a mess, and I think I need to get it looked at. I'm sorry to bug you," Lexie hurried on. "I just couldn't think who else to call."

She sounded pathetic and desperate. She was.

"I love bugs. I'll be right over."

True to her word, Shannon was at Lexie's house in less than fifteen minutes. Brock let her in, informing her that Mommy fell, and she hurried to where Lexie sat, icing her injury.

"I hope it's just a sprain," Lexie said, lifting the package of frozen peas for show-and-tell. Although, she was beginning to have her doubts. She'd sprained her ankle once in PE in middle school, trying out for the volleyball team. (Which was when she realized she wasn't and didn't want to be a jock.) It hadn't felt anything like this.

"Mommy says it hurts," Brock offered.

Shannon took one look at the purple balloon at the end of Lexie's leg with its tiny cartoon character bandage and made a face. "I bet it does. You definitely need to go to the emergency room," she told Lexie. "Guess what?" she said to Brock. "We get to take your mom to the hospital. She's got a big owie, and we're going to have a doctor fix it."

Lexie got her coat back on and Brock all bundled up, and then, with Shannon's help, hop-hobbled out to her car, which looked almost as old as Lexie's. Teaching was a noble profession, but not the way to get rich quick. Or even slow.

"After the doctor makes you better, can we put up our Christmas lights?" Brock asked. "May we?" he quickly corrected himself.

"Let's talk about that when we get back," Lexie said. Maybe Family Sam would send someone over to hang her lights. Maybe he'd feel bad enough or at least worried enough to offer that service for free.

Woodland General Hospital was a twenty-five-year-old facility but had tried to disguise its age with a fresh coat of paint. The emergency room had updated flooring and new chairs in the waiting area—just enough window dressing to tell patients *We're on top of things.*

The waiting area was sparsely populated, with a couple in their early twenties seated side by side, both wearing sweatshirts over pajama bottoms and busy on their phones, and two older women, maybe sisters, looking at them in disgust. Whether the problem was the pj's or the phones or the fact that neither looked sick, who knew?

One of the women did give Lexie a sympathetic look as she limped over after giving her information at the reception desk and getting a lovely plastic bracelet. Between the limp and the yelps, she looked pretty pathetic.

"Who knows?" Shannon said as they settled into their chairs with the stiff, Naugahyde cushions. "You might meet a gorgeous nurse. Or a doctor."

"Emergency-room speed dating?" Lexie joked, with a smile and a shake of her head.

"Stranger things have happened, and speed dating is better than no dating. Someone's getting happy doing Eventbrite singles' events. Not me, though. So far that's been a bust."

Which was a mystery to Lexie. With her pretty face and great curves her friend should have been a regular man magnet.

Shannon sighed. "I tend to meet my men...hmmm. Where do I meet men? Oh, yeah. Nowhere. I swear, I don't think there's one decent single man in this whole town."

"There's got to be some somewhere."

"I don't know. It's like mining for gold when the mine's gone dry. Or dead. Or whatever it is mines do."

"There's always Bumble or Hinge," Lexie said, pushing away the memory of her failed matchup attempts.

Shannon rolled her eyes. "Been there, done that. They always look so promising until you scratch beneath the surface. I found one cheater with a white no-tan line where his wedding ring had been, one condescending mansplainer, one stoner who asked to borrow money so he could pay for our drinks. And a partridge in a pear tree."

"There are still good men out there," Lexie insisted.

"Let me know when you find one, and ask him if he's got a brother."

"Grandpa Stanley is a good man," piped up Brock, who wasn't so busy playing an educational game on his tablet that he couldn't keep track of the conversation.

"Grandpa Stanley?" Shannon asked.

"Our neighbor," Lexie explained. "He's an older man."

"How much older?"

"Way much older."

"Oh, well. Hold out for a doctor, then."

The nurse who settled them in their curtained cubicle looked barely out of high school let alone college, the doctor was a woman, and the X-ray technician was middle-aged and wore a wedding ring.

"Strike three," Shannon said after he'd finished with them.

"That's okay. I'm not desperate."

"I am. It's been way too long since I've had *s-e-x*."

"What's that?" Brock asked.

"Nothing you'd be interested in," Lexie told him.

"I just read about a new dating app," Shannon said.

"Yeah?" Lexie prompted.

Shannon brought the site up on her phone. *"'Chemistry you can't flunk,'"* she read. *"'We'll find your perfect match.'"*

"I'm not sure there is such a thing," Lexie said.

She'd revved up her hope after the father fail had left and tried one of those sites but had quickly learned that people weren't exactly truthful about themselves online. The real thing rarely matched his picture, which was usually off by several years or pounds, and those dates often lacked conversation. Which always surprised her when it seemed the same men could chat up a storm from the safety of their keyboards. She'd finally concluded that if anything was going to happen for her, it would have to happen organically.

Whatever that meant.

The lack of eligible men on the hospital staff wasn't the bad news. The bad news was the result of the X-ray. Lexie did, indeed, have a chip fracture. This discovery was followed by the gift of a blue walking boot that was big and clunky and made her feel like Frankenstein's monster as she walked out of the hospital.

It could be worse. Her insurance would not only cover the visit and the boot but also a visit to a specialist, which would be next on the list.

"I can take you after school tomorrow if they can fit you in," Shannon said as they left with Lexie's new fashion accessory, a referral and a prescription for pain meds.

"Thanks." Lexie sighed. "I guess I should be grateful I didn't break it."

"I'm hungry," Brock announced.

"We'd better stop at Daisy's Dairy Delights on the way home," Shannon said. "My treat. How does a burger and a chocolate-mint shake sound?" she asked Brock.

"Yay!" he cheered.

So after picking up Lexie's pain meds, which Lexie was determined to take only at night and only for a couple of days, they fueled up at Daisy's.

"Thanks for coming to the rescue," she said when Shannon finally dropped them off.

"Happy to do it. I remember what it was like being new in town. Do you need a lift to school tomorrow? You sure aren't going to be able to drive wearing that thing."

"We can walk. It's only a couple of blocks," Lexie said. And it was, after all, a walking boot.

"It's supposed to rain tomorrow. I'll pick you up," Shannon insisted.

It was going to be bad enough wearing the boot around the classroom. Lexie took her up on the offer.

"Can we hang up our Christmas lights now?" Brock asked as Lexie hung up their coats. "May we?" he corrected himself.

Trying to climb up the ladder (still on her car roof) with the big boot didn't seem like a wise idea. Lexie's spirits, already a little low, took the elevator to the basement. Bad enough she had this stupid fracture. Now she had to disappoint her son.

Temporarily, she told herself. She'd find someone to hang the lights. Check with the hardware store. Put out a call on the Fairwood community page on Facebook. Maybe she could ask one of the teachers at school. Perhaps Ed Murrow would be willing to help her out. He was probably around fifty and seemed pretty handy, surely not too old to go up a ladder.

"Can we?"

She didn't bother to correct his grammar. Somehow, it didn't seem right when she had to disappoint him.

"Not today, honey. I can't go up a ladder with my hurt foot." Lexie stuck out her walking boot as a visual reminder. "But I'm sure we can find someone to help us later this week," she added, falling back on her mother's child-rearing philosophy that if you had to deprive a child of a treat you needed to have Option Number Two handy.

Option Number Two offered hope to take away the sting of disappointment. Anyway, they still had plenty of time until Christmas. The window of Christmas-light opportunity was far from closing.

Brock wasn't on board with Option Number Two. His eyebrows took a dip right along with the corners of his mouth.

"Oh, no. Here comes Prince Thundercloud. We don't like to see him, do we?" Lexie said. "He makes Mommy sad."

This ploy usually worked, but not today. Prince Thundercloud refused to leave.

"You promised," Brock said, his voice filled with umbrage.

"Yes, I did, and I will find a way to make sure we get our lights up. Meanwhile, I need to see an attitude adjustment," she said firmly. "Okay?"

Brock was still looking far from happy, the ghost of Prince Thundercloud lingering.

"Let's make you some ants on a log," she said, and started for the kitchen.

He nodded and followed her there, stood silently by while she washed a couple of celery stalks and cut them into pieces.

She set the peanut-butter jar on the kitchen bar along with the box of golden raisins and handed over a dull knife. "How about you get the log ready?"

He took the knife and globbed peanut butter onto the celery. "I could hang up the lights. I watched Grandpa Stanley do it."

Grandpa Stanley again. "Honey, he's not your grandpa."

"He could be."

Yes, and there could be a reindeer out there somewhere with a red nose. "Here, let's put some ants on your log," she said and opened the box of raisins.

He reached in and took several, spacing them out along the middle of the celery log, concentrating on his task.

"Very good," she said when he was done.

He took a bite. "I bet Grandpa Stanley would like to help us."

"Maybe, when he knows us better."

Okay, the ants weren't cutting it. They needed a better distraction. "How about we give Grandma a call and see how she's doing?" Lexie suggested.

Talking to her mother had been easy when she was a child, a trial when she was a teenager and a lifeline once she hit her twenties. Since losing her father, it had become a duty.

Not that she didn't love her mother or want to talk to her, but conversation since Daddy's death felt like trying to chat about the weather with a fellow passenger in one of the *Titanic*'s lifeboats. Still, those calls kept them connected and, Lexie hoped, reminded them that they still had each other.

"I'm sure Grandma would like to hear about how we decorated the house," she said, reaching for her cell phone.

Brock said nothing.

Lexie had about resigned herself to leaving a message on her mother's voice mail when Mom answered. "Hello, honey." She sounded as chipper as Brock.

"Hi, Mom. We thought we'd call and check in."

"That was sweet of you. How are you doing?"

"We've been having adventures. We got the house all decorated for Christmas. Here, I'll let Brock tell you all about it."

He took the phone and said a dutiful, "Hi, Grandma. We got lights. But Mommy can't hang them up because she's hurt and has a big blue shoe on her foot. I'm going to ask Grandpa Stanley to put them up for us." There was a pause, and then he held the phone out to Lexie. "Grandma wants to talk to you."

"What is Brock talking about?" her mother demanded.

"I took a fall in the hardware-store parking lot and wound up with a chip fracture."

"Oh, Lord. What next?" Her mother's favorite phrase. Ever since Daddy died she'd turned into an Eeyore. "Are you in a cast?"

"No, a walking boot." Too bad in a way. If she'd been in a cast, preferably full-body, maybe her mother would have roused herself from her doldrums and offered to come help her.

"What were you doing at the hardware store?" As far as Mom was concerned, hardware stores were the domain of contractors and bored husbands.

"We were getting the lights."

"That Grandpa Stanley's going to hang," Mom said as if Brock had just told her that a tall, invisible rabbit named Harvey was helping them out. "Who is Grandpa Stanley?"

"The older man next door," Lexie explained as Brock skipped out of the kitchen. "Brock finally met him and has taken a liking to him."

"Have *you* met him?"

"Not yet."

"I'm going to Grandpa's," Brock called from the front hall.

Going to Grandpa's? "Oh, for heaven's sake. Mom, I have to call you back."

"Alexandra, what's going on?" her mother demanded.

"Brock, you stay right here," Lexie called.

No answer. Of course not. Her son was a mini-man on

a mission. Once she got him back home he was going to be sitting on that kitchen chair for a lot longer than six minutes.

"Brock's on his way next door."

"To Grandpa's," her mother said, half disgusted, half confused.

"He knows he's not supposed to go out without me." That was it. She was going to have a lock installed at the top of the front door. "I'll call you later," she said and ended the call.

She clumped through the house as fast as she could, stopped at the coat closet only long enough to pull down her son's parka. Of course a little boy making a break for it wouldn't stop for something so insignificant as a coat.

Pulling her sweater tightly about her, she made her clumsy way down the front-porch steps and started across the lawn. Why was it, when you got pregnant, that no one ever warned you how hard parenting was?

Oh, yes, because then the entire race would die out.

Chip fractures, runaway sons... Honestly, could this day get any worse?

9

STANLEY WAS VERY BUSY—WATCHING A HOCKEY game on TV—when his doorbell rang. And rang. And rang.

Dog, his temporary houseguest, was thrilled with the idea of company and jumped off the recliner where she'd been sitting with him, raced to the door and began to bark.

Who the heck was on his front porch this late on a Sunday? Girl Scouts? Blue Birds? Someone selling magazines to put himself through college? Whatever they were selling, Stanley wasn't interested.

Okay, maybe if it was cookies, but it wasn't Girl Scout cookie season.

"I don't want any," Stanley called. Which was stupid. Nobody could hear him over the TV and the barking dog.

The doorbell continued to ring.

With a scowl, he pushed out of his recliner and lumbered over to the door. People should leave a man alone on the weekend when he was trying to rest.

He looked out one of the tall narrow windows that flanked his front door. No one selling anything. But something just as irritating.

He opened the door and frowned down on the kid from next door. What was he doing wandering around the neighborhood? It would be dark soon. And where was his coat? What kind of woman let a kid this age wander around the neighborhood without a coat? Or even with a coat?

Dog didn't care about any of those details. She was happy to greet their visitor, jumping up and pawing him.

The little boy giggled and knelt down to pet her, dropping the box he'd been holding. "What's your dog's name?"

"Dog. Does your mother know you're out?"

The boy nodded. He picked the box back up. It was a shiny cardboard one with a picture of a house lit with colored lights.

He offered it to Stanley. "Mommy can't hang up our Christmas lights. Will you?"

Stanley frowned and hid his hands behind his back. "Why can't your mom hang them?" What did he look like, the neighborhood handyman?

A soft chuckle floated on the air behind him.

His frown got longer. No, no, no. He did not hear a thing.

"She's hurt."

"Well, then, your dad."

"I don't have a daddy."

"Brock!" called an angry voice.

Stanley looked to see his neighbor coming his way. She was a pretty young woman, slender with long, reddish hair. She was carrying the boy's coat, but she herself was only in jeans and a thin sweater. And a blue walking boot. So that was why she couldn't hang the lights.

"Brock Arthur Bell," she scolded the boy, who gave a start and dropped the box. "What did I say about leaving the yard?"

The kid's lower lip began to wobble. "I just wanted to ask Grandpa Stanley to hang up our lights."

Grandpa Stanley?

The woman joined them on the porch and began stuffing her son into his red parka. "I'm sorry Brockie bothered you," she said to Stanley. "He was so enthralled with your Christmas lights that he wanted to put some up on our house. I'm afraid I fell in the parking lot at Family Sam's and fractured my ankle, so I don't want to try going up a ladder."

You can.

It felt like Carol was hovering right behind his shoulder. "I did not hear that," Stanley informed her.

"Excuse me?" The neighbor woman's face was turning red, probably not from the cold.

"Nothing," Stanley said. Meanwhile, the boy was kneeling in front of the dog, laughing while Butt Breath slobbered all over his face. "Dog, stop that," Stanley commanded, pulling on her collar.

Good grief. Dogs and kids and helpless neighbors. He had no idea what he had done to deserve this invasion of his privacy.

"I'm so sorry we bothered you," said the woman. "Come on, Brockie. We need to go home."

"But what about the lights?" The kid's face was scrunching up like he was going to cry. Next to him the dog whimpered in sympathy.

Stanley could hear the TV blasting at him from the living room. Some choir was singing "Deck the Halls." What the devil had happened to his hockey game? As if he couldn't guess. Carol again.

"Oh, for crying out loud," he muttered and scooped up the box. "I'll get my coat." He'd put the lights up, and then he'd be done with the neighbors.

"We have a ladder," Brock said, pointing to their car.

"So I see," Stanley said.

"You don't need to," she began.

"Yeah, I do," Stanley said, resigned.

"Well, thank you," she said. "It means a lot to my son. Come on, Brockie," she said to the kid, holding out her hand.

He didn't take it. "Can I walk over with Grandpa Stanley?"

Stanley was going to have to put a stop to this *grandpa* crap.

"May I?" his mother corrected, and Stanley suddenly remembered playing Mother, May I? as a kid.

This mother looked at him as if assessing his ability to get her son from his front lawn to hers. He obviously passed the test because instead of saying "No, you may not," she said, "All right. But once we're back at the house, you stay right in front of it. Do you understand me?"

The kid nodded eagerly and grinned.

Stanley, on the other hand, didn't. First he was the neighborhood handyman, now he was the nanny next door.

He grabbed his coat, Dog dancing at his heels, and then trudged next door with both Dog and Kid tagging along. It was freeze-your-ass-off cold out, and the air was damp, and Stanley had already hung one set of Christmas lights. Which he hadn't wanted to do. Wasn't Sunday supposed to be a day of rest?

There was no rest for his ears. The boy kept up a steady line of chatter. "We went to a hospital, and Mommy got her foot x-ed."

"You mean *x-rayed*."

Brock nodded. "Shannon took us. She's nice."

Mommy had a friend. Maybe that would lessen the amount of harassment she and the kid gave Stanley in the future.

"My grandma's in California," Brock continued. "My grandpa died, and he's with the angels."

So the boy was looking for a grandpa substitute. Well, he'd have to look somewhere else. At this point in life the last thing Stanley needed to be bothered with was a kid.

"Here," he said, handing over the box of lights. "Take these, and go wait on the porch." *And give me a minute of peace.*

The boy obeyed, walking off with the box, and Stanley trudged to the car and retrieved the ladder with Dog supervising.

"We're not going to get involved with these people," Stanley said to her.

As if the dog was staying? No, that wouldn't happen. Somebody would call and take her off his hands.

Back at the house, the kid was sitting on the front porch, his feet planted on the first step, his arms wrapped around the box of lights like it held treasure. Stanley supposed, in a way, it did. Kids were so easily pleased. Things that seemed small to grown-ups were huge to them.

He thought back to his own childhood, what a big deal it always was decorating the tree with his mom and dad and brother every year. And oh, the excitement of hanging up those Christmas stockings!

And oh, how pissed he'd been when he learned that his parents had lied to him about Santa Claus! He'd been all of five, and the news had been a crushing blow. Dad had lost his job at the plant, and they'd had to come clean. There would be no visit from Santa that year. There was no Santa, anyway, never had been. Stanley had been stunned, unable to take it in, even when he saw the proof of it on Christmas morning. The only presents under the tree had been socks and pajamas, new pants for his brother and him, along with boring knitted scarves and hats and winter coats a size too big from their grandparents. The Christmas stockings had felt like a joke, with hardly anything in them. An orange each and some Life Savers and a candy cane. No little toys, no fat bonbons. Not even any nuts. How could his parents have deceived him so?

"Life's tough," his dad had snapped when he made the mistake of complaining.

Christmas dinner had been at his grandma's. Turkey. Even back then he hadn't liked it. Grandma Clark had tried to save the day by serving cake and homemade fudge and sending some home with them. But it was too little too late.

If you asked Stanley, the whole Santa thing was sick and

wrong, anyway. Better to give the kids presents and take credit for it yourself. Why should a fat man from an old poem get the glory? It was dumb. And scarring.

His neighbor came out on the porch to join her son, a jacket on over the sweater, as Stanley was setting up her ladder. She began helping the boy take the lights out of the box.

"It's awfully kind of you to do this," she said to Stanley.

He hadn't had much choice. He grunted and walked over to them. "You've barely got enough to do the front of your roofline," he informed her, looking at them.

"That will be enough," she said. "I really appreciate you helping us. If it wasn't for this boot I'd do it myself, but I was a little nervous about going up the ladder with it. I was going to find someone to help me," she added.

"Well, you did," Stanley said resentfully. He took the light string and started for the ladder. The kid moved to stand at the foot of it, watching as Stanley climbed.

It looked like he wasn't the only one who was going to be watching Stanley's every move. The woman stayed there on the porch.

"I'm Lexie Bell," she said.

"Stanley Mann," he replied. Not that he wanted to make her acquaintance, but he did have some manners, after all.

"It's nice to finally meet you," she said. "We moved here from California, and it's taking longer than I thought to get to know our neighbors."

What was he supposed to say to that? Nothing, he decided and kept working.

He was spared from any more conversation when her cell phone rang. She pulled it out of her coat pocket and said, "Hello, Mom. No, he's fine. Our neighbor's here now, helping us hang our lights. Isn't that kind of him?"

Kind, yeah, that was him.

She moved to the far end of her porch, still talking away on her phone. These millennials—or whatever the heck she was—they ought to just have their phones implanted in their hands and be done with it.

She was gone, but her kid was still right there at the foot of the ladder. "I like you," he said.

Oh, brother. "Don't be so quick to like people you don't know," Stanley said. He wasn't in a hurry to like this kid or his mom. And he sure wasn't in a hurry to get better acquainted with them.

"Do you like me?" Brock prompted.

"I'll let you know," Stanley said, stretching to secure another section of lights.

"When?"

"When what?"

"When will you let me know you like me?"

"Later," Stanley said and worked a little faster.

Lexie Bell had just finished her conversation when Stanley came down from the ladder. He plugged in the lights in the outdoor socket, and the roofline of their house suddenly glowed with all manner of jewel colors. The boy jumped up and down and clapped his hands, and Lexie beamed at Stanley as if he'd worked a miracle.

"Thank you," she gushed. "How can we ever repay you?"

By not bugging me. "No need," he said. "If you open your garage door I'll put this ladder away."

"Oh, sure," she said and hurried inside.

A moment later, the door made its slow ascent, showing

a garage filled with packing boxes, stacked every which way, and a Chevy compact. It probably didn't have any cardboard under it to catch oil drips.

Not his problem.

Lexie stood in the doorway, which looked like it led to the kitchen, same as Stanley's house. "Put it anywhere," she said.

Stanley leaned the ladder against the wall. "There you go," he said and started to hurry away before she could find something else to say and trap him there in some verbal spiderweb.

"Thank you again so much!" she called after him.

The kid, who was turning into his shadow, started to run after him.

"Brock Arthur Bell, you come here right now!" she called.

"I have to go," the kid said to him.

"Good," Stanley muttered. He beat it back home, Dog trotting next to him. Back in the house the TV was still going, and the hockey game was playing once more. Of course.

He got a towel and wiped off Dog's muddy paws, then wandered through the dining room on his way to the kitchen to make himself something hot to drink. He couldn't help seeing the house next door through the sheers covering the window. Those lights did look nice. Lexie Bell should have bought enough to do the porch railing as well.

Not his problem.

"Brockie, you need to remember what we talked about on Saturday, about staying in the yard," Lexie said firmly as she sat across from her son at their little dining table.

He nodded but looked confused. "I didn't wander off."

True, he hadn't. And he had told her where he was going.

"But you didn't wait to ask my permission, did you?" she pointed out. "You just left, and without your coat."

His gaze dropped, a sure admission of guilt.

"You knew I didn't want to bother Mr. Mann." Brock looked momentarily confused. "Stanley," she clarified.

"He didn't mind," Brock said.

Oh, good grief, she was getting nowhere. "Well, it was still wrong to go running off like that without waiting for my permission. You need to spend some time thinking about that."

He heaved a sigh. "I don't want to sit on the thinking chair."

"Well, you have to," Lexie said firmly.

"I just wanted lights," Brock grumbled and made his way to the designated chair to begin his little-boy torture session.

"I know. But I want you to think about what you did wrong. Okay?" He plopped onto the chair, his back turned toward her, shoulders hunched.

"You'll thank me someday." Had she just said that? She was turning into her mother.

That was okay. She was glad her parents had worked so hard to discipline and mold her. All those times she was sent to her room, deprived of candy for a week, grounded— how she'd resented them! But she'd learned to respect her elders and work hard, and she knew that was thanks to her parents working so hard to turn her into a civilized, responsible human being. She wanted the same for Brock, wanted him to grow up to be a good man.

Her son, a grown-up. That felt a hundred years away. Only a hundred years to go until Brock was civilized and responsible. A long, lonely haul when you were doing the parenting all by yourself.

Millions of women managed it somehow, she reminded herself. She would, too.

Brock's time-out ended and, after another little talk, they feasted on chicken strips, mashed potatoes and carrots for dinner. And chocolate milk. Punishment was over. It was time to end the day on a good note.

Bath time was followed by story time and bedtime prayers. "God bless Mommy and Grandma and Grandpa in heaven and Dog and Grandpa Stanley," Brock concluded.

Lexie hoped their neighbor didn't mind being dubbed an honorary grandpa. At some point she'd have to explain to Mr. Mann about her father's death. She hoped he'd understand and that he wouldn't mind. He wasn't much of a talker.

Or a smiler. It didn't bode well for understanding.

Oh, well, the world was full of grandpas. They'd find a better one somewhere.

"How's your foot feeling?" Shannon asked when she picked up Lexie and Brock for school on Monday.

"Not too bad, really," Lexie said. The pain meds worked wonders.

"Let me know when you want me to take you to the specialist."

"I can probably get an Uber," Lexie said.

"Sure, why not? You're rolling in the big bucks, right?" Shannon teased.

"I don't want to be a pain."

"You won't be. Give me chocolate for Christmas, and we'll call it even," Shannon said with a smile. "You know, the kids are going to find that boot fascinating," she predicted.

She was right. They did and, of course, wanted to hear all about Lexie's fractured ankle. "Did you cry when you fell down, Miss Bell?" Mirabella, one of her favorite students, asked.

"I wanted to," Lexie said.

"But you didn't?" Mirabella was amazed.

"Maybe a little. It's okay to cry when you're hurt, isn't it?"

All the students nodded.

"I cried when my turtle died," volunteered a little boy named Jonathan.

"That's okay because it's hard to lose pets we love. I bet you gave him a very happy life while he was here with you," Lexie said.

"I did," Jonathan replied and looked up adoringly at her. Adoration, one of the perks of teaching little ones.

Later, in the teachers' lounge, her coworkers were equally fascinated as well as sympathetic. "You poor girl. Are you going to have to have physical therapy?" asked Mrs. Davidson.

"Probably, but first I have to see a specialist. I need to call and schedule that," Lexie said, thankful for the reminder.

She brought up the information on her phone and called the specialist the emergency-room doctor had recommended. Happily, the doctor could squeeze her in that afternoon.

True to her word, Shannon drove her to the doctor, who did, indeed, prescribe physical therapy.

"We can see you tomorrow afternoon," the receptionist at Healing Help Physical Therapy assured Lexie when she called them.

"No problem running you there," Shannon assured her. "I can play *Cookie Jam* on my phone while I'm waiting."

Thank God for Shannon.

Except late that night Lexie got a text from her.

Puking big time and have a fever. Going to have to call in sick. Sorry I can't take you to school or PT. Don't hate me. ☹

Her poor friend. She should take her some chicken soup.

Sadly, she couldn't deliver it since she couldn't drive. Not to Shannon's, not to school. Not with this big, clunky boot.

Lexie frowned at her Frankenstein's monster footwear. Well, they didn't call it a walking boot for nothing. She'd walk to school and then she'd have to take an Uber to physical therapy.

She heard a soft pattering against her bedroom window. It was starting to rain, something they didn't get a lot of in Southern California. She shut her eyes and envisioned a not-so-brisk three-quarter-mile morning walk to school in chilly, damp weather.

Ho, ho, ho.

It was early morning, and Stanley was wheeling his garbage can to the curb when he saw the neighbor and her boy walking his way. It was cold and gray, not what you'd call a nice morning for a walk. But with that gigantic blue boot on her right foot she'd have trouble driving.

She was young and fit, and the school wasn't that far away. The rain would probably hold off.

He quickly turned to walk back up his driveway before he got trapped in conversation.

Too late. "Grandpa Stanley!" the boy called. "Grandpa Stanley!"

This was followed by his mother calling, "Brock, no. Leave Mr. Mann alone."

Stanley picked up his pace.

Stanley! What do you think you're doing?

It was just the wind, but it sure sounded like Carol. Stanley didn't want to, but he turned around.

"Hi, kid," he said to Brock. Okay, he'd been friendly. Now it was time to go inside. A wet drop on his nose confirmed that, yes, he didn't need to be standing around in his driveway.

Except here came Lexie Bell, hobbling up behind her son. Couldn't be much fun walking around in that thing.

"I'm afraid Brock's taken a shine to you," she said, half apology, half what-else he wasn't sure. Carol had been the one who read body language and translated conversational subtleties.

"I guess," he said, at a loss for any better way to respond. Two more wet drops fell, hitting the bald spot on top of his head.

"Well, have a nice day," she said and started walking away. "Come on, Brockie."

There. The woman was perfectly fine walking to school.

A little rain never hurt anyone. Anyway, her coat had a hood, and that tote bag she was carrying looked waterproof.

Her son stayed put. "Shannon was going to drive us to school but she got sick. I don't think I like the rain," he added, scrunching up his face.

"It does that here in Washington," Stanley informed him.

"Brockie, come on," called Lexie Bell.

The boy heaved a dramatic sigh and started to trudge off after his mom.

Stanley frowned. Guilt was an uncomfortable thing.

Then he called, "Hey, you two. Come back here."

What a way to start his day.

10

"THIS IS SO NICE OF YOU," LEXIE BELL SAID TO STAN-ley as they drove off down the street. "I hope it's not too much trouble."

It was a pain in the butt. "You don't want to be walking around in the rain in that thing," he said.

"No, I don't. I really appreciate the lift. My friend was going to give me a ride this morning, but she's sick."

Which meant the woman would need a ride home, too. He sighed inwardly, resigned to his fate.

"What time do you get off?" he asked.

"Oh, Mr. Mann, you don't have to come get me," she protested.

If he didn't, he'd hear about it from Carol.

"It'll probably rain all day. You don't want to walk home in it. You don't even have an umbrella," he pointed out.

"You're right. It didn't rain that much where we lived. I guess I should invest in one now that we're up here."

"Yeah, you should," he agreed. "So, what time are you done with school?"

"You really don't have to bother. I have physical therapy scheduled right after. I'll just get an Uber."

"You're going to pay someone?" When she could get a ride for free? Stanley, not one to waste money, was horrified.

"Well, yes."

He shook his head. "Don't do that. What time do you get off?"

"I'll be ready to leave at three thirty. I'll pay you," she quickly offered.

"No need," he said.

Paying him would make about as much sense as calling some sort of taxi service. Who had that kind of money to fritter away?

He pulled into the drop-off lane and stopped, and she slid out.

"This was so kind of you. Thank you," she said as she opened the back door for her son.

"Thanks, Grandpa!" he called and hopped down.

"You go on in," she said to the boy. "I want to talk to Mr. Mann for a minute."

"Okay. Bye!" Brock said and ran off toward the front entrance.

"I wanted to explain about Brock," she said to Stanley. The few drops of rain had turned into a shower. She put up the hood of her coat. "My father died two years ago.

He was the only grandpa Brock had. I'm afraid he wants a grandpa desperately."

"Doesn't your ex have a dad?" There had to be an ex somewhere in the picture. The kid hadn't been hatched.

"I'm afraid there isn't an ex. Well, there is, but he's not part of our lives and neither are his parents," she said, her face reddening. "We were engaged but…"

Stanley held up a hand. He wasn't into soap operas. "That's okay. I get the picture."

"Anyway, I appreciate you being so nice to him."

Nice to him? Stanley was doing his best to discourage the kid. Now he had two pests in his life, Mama Pest and Baby Pest.

"You'd better get inside before you drown," he said.

"And I should let you get going. Thanks again."

He nodded. She shut the door, and he got out of there.

Back home, Dog was waiting at the kitchen door to greet him, tail wagging, when he came in from the garage. She'd already devoured all the food in her dog dish.

"You'd think nobody had ever fed you," he said to her.

Maybe nobody had in a while. Her owners had to be going crazy looking for her. Stanley checked his voice mail. Someone should have seen those posters.

No messages.

"Where the heck are your owners?" he asked the animal.

She sat on her rump, swept the floor with her tail and yapped.

He pointed a finger at her. "You're not staying." He called the animal shelter to see if anyone had been in looking for a white West Highland terrier. No. He looked down at the dog, who looked up at him and wagged her little tail some more. "I don't want another dog," he informed her.

She cocked her head at him as if trying to understand.

He ignored her and made himself some coffee. At least there was coffee. That was something in his life that hadn't been turned upside down.

Lexie had packed the children's day with activities ranging from working on learning the alphabet and all the sounds the various letters made to running one of their favorite math drills, which involved marching around the room, air punching while counting by twos. The storytime selection was *The Ninjabread Man*, a tale about a sensei's creation that comes to life and runs away.

Next came a craft project. She'd copied a pattern of a bell on red and green construction paper so the children could make their own Advent calendars.

"We're going to make paper chains to hang from our bells," she said, showing them the one she'd made as a sample.

"Bell, that's your name, Miss Bell," one of the children piped.

"Yes, it is. And what letter does the word *bell* start with?"

"*B!*" they chorused.

"And that makes the sound…"

"*Buh,*" came another chorus.

"Very good. Now, starting December first, every day we'll take off one link in our chain. Then we'll count how many links we have left, and that way we'll know how many days we have until Christmas."

The children wriggled with excitement.

"But we won't be in school until Christmas," Mirabella said, worried.

"No. But you'll all get to take your bells home with you when we leave for our winter break, so you can still take off the links," Lexie said.

She set them to work with safety scissors, cutting out the bells—a good motor-skills exercise for little hands. As the children worked she walked around the room, stopping at desks to help guide some of those little hands, offering compliments and encouragement as she went. "Good job following the lines, James... That's looking nice, Ilsa."

In addition to the Advent bells and Santa, Lexie had come up with a new favorite character, the Gingerbread Boy. She'd decorated the room with plenty of them before leaving school for Thanksgiving break, Brock helping her. There would be a hunt for the Gingerbread Boy, more stories about him, and on the last day of school, the children would find and decorate gingerbread boys (gluten-free for the children with allergies so everyone could enjoy the treat), all with the help of her two room mothers. It would be a month of learning, of course, but also of festivity. After all, Christmas was about joy, right?

The Christmas bell project went off without a hitch, and names were written on the bells and paper chains made, attached and counted. Lots of good learning there. By the end of the morning class, Lexie and her students were smiling. She took some ibuprofen and made her way to the teachers' lounge, humming "Joy to the World."

The afternoon slipped by as quickly as the morning had, and before she knew it, the school day was at an end and it was time for the children to collect their coats from their cubbies and line up at the door to go home. Another day successfully logged in. Lexie's ankle was screaming. Time for more ibuprofen.

She found her neighbor waiting for her when she and Brock walked outside. The rain had stopped but the trees were drippy, and the sky was still gray.

This was a variant Lexie hadn't thought to plan for when she took the job in Washington. Gray skies were rare in her corner of California. She'd never considered how much emotional warmth the sun provided. This constant gray was gloomy and made her feel a little gloomy, too.

Or maybe it was only that her ankle hurt.

"You're right on time," she said to Mr. Mann as she opened the back door for Brock. Rather an inane thing to say. Like he was a taxi driver or something. "Thank you for coming to get us."

"Where's the physical therapy place?" he asked, cutting to the chase.

"It's on Emerson Street. Do you know where that is?" Of course, he probably did. She was willing to bet he'd lived in this town for decades.

"Yeah, it's right around the corner from Main."

Main was the downtown street where the bank, the grocery store and drugstore and gas station were. It was dressed up for the holidays, the small trees in giant pots stationed along the sidewalk, all individually decorated. At the far end of Main were Daisy's Dairy Delight and a Taco Bell. Did every town in American have a Main Street? Probably.

On the corner of Main stood Great Escape, a small independent bookstore. The window display showed a Christmas tree made entirely of books with several teddy bears sitting nearby, each with a book propped in its lap.

Lexie had been in a couple of times since moving to town. On her last visit she'd learned that the owner, an older woman, had sold the store, and it would be passing into new hands soon. Lexie had been a little sad to learn this. She'd liked the woman and had been hoping to become better acquainted with her.

She'd also liked to have become better acquainted with her uncommunicative neighbor, to have been able to chat with him and ask him about his wife, and how long he'd lived in Fairwood. But Brock kept up a steady stream of chatter, telling Lexie all about his day, so Mr. Mann was neglected. He didn't seem bothered by that, though; he simply drove silently along.

He waited in his SUV while she met with the physical therapist for an assessment and was given her first easy exercises to do, Brock sitting on a chair nearby, then following her into the little gym area, taking it all in.

"I'll do exercises, too, Mommy," he promised as they left.

"That's a good idea," she said. "You can get strong ankles right along with me."

Back in the vehicle, conversation once more was between her and Brock with Mr. Mann their silent chauffeur.

He didn't speak until he'd pulled up in front of their house. "I'll give you a lift tomorrow if it's raining."

He sounded grudging, and she hoped it wouldn't rain.

"Well, thank you again," she said as she let Brock loose. "And please thank your wife for being so willing to share you with us."

The smile he'd almost been growing shriveled. "My wife's dead."

Something heavy landed in Lexie's chest, and she could feel her cheeks blazing. "I'm so sorry."

"It happens." He looked straight ahead, his face set in grim lines.

She couldn't think of anything to say, so she shut the door and gave a limp wave, which he didn't see, then followed Brock up the walk to the house. The poor man. No wonder he was so unhappy and unfriendly and un…everything.

It explained a lot. It also left her feeling at a loss for what to say next time she saw him. Where did they go from here? He obviously didn't want to talk about his wife. He obviously didn't like to talk at all. Awkward.

Oh, please don't let it rain tomorrow.

It rained.

Once more she found herself being chauffeured to school by her neighbor.

Their parting the day before hung between them like a thick, black curtain, and Lexie felt nervous about trying to part it.

She wanted to ask about his wife—how she'd died, when she'd died, what she'd been like when she was alive. But Lexie could imagine how that would go over. Perhaps it was just as well that Brock kept up a running commentary all the way to school, telling Mr. Mann about his teacher and the boy in his class who'd lost a tooth and gotten five dollars from the tooth fairy.

"Tooth fairy," Mr. Mann had grunted in disgust. Obviously, not a fan.

Brock moved on from the tooth fairy to Santa Claus and how he wanted to ask Santa for a dog, but Mommy said they couldn't have one yet.

"Every kid should have a dog," Mr. Mann said.

Oh, fine. Now her neighbor wanted to talk?

"Santa knows we're waiting until you're a little bit older," she said to Brock, and Mr. Mann shook his head in disgust.

Obviously an expert on children. "Do you have children, Mr. Mann?" she asked. Sweetly, of course. Manners were important.

"No," he said shortly.

No wife, no children. Did he have any family nearby? Did he have friends? She hadn't seen any signs of visitors at his place since she'd moved in.

Brock kept chattering. Fortunately, it was enough to keep the two grown-ups from having to make conversation. But she had to say something about his wife. Had to.

Once they reached the school, she sent Brock on ahead again. "I just wanted to say I'm sorry about your wife," she said.

"Things happen." If it wasn't for the scowl on Mr. Mann's face she'd have thought he'd resigned himself to his loss.

"It doesn't make it any less awful when they do," Lexie pointed out.

He didn't agree or disagree. Instead, he asked, "Do you have physical therapy today?"

"No, not until later in the week. And if it's not raining we can walk home after school today."

He nodded. She shut the door. He drove off. She breathed a sigh of relief and shot up a quick prayer for sun come afternoon. Stanley Mann was not proving to be a comfortable person to be around.

He was the antithesis of her own father, who had been upbeat and happy, determined to always look on the sunny side of life, as he liked to say. He was like those men you saw in old paintings from the fifties that made life look so perfect. To be with him anywhere was to feel at home. Mr. Mann would not have made it as a subject for any such painting. The way he reined in his lips so severely it was as if he thought his face would crack if he smiled. Had he always been like that? Surely not.

She thought about her mother. She'd smiled plenty when Daddy was alive, but when they lost him it was like she'd put her smile in the coffin with him.

Lexie sighed as she trudged into school. Life could be so hard sometimes.

But it wasn't awful all the time, and seeing the happy faces of her students reminded her that there was still much to appreciate. Life was what you made it, right? Life could be good in spite of the bad.

Mr. Mann's troubles were forgotten as she got busy with the children. There was music time, some math and language drills, and playtime when the children could go to different activity stations where they could enjoy dramatic play with various costumes, work on floor puzzles, bake imaginary cakes, or enjoy a taste of science, examining shells and rocks with magnifying glasses. She also provided a reading corner with favorite books, and a blocks center where children could create walls and houses. As always, the day went by in a hurry.

The sun did come out later, and her neighbor took her at

her word, leaving her to walk home after school. Clomping along in a walking boot may not have been the perfect ending to a perfect day, but it sure beat another awkward ride with Mr. Mann, and she was relieved.

She also felt a little guilty that she was relieved. Okay, so he wasn't the happiest person on the planet. It was understandable. The poor man had lost his wife. He needed to feel like someone cared.

"I think we should make some fudge when we get home," she said to Brock, who was skipping along beside her. "What do you think?"

"I like fudge," he said.

Maybe Mr. Mann liked fudge, too. Happily, she wouldn't have to ask him to run her to the store. She'd shopped before Thanksgiving, and she had everything she needed.

After a snack—that apple-a-day thing—she let Brock help her assemble the ingredients for chocolate-mint fudge, one of her favorites. Soon the house was filled with the aroma of chocolate. *The first baking smells of the Christmas season*, she thought and smiled. Maybe fudge would help their neighbor smile, too.

Okay, probably not, but she'd give him some, anyway.

As it cooled she got Brock started on his small amount of homework. Then she called Shannon to see how she was feeling.

"I think I'm going to live," Shannon said. "I'm planning on going to school tomorrow. Want a ride?"

"That would be great." Lexie suspected Mr. Mann would like a break from her as much as she would from him.

"I feel bad you had to walk to school in that boot," Shannon continued.

"I didn't. My neighbor wound up giving me a ride."

"Which neighbor? I thought you didn't know any of them."

"I don't really. It was the older man next door."

"You mean the hermit? Interesting. I guess he's not such a hermit after all."

"Oh, yes, he is."

But Lexie supposed that was what happened when you didn't have people in your life. What if Mom turned into a hermit? She'd never been as outgoing as Daddy. The last thing Lexie wanted to see was her mother becoming the female version of the never-smiling Stanley Mann. Hopefully, spending the holidays with her daughter and grandson would help Mom rediscover life.

Maybe having people to interact with would do the same thing for her reclusive neighbor. Fudge was a good way to begin.

While Brock dawdled over his homework Lexie walked next door to deliver her gift. His Christmas lights had come on, but no porch light glowed to encourage drop-in visitors.

She knocked on the door and immediately heard his dog barking. The porch light didn't come on, and the door didn't open. She knocked again. The dog barked. She could see lights on inside. She was sure he was home. She rang the doorbell. The only one interested in her presence on the front porch was the dog. Obviously, Mr. Mann had looked out the window and saw it was her and was deliberately hiding.

Rather a lowering thought, but she told herself not to take it personally. He probably wouldn't have opened the door even if Joseph, the Virgin Mary and all the shepherds were standing on his doorstep. Oh, well. She'd tried.

She was bending over to lay the plate on the porch when the light suddenly came on, and the door opened. There, with his dog prancing and barking at his side, stood Stanley Mann. Not smiling.

"Did you need something?" He made it sound like a crime if she did.

"No, I just wanted to give you some fudge." She held out the plate. "As a thank-you. For being so kind to us. It's been so nice to find a helpful neighbor."

He scratched an ear. "Uh, thanks."

As he reached to take the fudge the little dog rose up on her hind legs to greet Lexie. "What a sweetie," Lexie said, bending to pet her. "What's her name?"

"Dog," he said.

"Dog," she repeated. What kind of name was that?

"I found her. I'm waiting for whoever owns her to claim her."

"What if no one does?"

"Someone will." His tone of voice added *Someone better, or else.*

For a moment, Lexie was tempted to offer to take the dog, but she resisted, determined to stick to her resolve to wait until her son was a little older and would be more responsible in helping care for one.

Maybe Mr. Mann would decide to keep the dog after all. Maybe, come summer, he'd let the pup come over for playdates with Brock. Maybe by then they'd be good friends.

By this time next year I'll be married. That sure hadn't happened. Ah, yes, Lexie was so good at inventing perfect scenarios that didn't come to pass. She liked to think of it as being hopeful, but it was probably more a case of self-delusion.

Mr. Mann didn't appear inclined to stand around chatting. "I'd better get back," Lexie said. "I left Brock working on his addition, and I know he'll be needing help. Thanks again for everything."

"You're welcome," he said and managed a nod.

"Oh, and I don't need a ride to school tomorrow."

"Good."

Had he meant that as in good for her, or as in good for him? She decided not to ask. "Well, good night," she said and took a step back.

"Good night," he said, then he called the dog back in and shut the door.

Christmas lights, lifts to school, fudge, Stanley thought. *What next?*

11

SNOW, THAT WAS WHAT WAS NEXT. AT LEAST AC-
cording to Carol, who entered the quiet nothingness
of his slumber to give him a weather prediction. She was
still wearing that Santa hat, and now she had on her favorite jacket with the faux-fur trim, along with mittens, some
sort of ski pants and boots. Carol had never skied. Was she
taking up cloud-skiing?

"It's going to dump," she warned.

He didn't care. "If it does, I'm good. I've got snow tires."

And, speaking of good, Carol sure looked cute all dressed
up like a snow bunny. Tonight she looked about thirty.
Her hair was long again, hanging to her shoulders, and her
cheeks were rosy. She perched on the edge of the bed. If
he sat up and reached out, he could touch her.

He tried, but she danced away and floated up to hover in a corner by the ceiling.

"Your little neighbor will probably need you to drive her to physical therapy," she said. "And don't forget to shovel Mrs. Gimble's walk."

He and Carol had watched over the old woman ever since she'd lost her husband ten years earlier, and that wasn't going to change. Mrs. Gimble's daughter had moved back east with husband number two, and Mrs. Gimble was pretty much on her own. If Carol were still around she'd have been popping over there with cookies or to share a cup of tea, letting Mrs. Gimble ride shotgun when she went to the bookstore. Stanley had limited his involvement, but the old woman could hardly shovel snow by herself, so him doing it was a given.

"You'd better shovel Lexie Bell's as well so she can get to her mailbox," Carol continued.

"What, are you trying to kill me?" he protested. Hmm, probably not in good taste considering the fact that she was already dead.

"Your heart is fine, and you need the exercise. You're gaining weight. You've been eating too much junk food, Stanley."

"Not that much," he lied.

"Anyway, it's nice to help the neighbors, isn't it?"

Yeah, but how nice was up for debate.

"The lights you hung look lovely," she said, floating back down and hovering just out of touching range. "You have a good heart, Manly Stanley."

"Not so good anymore," he said. "It broke the day I lost you."

"I know," she said softly. "But it will mend. And I'm happy to see you've found someone to keep you company," she said, pointing to where Dog slept down by his feet. "A Westie, too."

Stanley crossed his arms over his chest. "I'm not keeping her. I told you before you di—er, left, no more dogs."

"Now, darling, you can't give up on enjoying animals simply because you know they'll leave you."

"Everyone I love leaves me," he said on a sob, feeling very sorry for himself.

"And new *everyones* come into your life," she pointed out.

"No one can replace you," he said, offended by how casually she dismissed her departure and his loss.

"I didn't say that. Stanley, you're being awfully difficult tonight."

"I am not," he insisted. "But you're not here anymore, and I can do what I damn well want."

"Am I going to have to get angry with you? Remember, I can be very scary when I'm angry."

He knew. He'd already seen.

Oh, no, there came the creepy red-hot flaming eyes again, and she was right in his face, and he didn't want to grab her anymore. And he sure didn't want her to grab him. He crab-walked to the other side of the bed.

"Carol, you gotta stop doing this," he protested.

She settled back on the foot of the bed, and the red died back to blue. "I want you to be happy, Stanley."

"How can I be happy without you?"

"By looking to the future instead of the past," she said. "You can do it. I have confidence in you."

"Will you come and visit me every night?" If she did maybe he could get through the days.

"No, dear. I'm only here to get you started down the right path."

She was beginning to fade.

"Don't go, Carol," he begged. "Let's talk some more."

But it was too late. She vanished, and it was only him and Dog, who was lying at the foot of the bed, whimpering in her sleep, her little paws pumping like she was chasing something. Maybe she was chasing Carol.

Like me, he thought. "If only you were real," he murmured and lay back down, burrowing into his pillow.

He shut his eyes.

A voice whispered, "Name the dog Bonnie."

Oh, brother, he thought. Easy for her to tell him to keep the dog. She wasn't the one who'd have to walk the silly thing and shovel the turds out of the back yard.

The next morning he awoke to a wet tongue licking his chin and bright eyes looking eagerly at him.

"You only like me 'cause I feed you," he informed the dog.

Man's best friend, that was what people said, but really, a dog would go with anyone who'd feed it. And if you and your dog were marooned somewhere with no food, Fido would have no problem taking a chunk out of your leg. Dogs bit and growled and peed on carpets. Got sick. Cost a fortune in vet bills. You had to let them in and out, take them for walks, buy them food and flea collars and dog licenses. They cost a small fortune, and then they died. That was the reality of dogs.

He pushed aside thoughts of wagging tails and furry

faces at the window looking for his return after a day of work. No dogs.

He let Dog out to go do her thing. She didn't stay out long.

"I know it's cold," he said as he let her in, "but you've got fur."

The silly thing just wriggled and barked, anxious to be petted.

"Yeah, you're a good dog," he admitted and obliged her.

He wiped her paws, filled her dog bowl, then checked for messages on his phone. Still no one calling to thank him for finding their beloved pet.

He poured himself a cup of coffee, then went to his computer to check the weather. The forecast had changed since the last time he'd checked. Carol was right. Snow was predicted for that very day.

"We'd better stock up," he said to Dog, who'd come to sit at his feet and keep him company.

Even though Stanley was in the store by nine, there was already a crowd. He wasn't the only one who'd seen the forecast. Although the Pacific Northwest usually experienced mild winters, every once in a while it got a dumping, and when that happened it was Snowmaggedon, and everyone panicked. Grocery-store shelves would get wiped clean faster than you could say "Where's the bread?"

Stanley didn't need to panic. He had all-wheel drive on his SUV, and his snow tires were on. Not that he wanted to go anywhere. No, he'd be perfectly happy tucked in his house. No need to interact with anyone. Snow was the solitary man's friend, and he could hardly wait to leave this crowd of panicked shoppers and get back home to enjoy his solitude.

He got milk for his cereal and more dog food, then rounded out his shopping by adding other essentials such as pizza and chips. And peppermint ice cream. Carol was going to come around whether he ate it or not, so what the heck. He went back home, put away his groceries, checked the news on his computer, read a Lee Child thriller and threw some clothes in the wash. Colors and whites together. Who cared if his white T-shirts didn't sparkle?

By midmorning the snow had arrived, drifting down in big, soft flakes that hugged the lawn, the streets and the rhododendron bushes in front of the house. His new neighbor would probably be getting out of school early.

"Walking in the snow in that boot will be awful," Carol whispered.

"She'll get a ride," Stanley said.

What if she doesn't?

"Oh, for crying out loud," he muttered and looked up the number for the school.

Early dismissal at noon. He left a message for her at the school office that he'd be coming to get her and the kid. Come noon he was waiting for them.

The kid spotted him first and raced up, slipping and sliding as he went, his backpack bouncing. He yanked open the rear door and jumped onto the back seat. "It's snowing!"

"Yeah, it is," Stanley agreed, not feeling the same enthusiasm.

"My teacher said we should all go home and make a snowman. I want to make a snowman. Will you help me?"

"There's not enough snow for one," Stanley said. If this

kept up it wouldn't be long until there was, but he kept that information to himself.

"When there is?" Brock persisted.

"I got stuff to do," Stanley informed him. He had to finish his book.

He checked his rearview mirror to see how the kid was taking this. He'd fallen back against the seat and was looking like Stanley had announced the end of the world. Too bad. Stanley wasn't going to freeze his ass off making a stupid snowman. Bad enough that he'd be out shoveling the white stuff the next morning.

Lexie had reached them now and settled into the front next to Stanley. "Oh, my gosh, you are a lifesaver. My friend offered to drive us home, but since she doesn't like driving in the snow, I was planning to walk to save her the extra distance."

"In that thing?" Stanley said, motioning to her booted foot. "You don't want to do that."

"You're right, I don't. Thank you."

"No problem," he said. Just a pain in the butt.

Happily, she didn't ask about Carol, and the conversation on the way back was mainly between her and the kid, who was still carrying on about making a snowman.

"I think we'll need a little more snow on the ground, Brockie. Let's wait till tomorrow. Will it stay?" she asked Stanley.

"Probably for a day or two. It never lasts long."

Although it would be fine with him if it did. He was stocked up on food, and he could hole up with his book and his TV cop shows. The world would settle under a blanket of quiet, and nobody would bug him. Well, once he had the walkways shoveled.

That evening, on his way to the kitchen to heat up some canned clam chowder, he glanced out the dining-room window and saw Lexie Bell's Christmas lights reflecting onto the snowy roof. He had to admit, there was something about holiday lights on a quiet winter's night that lulled you into thinking all was well with the world. Carol would have been at the window, enjoying the sight.

Carol. A familiar sadness fell over him, and suddenly the sight wasn't enjoyable. He heated up the chowder, then ate it right from the pan as he watched the news on TV. Things were never well in the world, and snow and colored lights couldn't change that.

"You can still make things well in your world," Carol whispered as he fell deeper into sleep later that night. Yeah, that was Carol. The glass was always half-full.

But for Stanley the glass had broken the day she died.

Early the next morning he groaned as he walked out with his snow shovel, Dog watching from the safety of the garage. There had to be six inches of the stuff. By the time he got done with his neighbors he wouldn't have any energy left for his own front walk.

So what? He didn't need to shovel his. He wasn't expecting company, and he sure wasn't going anywhere.

Anyway, two front walks were enough. "I'll probably have a heart attack," he grumbled.

Although maybe that wouldn't be such a bad thing. Then he could die and be with Carol.

Oh, boy, she'd be pissed if she heard him say that. Best not to even think it.

I should move to a condominium, he thought. *Or the Caribbean. No snow-shoveling needed there.*

Mrs. Gimble came to her front door as he was moving the last shovelful of the stuff from her walk. She wore slacks and a blouse with a cardigan that she was pulling across her chest for warmth.

"Stanley, you are a dear," she said. "Thank you so much."

"No problem," he told her. "I need the exercise." According to Carol, anyway.

"I won't need the walk cleared for myself, of course," she said. "I'm not poking my nose out the door until this stuff is all gone."

A good idea. Mrs. Gimble was now a little stick of a woman. If she slipped and fell, those twig legs of hers would snap like dry kindling.

"Of course, my Meals on Wheels lady will appreciate being able to get to the door. That is, if you wouldn't mind shoveling the front steps while you're at it."

Like he had a choice? "Sure," he said and got to it. There weren't that many stairs, anyway.

With Mrs. Gimble taken care of he turned his attention to the pest on the other side. He'd get her taken care of, then he could go in and… What did he have to do today? Work a sudoku puzzle, check his investments online. Try and find something on the sports channel, eat a solitary lunch. His usual routine.

He frowned. Carol and her lecture about life being like a savings account—she of all people should know how little he cared about what he had in savings now that she was gone. He had no purpose, no life. No one needed him.

Dog was waiting by the garage door and wagged her tail

and barked as he trudged past, on his way to take care of House Number Two. Well, okay. Someone needed him. At least for a little while.

Lexie was relieved that school was canceled. She sure hadn't wanted to walk to work, but the idea of riding with Shannon had made her anxious. The thought of Shannon even driving herself anywhere was not a good one, and Lexie was glad they could both stay safe at home. Shannon had made it safely to her place the day before but confessed to having almost collided with another sliding car before she safely slipped into her own driveway. She'd laughed about the adventure, but it had sounded hair-raising to Lexie.

Getting to enjoy the pretty, white stuff here in her neighborhood was a treat, though. *A snow day will be fun*, she thought, as she took a picture to text to her cousins in California. She and Brock could bake cookies, and he could try his hand at making that snowman he'd been talking about ever since he'd seen the first flakes.

She only wished she could show him how. This was his first year with snow, and she hated that she couldn't get out and enjoy it with him. She'd bought boots for both of them, but while his would fit great, hers would be useless.

"Breakfast," she called as she set Brock's bowl of oatmeal on the kitchen eating bar.

"Grandpa Stanley's outside," he cried as he raced over from the living-room window. He climbed onto a bar stool. "Can I go outside and help him?"

"May I go outside and help him?"

"May I?"

"What's he doing?"

"He's shoveling."

Shoveling. Lexie hurried to the window and looked out. Sure enough, there was Mr. Mann, working away, removing snow from their front walk. He was too old for that sort of thing. He'd have a heart attack.

She clomped out onto the front porch. "Mr. Mann, what are you doing?" she called.

"What's it look like I'm doing?" he called back, irritated.

"You don't need to do that."

"If I don't, who's going to?"

Not her. Not only was she on the injured list, she also hadn't thought to buy a snow shovel. Stupid.

"I'll get it done," she called. Surely she could find someone to hire. "Please don't go to all that trouble."

He kept shoveling. "Too late now. I'm half-through."

Brock was back. "I'm done with breakfast. Can I... May I go out and help Grandpa Stanley now?"

"I don't think he needs any help, Brockie." She wasn't sure he'd appreciate the company, either.

"Then, I'll watch."

"You can watch, but don't bother him," Lexie said. "Okay?"

Brock nodded eagerly.

"All right, then, let's get you dressed."

Brock ran for the stairs with a whoop, and Lexie followed, her gait uneven and clunky. Stupid boot. Stupid ankle.

At least she wasn't in a cast, she reminded herself. It could be worse. Things could always be worse.

Brock rushed through getting dressed and could barely

stand still long enough for his toothbrush to finish its al-
lotted two-minute brushing time. At last he was ready to
go, racing down the stairs.

He danced from one foot to the other as she got him
into his coat and hat and boots and tied on his muffler. He
took his mittens and ran out the door and down the steps
hollering, "Hi, Grandpa Stanley."

Mr. Mann didn't say anything, just acknowledged his
presence with a nod and kept shoveling. Brock was going
to drive him nuts.

"Brockie, see if you can make a snowman," she called
from the front door. That would give him something to
do besides bother their neighbor.

"Okay," Brock called back cheerfully and informed Mr.
Mann, "I'm going to make a snowman."

Mr. Mann grunted something. It might have been *Good*.
Or he might have been swearing under his breath.

It was obvious he wasn't wild about children. Happily,
Brock was oblivious. He bounded into the middle of the
yard, scooped up a handful of snow and sent it flying sky-
ward. Then he knelt down and began pushing it around,
a little human bulldozer.

Lexie had never made a snowman. Her parents had been
warm-weather people, beach lovers. It hadn't occurred to
them to take her someplace where there was snow, and it
hadn't occurred to her to ask. She'd been happy enough
with the beach, with weekends and vacations spent at her
aunt and uncle's place in Santa Monica, hanging with her
cousins, enjoying bodysurfing and bonfires and boys. Now
that she was in the Northwest, though, she intended to
learn how to cross-country ski. And make snowmen.

With her son happily playing in the snow, Lexie re-treated back inside where it was warm. She'd watch from the window.

She took a picture of him, texted it to her mom and then settled on the couch where she could keep an eye on her son and started checking out craft ideas online. Oooh, she could make bottle-brush trees. How cute would those be sitting on her counter? And how cute was this reindeer treat jar? She could make it with Brock. All she'd need would be pipe cleaners, googly eyes and pom-poms.

She looked out the window to make sure he was still safe in the front yard and not bothering Mr. Mann. All was well out there. She returned her attention to her cell phone. Tea-light snowmen. How adorable!

The kid was jabbering away. Stanley tuned him out. Thank God he was almost done with the front walk. He was sweating like a gym rat on a treadmill. As soon as he got back in the house he was going to grab some coffee and his book and not move. Well, after he made sure Dog did her thing.

Dog. Why hadn't anybody called him about the animal?

He gave his shovel one final push and dumped the load of snow on the lawn. Okay, mission accomplished.

As he turned to walk back to his house the Bell kid ap-peared in his line of vision. He'd plopped down in the snow in front of a small mound and was crying. Oh, good grief. What was the kid's problem?

Stanley walked over to where the boy sat. "What's wrong?"

"My snowman," the boy wailed.

"That's a snowman, huh?"

"I can't make him right."

There was an understatement. "Don't you know how to make a snowman?" Everyone knew how to make a snowman, for crying out loud.

The kid looked up at him, his mouth trembling, tears leaking out of his eyes, and shook his head.

"Did you ever make a snowman?"

Another shake of the head. "We never had snow where I lived." The words came out as a whimper.

Stanley remembered crying over a snowman once, too. He'd been a little older than this kid. His dad had gotten another job, and they'd moved to a new house in a new neighborhood that came complete with a neighborhood bully. The kid had knocked Stanley's snowman down and stomped it to death. It had been a crushing blow to see his work of art reduced to nothing but broken mounds and a carrot.

His old man came home from work at his new job and, after hearing about what had happened, had gone out with Stanley and helped him build a bigger, better one. He'd also given Stanley a few pointers in the manly art of boxing that served him well the next time the bully came around.

Who was showing this boy how to build snowmen and take on bullies?

Stanley laid his shovel aside. "Here, kid. You're going about it all wrong. You got to start with a ball and then roll it and make it bigger. Look."

He demonstrated. Hmm. Bending over wasn't quite so easy when you'd grown a gut.

He stood up. "Now, you keep rolling that around until it gets real big. That'll be his bottom."

"Okay," Brock said eagerly.

The eagerness didn't last, and kid was ready to quit way too soon.

"No, no. You gotta make his snow butt bigger," Stanley said.

"Snow butt," the boy repeated and burst into giggles.

Rolling such a big snow butt turned out to be a challenge, so Stanley helped him.

"Okay, there you go," he said when they were done. "Now we make his middle."

So it was back to rolling another ball of snow around the yard and then picking up some snow from Stanley's yard because it was fresh and untrammeled and why not.

"My mommy doesn't know how to make snowmen," Brock confided.

"I guess we'll have to teach her," Stanley said. "My dad taught me how to make snowmen."

"I wish I had a daddy," Brock confided. "Mommy says that sometimes things don't work out with daddies."

Not even an ex in the picture. *Good grief, this younger generation,* Stanley thought, forgetting he grew up in the era of drugs, sex and rock and roll.

"My mommy teaches kindergarten," Brock went on. "I'm not in kindergarten now. I'm in first grade. My classroom is next to Mommy's. My teacher's name is Mrs. Beeber. She has white hair like you."

"That means she's wise," Stanley said.

Brock considered this and nodded. "She's very smart. Like you."

Smart. Stanley smiled.

"Okay, this is big enough for his middle," he decided. "Let's put it on and see how he looks."

"Wow!" cried Brock as Stanley settled the second ball on the snowman. "Our snowman is really big."

"Yep. Nobody's gonna knock this guy over," Stanley said. "Now we just have to make his head."

Brock was dancing up and down by the time they settled the head in place.

"Arms," Stanley said and made his way over to the maple tree, the boy by his side. He broke off a couple of small branches. "These should work."

They did indeed. Old Frosty was coming to life.

"He needs a face," Stanley said, stepping back to admire their handiwork.

"How will we do that?"

"Well, you can use a carrot for his nose."

As if on cue, the kid's mom came out on the front porch.

"Mommy, we need a carrot," Brock cried, running up to her.

"And a scarf," Stanley called. "And you got any prunes?"

She looked at him, puzzled. "Prunes?"

Of course, the young had no need of prunes. "Never mind. I'll get some," he said and hurried back to his house.

Dog was dancing at the kitchen door when he went in, happy to see him. "You want to come see the snowman?" he asked the dog.

The bark and the tail wag looked like a yes.

Stanley grabbed a box of prunes. "Okay, come on, then."

Back outside they went, the dog bounding along, leaping as high as possible in an effort to clear the snow. Brock was already waiting, carrot and scarf in hand, his mom watching from the porch huddled inside a coat.

"So, we put the nose in the middle of the face," Stanley said, lifting the boy up so he could have the honors. "Then the eyes. Here you go."

Two prunes served as eyes, and six more made a smile. They wrapped the scarf around the snowman's neck, and that was that.

Lexie already had her phone poised. "Let me get a picture."

So Stanley and Brock stood by the snowman. Brock caught hold of Stanley's hand. Nobody had held his hand since Carol had died. It felt strangely comforting.

"That's perfect," she said happily.

Brock beamed up at Stanley. "Thank you, Grandpa."

"You did good," Stanley said and left it at that. "Now, get inside before you turn into a Popsicle."

"I can't turn into a Popsicle," Brock said with a giggle. "I'm a boy."

"And I'm an old man, and this cold is getting into my bones."

Stanley picked up his shovel, called Dog to come and walked back across the yards to his garage. He didn't realize it until he'd put away the shovel and gotten back inside the house: he was smiling.

He reined it in. He'd probably live to regret his good deed. Now the kid would really be a pest.

Sure enough, that afternoon his doorbell began ringing. Incessantly. And there was the kid again, this time with a plate of cookies cut in the shape of trees, frosted with green frosting and smothered in sprinkles.

"Mommy and me just made these," he informed Stanley. "I decorated them."

Stanley could tell. You could barely see the frosting under all those sprinkles.

Carol used to make those cookies. Stanley's thank-you was gruffer than intended, mainly because he was trying not to cry.

The boy's eyes got big. He looked like he wasn't sure whether he should smile or run away. He chose Door Number Two and scrammed.

Stanley felt suddenly sour. "Good. Maybe now the kid will leave us in peace for a while," he said to Dog, who was, as usual, standing right there next to him.

Dog didn't care about the complexities of human relations. Her eyes were on the plate of cookies. Her tail gave a hopeful wiggle.

"No, you can't have a cookie. They're not good for you." Stanley was going to have to buy some dog treats.

Dog treats. What was he thinking? This animal was not staying.

Except another check of his still-empty voice mail told him otherwise. "What's your story?" he asked Dog as he gave her another piece of jerky.

She stood on her hind legs and put her front paws on his pants.

He picked her up and carried her to his recliner. "What am I going to do with you?"

"Keep her," said Carol, who visited him that night to tell him how happy his kindness to the neighbors had made her.

"I always liked you in red," he said, taking in her red sweater. Darn, but she looked cute in that Santa hat.

She perched on the edge of the bed, her favorite spot. "Never mind my sweater."

"You're right. How about you take it off?"

She merely smiled and shook her head at him. "Your little neighbor's going to want to get a tree, you know."

"So?"

"She can't drive. Remember?"

Stanley frowned. "She'll find someone to take her."

"Who? She's new to the area with no family around, and she doesn't know anyone."

She has a job; she knows people.

"Stanley, she's taken a liking to you."

"That doesn't mean I have to be at her beck and call," he insisted.

"Stanley." It was the wifely-warning voice.

The best defense was a good offense. "Darn it, Carol. Enough already. What do I look like, Santa Claus?"

"No, you look more like the Grinch." Oh, no. Her eyes were starting to glow red again.

"I already risked a heart attack shoveling their walk."

"And made a snowman. And you enjoyed it."

"No, I didn't," he lied. "It was cold. Those two are pests."

"They need a father figure," Carol insisted.

"Well, that's not me." For crying out loud. What did he know about being a father figure?

As usual, she read his mind. "You were doing a pretty good job this afternoon."

"Carol, stop. Please. Leave me alone."

"Fine!" she snapped and vanished in a huff.

Crap. Now she wouldn't come back.

"Wait!" he cried. "I didn't mean it. Come back."

She didn't. He blinked awake and once more caught a hint of the scent of peppermint.

"I'm going crazy," he muttered.

Either that or he was developing a hyperactive conscience. Neither theory appealed.

It was only three in the morning. He got up, used the bathroom and then went back to bed. He punched his pillow, wishing he hadn't said what he'd said to Carol.

But, come on, hadn't he done enough of the holly-jolly Christmas crap? He wasn't a people person. He wasn't Saint Stanley. She knew that, and she would just have to be okay with it.

From the look of things the next morning, she wasn't.

12

CAROL HAD HANDED STANLEY A LEMONADE WHEN he'd come in from edging the lawn and demanded to know what he'd been doing flirting with Mrs. Gimble's daughter.

What the heck? "I was just talking to her."

Mrs. Gimble's daughter stopped by to see her mother every once in a while. They'd known her for years. Known the whole family ever since they moved to the neighborhood. It was hardly flirting to talk with the woman.

"And laughing."

"So? She said something funny."

"What?" Carol demanded.

"I don't remember. Good grief, Carol. She said hi. What was I supposed to do, turn my back on her?"

Carol's answer to that question was succinct. "Yes."

"You're always telling me to be more social," he reminded her.

She scowled and marched off to the living room, plopped on the couch and picked up her copy of *Woman's Day*. She began turning pages like she wanted to rip them out. Like she wanted to rip the magazine in two.

He followed and sat in the nearest chair, waiting for her to say something more. She would. He knew she would.

"There's social, and there's *social*."

"I don't understand."

"Oh, Stanley, don't be so dense," she said irritably. "She's divorced, you know."

"So? A lot of people are divorced."

"And she's looking for a replacement for her husband."

"So?"

"So, she was flirting with you. And you were flirting right back!"

"Oh, come on. We've known her since she was a kid. And I'm married."

"That doesn't mean anything. Ellie Jordan's husband left her for one of his college students, and one of Amy's friends had her husband stolen by her best friend. Who was divorced."

"Oh, come on, Carol, the woman doesn't want me," he said, amused. And a little flattered that she was jealous, he had to admit.

But it was silly for her to be. Even in his prime he'd never been more than average-looking. And now he supposed he was turning into an average middle-aged man. His hair was starting to thin, and his pectoral muscles were melting and sliding down, above the beginnings of a pot belly.

"You're still a nice-looking man."

He gave a snort.

"Are you getting a midlife crisis or something?"

"What?" He felt like he'd landed on an alien planet and was trying to learn the language and customs of its people.

"You've been being very secretive. Off running errands for hours. It doesn't take hours to go to the hardware store."

"It can," Stanley insisted.

Her eyes narrowed. "Is there someone else?"

"No," he said, shocked. "I'm working on something with John. And why would I want another woman when I've got you?"

Her gaze slid away from him. "I'm not exactly a size ten anymore."

So what if she wasn't quite as slender as she'd once been? "You still look great in a pair of shorts."

"And I'm getting gray hairs."

A few silver strands? So what? He loved those silver strands slipping into her hair.

"They make your hair sparkle in the sunlight."

He moved and sat beside her and put an arm around her shoulder. "If anyone needs to be worried about getting replaced, it's me."

"Women never trade their husbands in for younger men," she said irritably.

"Now, that was a sexist remark," he teased.

"It's true."

"Well, I'm not planning on trading you in, and I hope you're not planning on ditching me. I did see that new fifth-grade teacher eyeing you at the end-of-year party at Geri's house."

She made a face. "I'm being serious."

"So am I."

"I'm getting old," she said miserably.

"We both are. It happens. But we're still here, and we're both healthy, and we've got a lot of years left. And you really do look great."

She heaved a sigh. "I know I'm being completely illogical, but I'm having a hard time. I'll be fifty next month. Fifty, Stanley. I'll be half a century old. That's when things start to fall apart. You begin to become invisible. People throw over-the-hill parties for you and buy black balloons like it's some kind of joke, but I don't think it's funny."

"Well, then, I'll make sure nobody gives you black balloons."

She wasn't listening. "I'm getting wrinkles."

"Those are laugh lines."

"No, they're wrinkles," she insisted. She bit her lip and fell silent.

There was more going on here, something deeper. He knew it.

"What else is bothering you?"

She looked down at her hands. Sighed. "I think I'm done having periods."

Now he really had no idea what to say.

"Do you know it's been almost a year since my last period?"

He hadn't exactly been keeping track. Still, he remembered that first missed period. For a while there she'd thought that maybe, just maybe, a miracle had happened and she'd actually gotten pregnant. A home pregnancy test said no to that. Then the night sweats and mood swings had come, an unpleasant explanation of what was really happening.

She hadn't enjoyed the last few months at all. But lately, it seemed like those uncomfortable times were subsiding.

"What does that mean?" he asked. "Are you done with the night sweats?"

Her lower lip wobbled. "It means I'm done, period."

"Okay," he said slowly. Done, period. Done with periods. He wasn't getting it.

"It means I can never ever get pregnant."

They hadn't gotten pregnant the whole time they'd been married. This was nothing new.

But it was obviously something that still troubled her. He felt at a loss, unsure of what to say to make her feel better.

Tears began to slip down her cheeks. "I know it's silly, but at the back of my mind, I always had this fantasy that…" She took a shaky breath. "This is all so final. I just…have to adjust, that's all. I'm sorry. I'm not even being rational."

He snugged her up against him. "How you feel is how you feel. I'm sorry…" Now he was finding it hard to speak. "Aw, Carol, we should have tried harder to adopt. We shouldn't have given up. If I'd realized."

She shook her head. "No, don't you feel guilty because I'm having a meltdown. I'm the one who said no more. I know I need to be grateful that I'm still here. I love my job. I love my students."

"And they love you," he said. Many had come back to see her as young adults, telling her what college they'd chosen to attend or about that business they were starting. "You've guided a lot of kids over the years."

She nodded and took a swipe at her wet cheeks. "I know," she whispered.

"And you've got the nieces. They love you like crazy."

She nodded.

"So do I."

But it hadn't been enough. What they'd had hadn't been enough.

What came out next he really didn't want to ask because he was afraid of the answer he'd get. He asked, anyway. "Are you sorry you married me?"

She looked at him in surprise. "No, of course not."

"You could have married anyone." Maybe even married someone with kids. Her whole life could have been different.

She put a hand to his cheek. "I didn't want *anyone*. I wanted you. And we have been happy."

He felt so relieved to hear her say it that he almost cried. "We'll keep being happy," he said.

He'd work harder at doing things she wanted to do. He'd even take those ballroom-dancing classes she'd been wanting to take. Anything.

"I know. I'm being squirrelly," she said. "But I keep thinking what a turning point this is. It's like seeing a door closing."

"Which means another one's opening," he said. "Fifty's not that old, babe. You're still beautiful and healthy, and you love your work. You matter to all those kids you teach. You matter to your family. You matter to me."

She sniffed. Smiled at him. "Stanley, you are a dear."

"Age is just a number. You've got lots more years ahead of you, and you're going to be better with each one."

"Well, I don't know about that."

"I do. The best is yet to come."

"You're right," she said with a determined nod.

And now he had to make sure what he predicted happened. He already had a great surprise for her, but he knew he had to do more, so he did a very un-Stanley thing. He organized a birthday party, inviting the families and neighbors and friends.

"No black balloons or over-the-hill jokes," he instructed everyone.

"Stanley, no way can you do this all by yourself," Amy informed him. "I'm taking care of the food."

He hadn't been pleased with her assessment of his competence, but deep down he suspected she was right. Still, this was his idea, his wife, darn it all. So he asserted himself.

"I'm getting the cake," he insisted. "And I'm grilling burgers."

"Fine," she said, allowing him that much. "I'll take care of everything else."

He ordered a big sheet cake from the local bakery with lots of red frosting roses. He also ordered a dozen red roses from the local florist to be delivered on the big day.

He'd half wanted to surprise Carol, but he suspected she'd want to look her best, so he gave her a few days' notice. "We got company coming Saturday afternoon."

"We do?"

He could see the excitement in her eyes. Carol loved having company. He felt downright proud of himself.

"Yep. Thought you'd want to get your nails done or something."

"I just might," she said. "And what's this party for?" she asked coyly.

"Someone special I know is having a birthday," he answered.

"You're throwing me a party? Oh, Stanley, that is so sweet of you," she said and hugged him.

"I thought so," he said, making a joke of it.

But his stress levels had been no joke. Calling people and organizing the whole thing, figuring out how much hamburger and how many buns to buy, borrowing card tables and chairs to set up in the back yard—he was glad he didn't have to do this on a regular basis.

The big day came, and the hordes of guests arrived, bringing gifts and cards, crowding onto the patio and spilling into the back yard, guzzling beer and soda pop by the gallon. Kids running everywhere. Chaos. Stanley was glad to be tied to the barbecue where he didn't have to be in the middle of it all.

Carol was in her element, beaming as if he'd given her diamonds. Well, wait until she saw the surprise.

After dinner, as she was cutting her birthday cake, he slipped inside the house and called his buddy John. "Okay, bring it over."

"Be there in ten," said John.

Stanley wandered back out onto the patio. He checked his watch a couple of times and finally, with a couple of minutes to go, sauntered up to where Carol stood talking with one of her former students, her sister positioned next to her.

"Time for presents," he said. "Come on out to the front."

"Presents, yes, good idea," said Amy. "Don't you want her to open them here?"

"Not this one," he said and took his wife's hand.

"Hey, everyone, presents," Amy called and started a parade of people following them through the house and out onto the front porch.

Right on cue, John drove up to the curb in a refurbished shiny red 1969 Ford Mustang sporting a big red bow on its hood.

Carol gasped and covered her mouth with both hands. It was exactly the reaction Stanley had been hoping for, and his heart swelled.

"Happy birthday, babe," he said as all their friends oohed and aahed and clapped.

"Oh, Stanley," she breathed.

"Now you know where I was and what I was up to."

"You are amazing," she said and hugged him.

"Let's go check it out," he said.

"Oh, yes!"

She ran down the front walk, him strolling after, feeling very proud of himself.

She walked around the hood, and John got out and handed her the keys.

"John, it looks great."

"Yeah, well, you should have seen it when we first got it," he said.

Stanley joined them. "Take it for a spin."

She took the keys, hopped in and started it up. He hadn't seen her this happy in a long time.

The windows were already down to take advantage of

the July sunshine. Stanley leaned his arms on the window of the driver's side. He motioned to the radio.

"Turn the radio on," he suggested.

She did and her favorite rock-and-roll classics station started playing the Eagles' "Life in the Fast Lane."

"Yow!" she squealed and cranked it up. "Get in, Stanley."

He ran around to the passenger side, hopped in, and she laid rubber, and they roared off with everyone clapping and waving.

"Stanley, this is the best present ever," she said, her voice filled with joy. "I feel like I'm eighteen again."

"You look as good as you did at eighteen," he said.

She smiled and shook her head. "You are so full of it, but you know what? I don't care. You're right. Fifty is just a number."

"It's a good number. We're gonna have another fifty together."

And he was determined to make sure they were good ones. "I still have some vacation time left," he said. "We should take a road trip before school starts again. See how this baby handles on the open road."

"That's a great idea."

"Where do you want to go?"

"Let's drive down the coast." She pointed a finger at him. "I'm doing all the driving."

"Absolutely," he said. "It's your car."

They took their drive down the coast that summer, visiting beach towns along the way. They had such a good time they took another road trip the next year. And the year after. And for her fifty-fifth birthday they took a cruise in the Caribbean and swam in turquoise-blue waters. They both had so much fun they signed up for another cruise, this time to Alaska, where they gaped at the glaciers in Glacier Bay and took a dogsled ride in Juneau and rode an old-fashioned train to Skagway. All memorable experiences made doubly memorable because he was with her.

They'd even taken a trip or two with friends.

Then for her sixtieth he'd thrown another party.

"You're becoming a real party animal," Amy had teased him.

Not really. He did it because Carol loved to entertain, and he loved Carol. If it weren't for her he'd probably be a hermit.

13

STANLEY HAD AWAKENED SHIVERING, WITH DOG licking his face. All the bedcovers were pulled off him and dangling from the opposite side of the bed. For a moment there he thought *Carol*. But no, he'd done that himself, tossing and turning after she left in a huff.

He'd pulled on his bathrobe and went downstairs, turned up the thermostat and walked through the living room on the way to the kitchen just like he did every morning. And everything had looked the same, just like it did every morning.

Until this. There was his sudoku-puzzle book lying facedown on the floor, half-torn.

"Dog, you won't get any treats if you pull stunts like this," he scolded as he picked it up.

The dog looked at him as if to say *What are you talking about?*

He held it for her to see. "Half-torn."

She whimpered and started for the kitchen and the back door.

"I should make you stay out there," he muttered as he followed her.

But he didn't have the heart to get mean with her. She hadn't chewed up so much as a sock since she'd been with him. Everyone was allowed one mistake. Still, it was very strange.

He felt cold as he opened the door for the dog, but that was only a bit of wintry gust coming in. That was not Carol. And ghosts couldn't move things. Could they?

He needed coffee. He let the dog out, then flipped on the kitchen light.

Except it didn't come on. The coffee maker was dead, too. A tree must have fallen in the night and caused a power outage. No underground lines in the town of Fairwood, so that stuff happened a lot.

He went back to the living room and peered out the window. The house across the street had sold but was still standing vacant, so no lights were on there. The millennial workaholics were already gone. They never left any lights on in their place, so you couldn't judge by them. But farther down across the street he could see lights coming from inside the house. Same was true for Mrs. Gimble. Even Lexie Bell had power.

He went out to the garage. Once there he found no problem in the fuse box. Something was amiss.

Or, rather, someone. "Okay, Carol," he said as he went

back into the house. "Not funny. Put the power back on. I want my coffee."

Nothing happened.

"This isn't fair. Come on."

Nothing happened.

"Okay, okay. I'll take her tree-shopping."

Suddenly everything began to hum back to life.

"But only if she asks."

The power flickered.

"I said I'd do it!" he shouted.

The power clicked back on and the microwave began to flash the time. It was stuck at 3:00 a.m., probably about the time he'd been having his nocturnal squabble with Carol.

Coincidence, he told himself. It was all coincidence.

He reset that and the clock on the stove and made himself some coffee, using what was left in the coffee canister, which had run mysteriously low. He let the dog back in and fed her, then got dressed in his favorite old sweats and Seahawks sweatshirt and sat down at the computer to check his stocks and read the morning's news. Dog settled at his feet.

All nice and cozy. Why did some people think you needed a whole troop of extras in your life, anyway? Besides, what was the point? He could barely stand his own company these days. Why would anyone else want to hang out with him?

"We're fine just the two of us, aren't we?" he said to Dog.

Just the two of them. The minute the words were out of his mouth he knew he was going to keep the animal. Unless, of course, her owners called to claim her. No one had called yet. At this point, it was likely no one would.

SHEILA ROBERTS 171

"Their loss, right, girl?" he said to the dog, and she agreed by nudging his hand.

He got the hint and petted her. "I should name you. You want a name?"

Name her Bonnie.

Okay, he could do that.

He didn't see Carol that night, but she did whisper in his ear, "You're making progress, Manly Stanley."

Bah, humbug.

By Monday morning the snow was beginning to melt, and the snowman in the Bell yard was slumping and falling apart. The streets and sidewalks were still slushy, though.

Stanley was backing his car out of the driveway to make an early-morning run to the store to replenish his supply of coffee when he spotted the pests next door walking down the street. Lexie Bell had tied a plastic bag around her injured foot. How long did she think that was going to last? That walking boot would tear the plastic to shreds in no time.

Accepting the inevitable, he let down his window and called them over. "You don't want to walk to school in this," he said.

She smiled as she got in. "You're right. We don't. I should sign Brock up to take the school bus, I guess, but that seems silly when we live so close."

"Not close enough for walking in this mess," Stanley said.

"My friend Shannon offered to give us a ride, but I think the streets are still kind of slippery, and I didn't want to make her drive any farther than she had to."

"Better to stay off the streets if you don't know how to

handle snow and ice," Stanley said. But slush was no problem, especially for someone like him, who'd lived in the area all his life.

"You know how, don't you, Grandpa?" piped the kid.

"You bet your a—" *Ass* was probably not a good word to use in front of a little boy. Although he'd hear worse on TV. Still, Stanley censored himself. "Boots," he finished. Then, just to be clever, refined it to "You bet your snow boots."

"I'm wearing my snow boots," Brock said.

"So I see."

"It's awfully kind of you to come to our rescue. I'm sure this will be completely gone tomorrow, and then I'll get a ride with my friend," said Lexie Bell.

Stanley nodded. That suited him fine.

"How's the ankle doing?" he asked.

"I guess I need to resign myself to the fact that it's not going to heal overnight. The physical therapist thought the doctor might let me graduate to a brace before Christmas, which would really be great. I sure hope I can get back to physical therapy soon."

"Make an appointment for today. I'll take you."

Oh, no. Had that really just come out of his mouth? He wished he could stick out his tongue and pull the words right back like a frog catching flies. Carol was probably dancing for joy on some cloud.

"I couldn't ask you to drive me."

"You didn't. I volunteered." Like a dope. "Give 'em a call."

She did. "They can take me at four."

"I'll pick you up at school at quarter till," he said.

"That will be great," she said.

For her, not for him. What a pain in the butt.

But at three forty-five there he was, sitting outside the school, waiting when she and her kid emerged together.

"I can't tell you how much I appreciate this," she gushed. "You're being so kind to us."

He could hardly say the reason for that was because his wife's ghost was making him, so he said nothing.

"It's really great to start getting to know our neighbors."

Who said that was what they were doing?

"It's hard starting over in a new place," she confided.

Stanley didn't look her way, but he could still see her out of the corner of his eye. She was smiling at him like they were now best friends. He hunched into his coat like a turtle pulling into its shell.

"I guess that's the one thing I miss about California," she continued. "All my old friends. And my family. My aunt and uncle are there, and my cousins. And my mom." She sighed. "It's been two years since Daddy died, and she hasn't been doing very well without him. Of course, I get that. It hasn't been easy not having my father around. But still."

Why was this woman telling him all this? He wasn't a counselor. He kept his mouth shut, determined not to encourage any more sharing. It didn't work. She shared, anyway.

"I tried to get her to come up this summer and see the new house, but she made up some lame excuse."

"Maybe she wants to be alone," Stanley said, forgetting that he wasn't going to say anything. Well, the woman needed someone to defend her. "Not everyone wants to be around people." He sure didn't.

Yet here he was, chauffeuring Lexie Bell and her boy all over town.

"But I'm not people. I'm her daughter," Lexie protested. "Oh, well. She's coming up for Christmas. We'll make sure she has a wonderful time. Won't we, Brockie?"

"Yep," agreed the kid.

Whether the woman wanted it or not. Stanley thought of his sister-in-law. Any day she'd be calling him, determined to make sure he had a wonderful time at Christmas. Heaven help him.

He parked in front of Healing Help Physical Therapy, kept the engine running so he could keep the heat on, and prepared to wait in the SUV and read some more of the Lee Child thriller, which he'd brought along.

But then the kid said, "Come on, Grandpa," when he saw Stanley not moving to get out.

Stanley frowned. Surely his presence wasn't needed in there.

It won't hurt you to go in.

"Fine," he muttered, and turned off the ignition, grabbed the book, and got out.

"I hate you to have to wait," Lexie said as they entered.

This required a polite response. "It's okay. I brought a book," he said, and held up the paperback.

Stanley soon realized he wouldn't be doing much reading. Instead of following his mom around, the kid opted to wait in a chair next to Stanley while she got put through her paces on the equipment. Even though the boy had a spelling assignment, which he should have been fine doing on his own, he was determined to bring Stanley into the experience.

"Lap," he said out loud, as he filled in blanks in one column to match the words in another. *"Nap. Cat.* Do you have a cat, Grandpa?"

"No, I already have a dog," Stanley said. Yep, that confirmed it. Bonnie was staying.

"Dog," Brock said and giggled.

"Her name's Bonnie now."

"Bonnie." The boy considered this. "That's a nice name."

"That's what my wife thinks—er, would think."

Brock looked at him. "What's her name?"

"Carol."

"Grandma Carol," the kid said, trying it out.

"She's gone." It still hurt to say it.

"Is she in heaven with my grandpa?" Brock asked.

"She should be." Stanley wished she'd hurry up and go there.

Except then he wouldn't see her again. Fresh sadness settled over him.

Their conversation was cut off by the appearance of a man leaving. He was Stanley's age and wore a jacket over a pair of jeans and old army boots. George Mathews from the bowling league. Stanley braced himself.

He smiled at the sight of Stanley. "Stan, haven't seen you in ages. What are you doing here?"

"Waiting for someone. Why are you here?"

George rubbed his shoulder. "Stinkin' rotator cuff. Hoping they can get me good as new in time for the spring league. When are you coming back?"

"I don't know." *Probably never.* "Kind of busy these days."

"Yeah? Who's this?"

"This is Brock," Stan said.

"Hello, there, Brock."

"My mommy's getting therapy," Brock told George. "Grandpa Stanley and me are waiting for her."

"Didn't know you had kids," George said to Stanley.

"Just friends," Stanley said. They weren't really friends, but he could hardly say *pests*.

"Grandpa and me made a snowman," Brock continued.

"Pretty cool," said George. Then, to Stanley, "Wish my grandkids were still at an age where they liked to do that. They're all in high school now, and all they want to do is look at their phones." He shook his head, then said, "Oh, well. What are you gonna do? Enjoy this while it lasts, my man. They grow up way too fast. And hurry up and get your butt back to the alley."

"Will do," Stanley lied, and George gave him a friendly salute and left.

Then it was back to spelling. Stanley half listened and idly watched as a therapist worked with Lexie. The guy looked to be about her age, and there seemed to be some friendly chatting going on. She was a pretty little thing so he was hardly surprised to see the guy showing some interest.

She seemed nice enough. What had happened with her and Brock's dad?

What did it matter? It was none of Stanley's business. The kid had fallen quiet. Stanley opened his book in the hopes of getting a chance to read some of it.

The silence didn't last. "My bonus word is *antlers*," Brock informed Stanley. "Reindeer have antlers. Reindeer pull Santa's sleigh."

Santa again, Stanley thought in disgust. He was spared

from any conversation about reindeer and Santa as Lexie was done and ready to leave.

Stanley was ready also. He'd go home, drink some eggnog, make himself some toast with peanut butter, read his book in peace and quiet.

So, why, when he was anxious to get home, he opened his big mouth and asked Lexie Bell if she needed to run any errands, he would never know.

"I could stand to get a few things at the grocery store," she said.

What the heck. He could stand to buy a few more cookies.

So they went to the grocery store. She purchased the kind of good things responsible parents bought: apples, lettuce, milk. He bought chocolate chip cookies and chips. Why not? Bonnie didn't need lettuce and neither did Stanley. Bonnie. He doubled back and purchased a box of dog biscuits.

"Thanks for being willing to detour," Lexie said as they left the store. "I was pretty well stocked up, but I don't like to run out of produce."

"Can't have that," he agreed. Hey, he managed a carrot once in a while.

Their route home took them by the tree lot.

"Trees!" cried Brock. "Can we get our Christmas tree now?"

"Oh, sweetie, not now," said his mom. Stanley could hear the embarrassment in her voice.

"But you promised," the kid said.

"I know. And we will."

"When?"

"When I get things worked out," she said.

"I want a tree," Brock whined.

"You getting a live tree?" Stanley asked. *Oh, yeah. Open the door wide to more errand-running.*

"I was planning on it. I'm sure my friend can take us later this week. Or I can get an Uber."

That again. This woman needed to learn the value of a dollar.

"Wait too long and all the good ones will be gone," Stanley said. Good grief. Just whip him with a string of Christmas lights and be done with it. He could feel her gaze on him. "May as well stop now. I've got rope in the back."

"Really?" She sounded so...grateful.

"Why not?" *Because I want to go home and relax, that's why not.* Well, it was too late now. He could almost see Carol smiling.

"That would be fabulous."

"Yay!" hooted Brock from his seat in the back.

And so it was that Stanley Mann found himself walking through a forest of cut trees in Grandma's Memories Tree Lot, helping Lexie Bell and her son pick out the perfect tree for their new home, offering sage advice and tapping various candidates on the ground to see if any needles fell off. Boy, did that bring back memories.

14

OVER THE YEARS STANLEY AND CAROL HAD ALL kinds of trees: ones so tall he had to saw off several inches once they got them home in order to fit inside, cheap ones, pricey ones, flocked, and bare. Some they found at tree farms and cut themselves, most they picked up at tree lots. One year Carol wanted a Charlie Brown tree, and they found a perfect candidate when they were snowshoeing in the Cascades.

"That one is perfect!" she'd cried. "It's so scruffy and sad."

There was an understatement. "It's half-dead," he'd pointed out.

"Then, let's take it home and give it a purpose before it goes to tree heaven."

Both families had teased them about it. "This the best you could do?" joked his brother-in-law, Jimmy.

Carol had jumped to his defense. "It was exactly what I wanted. You know, you don't have to be perfect to be loved."

Thank God for that, Stanley had thought. With his hermit tendencies he was hardly the perfect man for Carol.

They finally switched to artificial trees. Less hassle, but it was never quite the same as getting a real one.

The first Christmas tree they ever bought was at a tree lot that turned out to be run by one of Carol's old boyfriends.

"Carol," he'd greeted her as they walked onto the lot. "Merry Christmas. How are ya?"

"I'm good, Dan."

"You look good," he said, sounding way too friendly for Stanley's taste.

She put an arm through Stanley's and moved him front and center. "This is my husband, Stanley."

Dan stuck out a mittened hand. "Nice to meet ya."

"Same here," Stanley lied as he took it.

Was this the jerk she'd told him about? Couldn't be. The guy wasn't as tall as Stanley, but judging from his shoulders and those tree-trunk thighs, he probably worked out. Stanley vowed to join the gym in the New Year.

"I heard you got married," Dan said. "You're a lucky dog," he told Stanley. "Half the guys in our class wanted to date her."

"You got to," she said, her voice light.

"Yeah, for about two seconds. You happy? I'm still single," he added with a grin.

Stanley frowned. Was that supposed to be funny?

"I'm ecstatic," she replied and hugged Stanley's arm.

"Well, darn. Guess I'll have to settle for selling you two a tree."

"That's what we're here for," she said.

"You got any fresh ones?" Stanley asked.

"They're all fresh," Dan the Tree Man replied, insulted.

Stanley walked up to one, grabbed it by the trunk and gave it the old needle test, banging it on the ground. A shower of needles fell.

"Hey, not so hard," protested Dan.

"Fresh, huh?" Stanley challenged.

The guy frowned at him. "Any tree's gonna lose needles if you treat it like it's a hammer."

Carol moved on to another. "Here's a pretty one. I bet it's fresh," she said, ever the diplomat.

Before Stanley could touch it Dan grabbed it and gave it a gentle tap. "See? Perfectly fresh."

"We'll take it," Carol said.

"I think we got took," Stanley muttered as he tied it on the roof of the GTO. "He could have at least given you a discount for old times' sake."

"Maybe he would have if you hadn't insulted him."

"I didn't insult him. I just tested to see if the needles would stay on. It's not fresh if they fall off. I don't care what he said."

"I think you were a little jealous."

"So you went out with him, huh?"

"Not for long, so there's no need to be jealous."

"I wasn't."

"Good. Because he's not half as cool as you. Or as...

manly. Manly Stanley," she finished with a grin. Then she sobered. "There's no one I'd rather be with than you."

"Sometimes I wonder why," he admitted.

"Well, for one thing, you're easy to talk to. You actually listen. And that's more than I can say for a lot of the guys I dated."

Stanley had never been one to talk about himself a lot. He preferred to listen, especially to Carol. He appreciated her wit and her positive take on life, always enjoyed hearing the stories about the shenanigans of her pupils at school. She was so easy to be with.

Obviously, other men still wanted to be with her.

"That Dan wasn't the jerk you told me about, was he?"

"No. Who knows where *he* is."

Her comment got him wondering. He looked at her suspiciously. "Wait a minute. You knew your old boyfriend had this tree lot?"

"Yeah. Amy told me."

Stanley frowned. The last thing he'd have chosen was to go see some old boyfriend of Carol's.

"He wasn't really a boyfriend," she explained. "More like a friend I went out with a couple of times."

Had the guy kissed her? It didn't matter, Stanley reminded himself. He was the one who'd gotten her, and he was the one who was kissing her now.

"It's nice to give old friends business," she said.

Stanley wasn't so sure he wanted to bring any old *friends* into their life.

He gave the rope a final tug. "If any needles fall off, we're not doing business with him next year."

She just giggled.

Now that they had a tree, they had to get ornaments. Together they picked out red and blue and gold balls at the hardware store to go with the ornaments Carol already had. Her collection had been acquired over the years, all of them from her grandmother.

"She gave me one every year, starting when I was a baby. They all mean something to me," Carol said as she hung up a pink one that said *Baby's First Christmas*. "I love having special mementos to mark the years."

He liked the idea of that and vowed right then to find something special for her, something to mark their first year of marriage.

They'd hung the lights, the chains of gold beads that her mother had passed on to her and all their new ornaments and were admiring their handiwork when she said, "I have one more."

She disappeared down the hall to their bedroom and came back with a little wrapped box that he hadn't seen anywhere.

"Where'd that come from?" he asked.

"Santa's elves. Open it."

He did and found a metal Hot Wheels ornament shaped like a GTO. It was even red like his car. "Wow," he said. "This is really cool." How he wished he'd thought ahead to do something for her!

"Your first memory," she said. "Where do you want to hang it?"

He picked a bough at the front of the tree, smack-dab in the middle. "Here, where I can see it every day and think about what a great wife I have. Not that I need a reminder," he hastily added.

"I should hope not," she teased.

The tree made their small apartment festive. So did the cookies she baked—sugar cookies cut out to look like trees, frosted with green frosting and decorated with colored sprinkles.

"My family makes these every year," she said when he came into the kitchen to sample one.

"My mom makes these. I love 'em," he said and took a bite. "Oh, man, that's good."

"Lucky for you I like to bake," she said.

"I'd be a lucky man to have you even if you didn't like to bake," he said and slipped an arm around her waist.

Christmas Eve was spent visiting with both the families, opening presents, eating two Christmas dinners and attending a candlelight service, but Christmas morning was theirs alone. Stanley made his one specialty—pancakes from a mix—and they enjoyed them with hot chocolate.

After breakfast they opened the presents they'd bought each other. She'd given him a tool set, and he'd given her some Jean Naté perfume and a book by Elizabeth Peters, one of her favorite authors.

But the gift she was most thrilled with was the one he'd made over in his dad's garage. It was a flat wooden heart. In the middle was carved *Stanley + Carol. Forever.*

"Oh, Stanley, I love it," she cried, throwing her arms around him.

"Where are you going to hang it?" he asked, echoing her question to him when she'd given him his ornament.

"Right here, next to yours." She hung it and turned to him. "I do so love you."

"I love you more," he said and kissed her.

He never got tired of kissing her. Or making love to her. Being together, loving each other, that was the best Christmas present of all.

After, as they lay there, her in his arms, he kissed her hair and asked, "Happy?"

"Very," she said. "This is a perfect Christmas."

"Yes, it is," he agreed and thought how it didn't matter what was under the tree. He was holding the best present a man could have in his arms.

15

THE FIVE-FOOT TREE LEXIE FINALLY SETTLED ON was nice and full and had good color. Stanley, assisted by one of "Grandma's" helpers, loaded it onto the SUV and tied it down.

"Can we decorate it tonight?" Brock asked.

"May we decorate," his mother corrected.

"May we?"

"It's getting a little late," said Lexie. "Let's do that tomorrow. Mr. Mann, would you like to come over and help us and stay for dinner?"

A home-cooked meal? It had been a long time since he'd had one of those.

But it came at a price. Going next door for dinner was probably not a smart idea. He'd only get further enmeshed with these two.

"I make great lasagna," she said. "And I'd like to thank you for how much you've helped us."

Oh, man. Lasagna.

"My cheese bread kills."

"Kills?"

"It's really good," she explained.

Cheese bread, too. Really good cheese bread.

"And Caesar salad." She pointed to the grocery bag at her feet. "I've got romaine."

Who cared about the salad?

Cheese bread and lasagna, though. *Say yes*, urged Stanley's taste buds.

"Okay," he said.

"Great. Does six o'clock work for you?"

"Sure." What the heck, he had to eat. And it was only dinner.

And tree-decorating. He shouldn't have listened to his taste buds.

"More progress," whispered Carol later as he was drifting off to sleep.

That wasn't what Stanley called it. He called it *entanglement*. More involvement, more having to pretend he was happy with the season, happy with his life. He should have declined the offer.

"Lasagna, Stanley. Your favorite."

There was that. But this wasn't just about lasagna. This came with social strings attached. Ugh. Cheese in a mousetrap, that was what Lexie Bell had offered him.

Carol's final words were "Don't show up empty-handed," and that popped his eyes back open.

He had no idea what he should bring to his neighbor.

Not cookies, since she baked. Not wine, since she had a kid and he wanted to bring something they could all enjoy. What, then?

This social stuff had been Carol's department, not his. Not only did he have no idea what to bring but he also had no idea what he and this young woman would find to talk about stuck together for a whole evening. She was Twitter and Facebook, and he was TV and puzzle books.

What was the point? He didn't need to go over to Lexie Bell's house. He could buy lasagna in the freezer section of the grocery store.

That settled it. He was staying home. Happy with his decision, he finally fell asleep.

His dreams that night put him in a winter wonderland, but Stanley found himself poorly dressed for the weather in nothing but his tighty-whities and a Santa hat, standing at the top of a mountain. Next thing he knew he was sledding down the slope on some kind of racecourse, out of control. In and out of trees he careened, branches whapping him as he went. Somewhere along the way he lost his Santa hat, and that seemed to bother him even more than the fact that the rest of his clothes were missing.

He shot out of the trees into the open where crowds of cheering people stood on both sides of the course, rooting for him. There was his bowling team. Unlike him, they were dressed.

"Go, Hambone!" yelled George Mathews.

Standing next to George was Frosty the Snowman. "You're gonna freeze your ass off," he called.

Stanley already was. He rushed past a herd of senior church ladies, waving, each one holding a casserole dish.

And there was the Grinch. "You're headed for disaster if you go next door, fool," he called.

Carol elbowed her way through the crowd, pushing the Grinch aside. "Don't listen to him, Stanley!"

A finish line just like the ones in the Winter Olympics loomed ahead, and there, along with a crowd of elves, stood Lexie Bell and her kid, both dressed in red parkas and ski pants and snow boots, both wearing reindeer antlers.

"You can do it, Mr. Mann," Lexie called. "Strong finish!"

Except at the last minute he fell off his sled and someone else swooshed by him. Santa Claus.

"Ho, ho, ho! I won," he taunted. "You are such a loser, Mann."

Suddenly a crowd of little demons wearing Santa hats and bearing huge pitchforks were surrounding him. "You're a loser," heckled one. "Nobody really wants to see you." He gave Stanley a poke with his pitchfork, making Stanley yelp.

"It's too late for you," jeered another. "You're never gonna change." He, too, gave Stanley a poke.

"Cut that out!" Stanley protested.

"Why?" joked the first one. "Your attitude sucks, and you deserve it."

A third demon stuck his pitchfork right through Stanley's hind end, turning him into a kebab. He lifted Stanley in the air like some sort of prize, and they began to parade off through a snowy forest.

"Where are you taking me?" Stanley cried. Amazingly, he wasn't in pain, but the humiliation sure stung.

"Someplace you'll feel right at home," said one.

They marched him to the edge of a precipice. A huge fire raged below them.

"Toss him in," cried one of the demons, and the one who had him skewered hurled his pitchfork like a javelin, sending Stanley the Kebab flying, screeching all the way.

He awoke just before he hit the flames and bolted upright in bed, startling Bonnie awake. It felt like the Little Drummer Boy was banging around in his chest. He swallowed and drew the dog up against him.

"What the heck did that mean?" he asked.

The dog had no answer. She flattened out against him and went back to sleep.

He knew, though. *Bad dreams. Not playing fair. Dirty pool, Carol.*

He lay back down, pulled the covers up to his ears, rolled onto his side and muttered, "I'm not going."

Then came the whisper. "Don't be a chicken."

His eyes popped open, and he searched the darkness for some hint of Carol. He sniffed. No peppermint in the air. Still, she was there somewhere, he knew it, waiting for him to shut his eyes again so she could catch him unawares.

Okay, if she wanted to play that game he'd wait her out. He'd stay awake. He turned on the bedside lamp, picked up his book and began to read. After ten minutes his eyelids drooped.

No, no, stay awake. He blinked and stared at the page. The printing was beginning to blur. His eyelids felt like they had ten-pound weights attached to them.

The weights won and he was back on that snowy mountain, all by himself. It was such a vast expanse of nothing, and looking around, he felt small and scared. Abandoned.

Carol didn't show herself, but he could sense her next to him. "You don't have to feel like this, Stanley. You can have people in your life."

Next thing he knew he was walking toward a lodge nestled among snow-covered fir trees. The lights inside beckoned him, and as he drew closer he could hear laughter and Christmas music. He smiled and picked up his pace. Once on the porch, he opened the door and was greeted with a blur of light that seemed to reach out and warm him.

He never saw beyond the light, but he woke up feeling... He wasn't sure what he felt. A little nervous, half-wishing he could stick with his decision to back out of that dinner invitation. But he knew he wasn't going to, because mixed in there somewhere was a feeling of anticipation, a thought that yes, homemade lasagna and cheese bread that *killed* would probably top what he found in the supermarket freezer. And the girl would need help putting up that tree.

Someone needing him. The thought made him feel rather...mellow.

After breakfast he went to the grocery store and bought a two-liter bottle of root beer. And vanilla ice cream. It seemed like the right kind of thing to take over to Lexie Bell and her kid. After all, who didn't like root-beer floats?

The subject of romance (or the lack thereof) was one that two single women were bound to discuss frequently. As Shannon drove Lexie and Brock to school, she informed Lexie that she was meeting up with someone she'd found on her new favorite online-dating site.

"So, he's got potential?" Lexie asked.

"I hope so. From the looks of him I think he could have.

You really should check out that site. The people on it are more…real."

"I'll see how it works for you," Lexie said.

So far she hadn't had much luck when it came to online dating. She'd taken a couple of stabs at it, had a few dates, but nothing had worked out.

Of course, she wanted to find someone fabulous to share her days. And nights. Someone who would love both her and her son. But she was beginning to think that in order to change her luck she'd need to find a four-leaf clover, wear a rabbit's foot every day, hang a lucky horseshoe over her front door (where did you even find a horseshoe if you were a city girl?), capture a ladybug and get it to show her the end of the rainbow. Maybe then romantic good fortune would smile on her.

"I'll find out if he has a friend," Shannon promised.

Lexie wasn't holding her breath.

Oh, well. She had her son, she had her house, she had her teaching job, and she was making friends and had found a great bestie in Shannon. Her life was good. And if it never got better than that, so what? *Good* was a lot more than many people had.

And so what if she didn't have a date that night? So what if the company coming for dinner at her house was old enough to be her father? At least she had company coming.

She started baking the lasagna at five, and by five thirty she and Brock had set the table and she'd made the cheese mixture for her cheese bread. When their neighbor knocked on the door at six, the lasagna was out of the oven and the house smelled like an Italian restaurant.

He handed over a large bottle of root beer and a freezer

bag with a carton of ice cream in it. "Thought you guys might like root-beer floats."

"That will be perfect for dessert," Lexie said.

Especially since they'd eaten all the cookies she'd baked. When she'd extended her dinner invite she hadn't thought ahead to dessert. Even when she was cooking she hadn't. Probably because she'd been thinking about horseshoes and four-leaf clovers.

"May I take your coat?" she offered. Except her hands were full. "Umm. Just a minute. Brockie, you can put the pop and the ice cream on the kitchen counter. Okay?"

"Okay," he said eagerly and started to dash toward the kitchen with the goodies she'd handed him.

"Walk," she called. "You don't want to shake the pop."

Brock slowed down, and Lexie took Mr. Mann's coat and hung it in the hall closet. "Come on in and sit down," she said, motioning to the living-room couch.

He nodded, came in and perched on the edge of her couch, set his hands on his thighs as if bracing to get right back up again. Looked around. He didn't say anything more, and she wondered if he'd used up all his words for the day just telling her about the root beer and ice cream.

"Dinner's almost ready," she told him and went to the kitchen. "I hope you're hungry," she called.

"I am."

She'd hoped he'd add something more, but that was the end of that conversation. There was really nothing cozy about being with Mr. Mann, and yet Lexie still felt drawn to him. She was sure that, deep down, like her, he was looking for connection.

Brock took over the conversational duties. He went in the

living room and perched on the couch next to Mr. Mann. "Do you like cheese bread?"

"I do."

"I do, too," Brock said. "I helped set the table."

"It's good that you help your mom," said Mr. Mann.

Their tight-lipped neighbor was voluntarily saying something. Brock obviously knew how to draw him out.

She set out the food and summoned her son and her guest to the table. She watched Mr. Mann out of the corner of her eye once he dug into the lasagna. Would they possibly connect over pasta and tomato sauce?

He chewed, nodded his approval like some judge on a cooking-competition show and swallowed. "Really good."

It had been a long time since she'd had a compliment. She grinned and actually wiggled a little in her seat, like a child who'd just been patted on the head.

"My wife used to make lasagna," he volunteered. "This is almost as good as hers."

Thinking this was a possible invitation to offer condolences, Lexie said, "I am sorry about your wife."

He'd almost been smiling. The smile factory shut down, and he took another bite.

"How long has she been gone?"

"Three years."

"I don't think my mom is ever going to get over losing my dad," Lexie said. Not that she had herself, but she was doing better than her mother.

"You don't," Mr. Mann said simply.

"I worry about her," Lexie confessed. "She doesn't do any of the things she used to or see her old friends."

"Maybe she doesn't want to."

"But she needs a life."

"Yeah, well, everybody's got the right to live their life the way they want."

He said this with so much authority it was almost enough to convince Lexie that he was right. Almost, but not quite.

"When you have other people in your life, you have to keep living," she insisted.

"Maybe not everyone needs other people in their life," he said.

"Everyone needs someone," Lexie insisted. "It's why we're all put here together in the first place."

Mr. Mann merely shrugged and bit off a chunk of cheese bread.

"My grandma's coming to visit for Christmas," Brock announced.

Mr. Mann grunted. "Figures. That's when everyone's supposed to get happy, whether they want to or not."

After finishing his sentence, he did a very odd thing. He shot a quick look up toward the ceiling. What on earth was he looking for up there?

"Isn't Christmas a perfect time to get happy? To think about the good things in your life?" Lexie countered. "Christmas carols, presents, peace on earth, goodwill toward men?" He wasn't on board yet. "Christmas cookies?" she prompted.

He almost smiled at that. "Yeah, cookies are all right."

"I like cookies," Brock said.

"We need to make more, don't we, Brockie?" Lexie said. "Do you have a favorite cookie, Mr. Mann?"

His expression turned wistful. "My wife always made

these chocolate cookies with a chocolate-peppermint frosting. They were the best."

"If you find that recipe, I'd love to try them," Lexie said.

He shrugged. "I don't know where she kept it." And he obviously didn't want to go looking.

She didn't press him. Instead, she moved them on to new conversational territory. "I'm glad you brought makings for root-beer floats, since I didn't have anything for dessert tonight."

"We used to have those sometimes when I was a kid growing up. When I was a teenager we got 'em a lot. Hamburger joints, the best place to take a date when you didn't have a lot of money." A smile tugged at the corner of his lips. "I used to take my wife to a place in Ballard called Zesto's."

"You fell in love over root-beer floats," Lexie finished for him, hoping to hear more.

"Long before that. I fell in love with her the first time I saw her."

"That is so sweet."

"She was sweet." He lost his smile and stuffed the last of his cheese bread in his mouth.

"I bet she was." And now it was time to move on before the poor man shut down. "Brockie, help me clear the table, and we'll get those floats made."

Mr. Mann dutifully ate his, but his smile stayed in hiding.

After dinner it was time to set up the tree, and she was glad of his help, both in bringing it in and getting it straight in the tree stand. Brock stood by, anxiously awaiting the moment when they could begin to decorate.

He was thrilled when Mr. Mann handed him a section

of the lights and said, "Okay now, your mom will tell us where she wants these. Hold it up high."

So the two of them did Lexie's bidding, moving the string up and down and around the branches as she directed.

"And now the ornaments," she said, and Brock dived for the box she'd brought in from the garage.

"I guess it's kind of silly to put up a real tree and bother with lights when you can get artificial ones with the lights already on them," she said as she handed a glass snowflake ornament to Mr. Mann. "And it's a lot cheaper in the long run." She was still in sticker shock over how much she'd spent at the tree lot.

"Easier, too," he said.

"But I thought it would be fun to pick out a real tree."

"It is," he agreed. He half smiled. "I remember a couple times going with the wife to a tree farm and cutting our own tree. Your boy would love that."

"Next year we'll probably buy an artificial one that we can bring out every year," she said. "That will be more budget-friendly. And being on a beginning-teacher's salary, budgeting is important."

"You'll make more as time goes on."

And Brock would keep growing and needing more. Not that she'd ever begrudge him a penny. She watched as her son looked for the perfect spot to hang the little *Baby's First Christmas* ornament her parents had given her five years earlier, and her heart tightened. Her boy was the best thing that had ever happened to her.

She grabbed her phone and took a picture, capturing his look of concentration as he hooked it on a bough. Then caught him again as he beamed at her.

At last the tree was done, a happy one sporting colored bulbs and balls, homemade works of art, and the Patience Brewster ornaments Lexie had collected over the years.

"Our tree looks pretty," Brock said, taking it all in. He turned to Mr. Mann for confirmation. "Doesn't it?"

Their guest nodded approvingly. "Yeah, it does. Don't forget to keep water in the tree stand," he cautioned Lexie. "You're putting it up pretty early, and you don't want it to dry out and become a fire hazard."

"I won't forget," she promised.

Then he was out of things to say. He cleared his throat. "Guess I'll get on home. Bonnie needs to go out."

"Bonnie? Oh, your dog. You named her."

He shrugged. "Nobody's called to claim her. Looks like she's mine. Well," he finished briskly, "thanks for the dinner."

"Would you like to take some home with you?" she offered.

"No, that's okay."

"It'll only take a minute to wrap a piece."

He was already moving toward the door. "No, thanks."

She followed him and pulled his coat out of the closet, and he shrugged into it, gave a brisk nod, said good-night and then was gone.

But he'd come over and helped them decorate their tree. They'd actually had a conversation. Maybe, just maybe, she had made a friend in the neighborhood.

She got Brock in the tub and went back downstairs to put away the ornament boxes, humming as she went.

Her cell phone rang. *Mom*, she thought with a smile.

"Mom, we've just had the nicest time with our neighbor," she said. "He came over for dinner and helped us put up our tree."

"That was nice of him," Mom said.

"He's a little gruff and hard to get to know, but I think he's got a good heart. You'll get to meet him when you come up for Christmas."

"About Christmas," Mom began, and Lexie's smile fell away.

Oh, no. Don't say it.

16

"DARLING, I'M NOT FEELING UP TO MAKING THE trip," Mom said.

An avalanche of disappointment dumped itself onto Lexie. It wasn't as if she was asking Mom to fly to Europe or drive twelve hours. It was barely over a three-hour flight from LAX to Sea-Tac airport, and then only another forty minutes to Fairwood, and Lexie had planned to pick her mother up at the airport. All Mom had to do was sit on a plane and then sit in the car.

"Oh, Mom. You promised."

"I know. I'll come up in the summer."

"It won't be the same. I wanted you to share Christmas with us in the new house. Brockie will be so disappointed."

Her mother's only response to this bit of guilting was to sigh.

It took a lot to make Lexie mad, but she could feel her temper rising. There was mourning, and there was self-ishness.

But you could hardly call your mother selfish, especially when she wasn't normally. Not that anything had been normal since Daddy died.

Lexie tried begging. "Mom, please. We've both been looking forward to you coming up." The Christmas before had been hard. She'd been hoping they could make some new, happy memories this time around.

"I know you have, but I'm not feeling well."

Not feeling well. What did that mean? "As in you're sick?"

"I'm not myself. I'll make it up to you next year. I really will. I'm just not in a holiday mood."

Lexie took a deep breath. It was what it was, and there would be no changing her mother's mind about coming up. *Okay, adapt or die.*

"All right. I understand. We'll come spend Christmas with you."

They could have their own little Christmas early, enjoy their tree, then go to Mom's. The tickets would cost a small fortune, but that was what plastic was for.

"No, I don't want you to do that."

"Mom, you can't be alone on Christmas," Lexie protested.

"Your Aunt Rose will look in on me."

Look in on her. Like she was an invalid. Maybe in a way she was. She and Daddy had been a unit. They'd done everything together. One would take a breath, and the other would exhale. It was a wonder her mother was breathing now.

"You enjoy your holiday in your new house," Mom said. "We can Zoom on Christmas Day."

"That's hardly the same as having you here," Lexie grumbled.

Then she frowned. Maybe she was the one who was being selfish.

She gave up. "All right, we'll Zoom."

"I've disappointed you, haven't I?" Mom's voice was filled with regret.

"Yeah, you have," Lexie said. She wanted to add *I lost him, too. Snap out of it, Mom. You've still got people who need you.* She bit down on her lip. Hard.

"I'm so sorry. You know I love you more than anything."
Except Daddy and his memory.
Lexie sighed. "I love you, too."

And because she did, she was going to have to be patient and let Mom work out her issues. Heaven knew she'd had issues of her own when her relationship with the husband fail ended. It took time to get over losing someone, and when you'd been with that someone as long as her mother had been with her father, the time increased exponentially.

Once Lexie had her baby who needed her, she'd had to close the door on the past and move forward. It was the same when her father died. She still missed him, but she had to keep living, and she was determined to make life good for her son. She wished her mom could share that determination.

Maybe Mom thought Lexie didn't need her. If she did,

she was wrong. A girl always needed her mother, no matter what age she was or where she was in life.

And Brock needed his grandma. Not that sleepwalking woman he'd come to know, but the energetic, involved woman she'd always been.

When Lexie was growing up Mom had dished out the fun like cookies: water-balloon fights in the summer and experiments in making Popsicles and ice cream; crazy Halloween parties where she'd don a sheet with holes to see out of, pretend to be a ghost and chase Lexie and her friends all over the house.

Then there was Christmas. Every year Lexie not only got treats in her Christmas stocking but there was always a letter from Santa, thanking her for minding her parents and telling her how proud they were of her. The Christmas stockings continued even when she was a teenager, and in addition to candy, teen-girl treasures such as nail polish, lip gloss and gift cards for token amounts started appearing. And always there was Santa's letter, encouraging Lexie to remember how loved she was and to always let her light shine. Daddy had always been the one to sneak outside Christmas Eve night and jingle some bells and call "Ho, ho, ho!" but Mom had been the architect of those letters. Lexie had saved every one of them.

After Brock was born Mom had started the tradition with him, too, but then Daddy died and so did the tradition of the letters from Santa. So did the laughter. Lexie had hoped this would be the year her mother took even a tiny step toward living her life again. It wasn't going to happen.

She said goodbye with as little rancor as possible and then went to fish Brock out of the tub. She put on a smile for her son and pretended everything was fine. She listened to his prayers and felt like she had an anvil on her chest when he asked God to bless Grandma. He was looking forward to his grandmother coming up for Christmas. It was not going to be fun breaking the news to him that she wasn't coming.

Lexie decided that news could be postponed. Who knew? Her mother could change her mind at the last minute. Or not.

Either way, she had to keep moving forward, and she'd make the holiday special for her son, no matter what.

She tucked Brock in, kissed him good-night, then went downstairs and made herself a mug of hot chocolate. Then she grabbed the TV remote and brought the Hallmark channel to life. At least there things turned out the way you wanted.

Stanley loved lasagna, but lasagna didn't love him anymore. By the time he got home, he had a three-alarm fire going in his gut. He popped a couple of antacids and washed them down with a glass of milk.

"I shoulda stayed home," he said to Bonnie, who had trailed him out to the kitchen in the hopes of getting a dog treat.

But she'd already had her treat for the day. "I'm not going to spoil you," he told her.

And yet there she was, looking up at him with those bright little eyes.

"Okay, one more, but that's it," he said.

He dug one out of the box. Made her sit for it, then handed it over. She snapped it up and downed it in only a couple of chomps. Kind of like he'd devoured that lasagna earlier. A home-cooked meal had been a real treat.

Speaking of home-cooked meals. He frowned when his phone rang and the caller ID told him it was his sister-in-law, Amy, again.

"She's a pest," he informed Bonnie. A much more irritating pest than his neighbors would ever be. He knew she wouldn't give up calling him, though, so he decided to take the call and be done with it. "Hello, Amy."

"Oh, my gosh, you actually answered your phone. I'm in shock," she said.

Her greeting didn't produce any warm fuzzies. Quite the opposite. The cold pricklies took over.

"What do you want?" As if he couldn't guess.

"To see you."

Not really. They'd always rubbed each other the wrong way. Amy was only calling him out of a misplaced sense of duty.

"I look the same," he said. A little heavier, but she didn't need to know that.

"Funny, funny," she said, not in the least amused. "I let you off the hook for Thanksgiving, but I'm not going to for Christmas. You need to come down for Christmas dinner."

No, he didn't. It would be a repeat of Thanksgiving, only substitute red velvet cake for pumpkin pie. He still didn't like turkey, and he wasn't so crazy about cake that he was willing to drive all the way to Gresham for it.

"You can spend the night, you know," she added as if reading his mind.

"I'll pass, but thanks for the offer." There. Nice and polite.

There was momentary silence on the other end of the call as Amy worked out her next plan of attack. Then, "You know Carol wouldn't want us to lose touch."

Stanley rubbed his forehead. Amy was probably right on that one. Except he'd only gone to all those gatherings to please Carol and to make sure she got her family fix.

"Yeah, well, maybe next year," he said. Maybe by next Christmas Amy would have forgotten him. He only heard from her on Thanksgiving and Christmas, and if he kept turning her down, eventually those calls would dry up.

"I don't know why I bother," she said in disgust.

"Me, either," he said. "It's okay by me if you don't."

That pissed her off, and she ended the call, leaving Stanley to listen to the dial tone. He smiled and went in search of his recliner and TV. Amy was probably envisioning him feeling all hurt and insulted that she'd ended the call without so much as a goodbye and good luck. Actually, he felt amused. Amy always was a drama queen. She was probably working herself into a lather now and putting on a good show for her husband. The thought made him chuckle.

Carol wasn't laughing when Stanley rolled over in bed and found her head on the pillow next to his. "That wasn't very nice."

Oh, no. Not having this discussion.

He rolled away, facing the window only to find her already on that side of the bed, bending over him. She was wearing a silky blue nightgown that matched her eyes. *Wow.*

"Is that new?" he asked.

"New in your dreams. Now, don't change the subject."

"Oh, come on, Carol. You know your sister is a pain in

the butt. The only reason she's bugging me to come visit is out of guilt. I'm not driving all the way to Gresham on Christmas Day. It's a long trek." And when you moved that far away you couldn't expect people to come visit.

"It is a distance," Carol admitted. "But she does care about you, Stanley."

He supposed, when it came right down to it, she did. He shouldn't have been so ungrateful.

But he still wasn't driving all that way for Christmas dinner.

"So what *are* you going to do?"

"I'll think of something."

"Maybe something with your neighbor," she suggested.

"Maybe," he said, not making any promises.

Carol smiled at him and bent over, close enough to kiss him. Maybe she was going to. To be able to kiss her one more time would be a taste of heaven.

"Lexie and Brock have taken quite a liking to you, Manly Stanley."

"Huh?" He pulled his thoughts back into the conversation with an effort.

She drifted away to the far end of the bedroom. "Did you have a good time tonight?"

"It was okay."

"Enjoyed the lasagna?"

"Almost as good as yours, babe. And the cheese bread was really good."

"It was kind of you to help set up their tree."

"Lexie could hardly haul it in with that boot of hers."

"And stay to decorate it."

"I was only being polite."

Carol grinned at him. "Oh. Was that it?"

"Yes."

"Admit it, Stanley. You enjoyed yourself."

"I guess. But I'm not making a habit of hanging out with those two."

Carol's expression became stern, and suddenly the bedroom felt cold. Stanley pulled the covers up to his chin.

"You've been making such progress. Don't disappoint me."

"I would never want to disappoint you," he said earnestly. He'd lived to make her happy.

"I know," she said. "And I know you're doing these things now to make me happy, but it's not about me, really."

"Of course it is. Who's haunting who?"

She giggled. "I am having fun. But this is about you, darling. I am going to make sure that you wind up with a good life."

"I'm fine," he insisted. He wasn't, and they both knew it. He'd never be fine without her.

"You're surviving. It's not the same as really living. You have to start participating in life."

"I am, already. What more do you want?" he demanded, irritated.

"I want you to start allowing yourself to enjoy being part of the human race." He opened his mouth to speak, but she held up a transparent hand. "I know you're not an extrovert, but you're not really a hermit, either. I'm not going to rest until you realize that there's a part of you that needs people, that wants people in your life. This is all a little bit like starting an exercise program. You're doing these things because you have to. I want to see you come to realize you

don't have to but that you like to. You've made a beginning. Don't drop the ball now."

"Oh, for crying out loud," he muttered.

"Good night, Stanley. Pleasant dreams," she said and
vanished in a cloud of sparkles.

Pleasant dreams. After that little speech, he'd probably have
nightmares. He got up, went downstairs to the kitchen and
took two more antacids.

17

SHANNON CAME OVER FOR DINNER AND A CRAFT-ing night after taking Lexie to her physical-therapy appointment on Monday. Lexie served up homemade veggie soup and used up the last of the French bread to make more cheese bread. She'd ordered online what they needed for their pine-cone centerpiece project, and the box of supplies had come that very afternoon.

Once Brock was in bed and it was just the two women, Lexie asked how Shannon's date with her latest possible match had gone. "Spill. I want deets."

Shannon squirted a dab of hot glue on the back of a pine cone. "He's really nice."

Nice. Where were the rave reviews? "And?" Lexie prompted.

"He likes to play tennis, so that's good, and he's a foodie."

"Sounds like you guys have got stuff in common."

"We do, but I don't know if he's a keeper."

"If he's really nice…"

"There's more to life than nice," Shannon said, concentrating on securing her pine cone to its base. "I want to feel some sizzle when I'm with someone."

"So he didn't kiss you?"

"He did, and it was okay."

Just okay: that wasn't okay. "No fire, huh?"

"Barely a spark. He wants to see me again, but I'm gonna cool things."

"You're not going to just ghost him, I hope," Lexie said.

"No. I'm gonna use the *f*-word."

"Men hate it when you only want to be friends."

"I know," Shannon said with a sigh. She picked up another pine cone and examined it. "But what can you do? I mean, he *would* make a great friend. But I want a great friend plus great sex. I want to end up with somebody who sets me on fire, who sets the whole bed on fire. Is that asking too much?"

"I don't think so," Lexie said.

Except maybe it was. Could a man be fun to be with, great in bed and undyingly loyal all at the same time? She wasn't sure. She heaved a sigh.

"Yeah, maybe I'm dreaming," Shannon said.

"There's nothing wrong with dreams," Lexie was quick to say.

Except she wasn't so sure they came true. Her big dream had turned into a nightmare. She'd found someone she thought was perfect and gave him her heart, and look what had happened.

"If you really believe that, how come you're not looking harder?" Shannon challenged.

"I guess I'm not as brave as I once was."

Having her little boy to love had gone a long way toward helping her heal, but there was still a fissure that could crack her poor heart in two if she entrusted it to someone only to get rejected again. She longed to have a wonderful man in her life, really wanted that happy ending, that one true love like her mother and grandmother had both found, but maybe there was no such thing anymore. Maybe nobody really cared about *happily ever afters*. Maybe there was only *happy* now. Maybe you had to think of love like it was chocolate. You enjoyed it while it lasted, and when it was gone, it was gone.

You could always go out and get more chocolate. How many times could you go out and find true love? And if it kept vanishing and you had to go looking time after time, was it really love?

She frowned at her half-finished wreath. "Why is love so complicated?"

"I don't know," Shannon said. "I asked my mom that once."

"What did she say?"

"She said 'Don't ask me.' Mom's been married twice, and it's not looking good for Number Three."

"Some people figure it out. My parents did. And I think our neighbor did. His wife's been gone three years, but I can tell he still misses her. He can hardly bring himself to talk about her."

Similar to her own mother. But at least Mr. Mann was getting out there and making an effort in his own stiff way.

"That's so sad. And so romantic all at the same time."

Stanley Mann, romantic. Lexie had trouble envisioning it. He could barely manage friendly.

Getting to know him was like befriending a feral animal. There was a lot of coaxing involved. But the coaxing was working. He was warming to her and Brock and each time he was with them he revealed a little more of himself. There was a lot of good hiding under that crusty exterior.

Inch by inch, Lexie Bell and her kid kept encroaching further into Stanley's life. First it was cookies, rides, tree-shopping, then it was tree decorating. Next the kid was asking if Bonnie could come over to his yard and play.

The dog needed something to do besides watch TV and supervise Stanley as he worked his sudoku puzzles, so he let her go. But then he found himself walking over to say it was time for Bonnie to come home. And standing on the front porch, yakking with Lexie Bell. Not about anything much—him asking if she was keeping her tree watered, if she needed anything from the store. Her talking about Brock, how he was liking school and starting to make friends. Oh, and his Winter Holiday program was coming up at school. Would Stanley like to go? Not really, but he'd wound up saying yes, anyway.

He wasn't sure, but right after he'd agreed he thought he heard his wife whisper, "Good for you, Stanley."

Good for somebody. Those two were sucking up his time faster than a new vacuum cleaner.

They weren't the only ones. It seemed that Mrs. Gimble was somehow starting to take up more of his time also. It all began with a conversation at her mailbox. Even though she had someone to deliver meals, she was itching to bake. Could he pick up some vanilla extract at the store? Why not? He had to go to the store, anyway. Next he got a call. She was out of her pain medicine, and the friend who usually picked it up for her was sick. Was he, by any chance, going by the drugstore? And, while he was out… She'd reserved a book at the library. Would he mind picking it up?

Yeah, he minded.

Okay, not that much. He had to go out sometimes, himself, so really, it wasn't that big of a deal to run errands for the old woman.

Or for Lexie. It seemed like every day she was wanting to bake something Christmassy: red velvet cupcakes for the teachers' lounge, gingerbread cookies for her class. Oh, but she needed gluten-free flour. If he was going to the store…

He always got a treat as a reward, so why not? Good grief. He was no better than his dog. Anything for a treat.

But who could blame him? It felt like forever since he'd enjoyed home-baked goods. Carol had been quite the baker. And a great cook. He sure missed her chicken pot pie.

Had she been whispering to Lexie Bell in her dreams? he wondered when Lexie invited him for dinner on Thursday after he'd dropped off white chocolate chips. "I'm making a chicken pot pie," she said as they wound up having yet another front-porch yakfest.

The very mention of his favorite dish made his mouth water. "You know how to make that?"

"My mom's recipe. Flakiest crust you'll ever eat," she added.

He had to eat, and Carol wanted him to get out more. He agreed to dinner.

"Do you like it?" Lexie asked when he sat at her dining table, wolfing it down.

He nodded, swallowed. "It's as good as what my wife used to make."

She smiled at that. "I'm glad to hear it. My mom taught me how to make pie crust. She always said the secret to good crust is not handling it a lot, but I watched a cook online who said the secret is really in chilling it."

He nodded. He didn't care what the secret was. All he was interested in was the end result.

"Well, it's good," he said.

"I added thyme."

"Like in the old Simon and Garfunkel song."

She looked questioningly at him.

"Parsley, sage, rosemary and thyme?" he prompted. "'Scarborough Fair'?"

She nodded and pretended to know what he was talking about.

"Never mind," he said.

"We have pudding for dessert," Brock volunteered, not wanting to be left out of the conversation. "I held the beaters."

"That's good. You'll be able to cook for yourself when you move out."

Brock looked as puzzled now as his mother had over the mention of the Simon and Garfunkel song.

"When you grow up and have a house of your own," Stanley explained.

"I'm going to live with Mommy all my life and take care of her," Brock said.

Stanley chuckled at that. "Yeah, I said that when I was your age, too. Then I grew up and met a girl."

Brock made a face. "Girls."

"Yeah, I said that, too," Stanley told him.

"I like Shatika Wilson," Brock confessed after a moment. "She has a turtle *and* a cat."

"A wealthy woman," Stanley observed.

"Can we have a cat?" Brock asked Lexie.

"May we have a cat?" she said. "And now you want a cat instead of a dog?"

"We have Bonnie. I don't need a dog anymore."

Lexie looked at Stanley as if to say *What can you do?*

Yeah, what could you do? The kid had adopted both him and his dog.

"How did your day go, Mr. Mann?" Lexie asked.

Still calling him Mr. Mann while her kid called him Grandpa Stanley. It seemed a little weird. "Call me Stanley," he said.

She looked pleased. "Stanley. How did your day go?"

"It was all right. Had to run an errand for Mrs. Gimble. You haven't met her yet."

"She waved at me once this fall when she was at her mailbox," Lexie said.

"She doesn't get out much," Stanley said.

"That's too bad."

He shrugged. "It happens when you get older." A lot of stuff happened when you got older. Aches and pains, hemorrhoids, wrinkles. Potbellies. He'd put some work into that, he thought, and half smiled.

Losing the love of your life. His smile vanished, and his throat suddenly felt tight.

He cleared it. "How was your physical therapy?" he asked. Her friend had taken over chauffeur duties, and that had been a relief. One less thing he had to do.

He could almost hear Carol mocking "Yes, because you are so busy."

"I have another doctor appointment for right before Christmas. I'm hoping I'll be able to get out of this boot and into a brace."

"If you need a ride."

"I'm sure Shannon can take me."

Yep, she didn't need him for that. Oddly, he felt a little... hmm, what? Rejected? Nah.

"Well, if she can't and you need someone," he told her. What was he saying?

"Thanks."

"You should have my phone number for just in case you, uh, have an emergency or something," he said.

She smiled at him as if he'd given her a bouquet of roses. "That's so nice of you."

He wished she'd quit saying stuff like that. It was embarrassing.

"Well, you never know when you might need something."

She happily put his number in her phone and then gave him hers, too. "Just so you have it," she said. "Not that I'd be any help in an emergency," she added, sticking out her booted foot as exhibit A.

"I may have a cookie emergency," he joked. She giggled, and it lifted the corners of his mouth.

"Now, how about we have our pudding?" she said.

"Yes!" Brock hooted.

So pudding it was. Chocolate, with freshly whipped cream, not the crap from a can. Someone had raised this girl right.

"Good," Stanley said in approval after the first bite. "Nice to see someone using real whipped cream."

"Oh, yes. Another thing my mom taught me," Lexie said.

She suddenly looked sad. What was that about?

None of his business, that was what.

After dinner Brock asked Stanley if he'd play Candy Land with him.

Stanley had played the classic board game as a kid, himself. "That game's been around forever," he said.

"No, it hasn't," Brock said. "We just bought it this summer."

"I mean the game itself." He turned to Lexie. "The woman who invented it had polio. She came up with it when she was in the hospital, made it up to entertain the kids who were in there."

"So can we... May we play?" Brock asked.

"Yeah, I guess I've got time for a game," Stanley said.

With a whoop, Brock ran to fetch the game from a cupboard.

"It's really nice of you to stay and play with him," Lexie said.

Stanley shrugged like it was no big deal.

"I never knew the history of that game," Lexie continued as she began to clear the table. "That is so inspiring."

"She was a teacher, just like you."

"Except I'll probably never do anything big like that."

"You never know. You're still young. You got lots of time. Anyway, you're already doing something big. You're teaching kids. And you're raising one."

She sighed. "It seems like such an overwhelming job sometimes. I wish I wasn't doing it alone."

"So why are you?" None of his business.

Lexie concentrated on rinsing off a plate and loading it in the dishwasher. "I think I might have mentioned that things didn't work out with Brock's dad," she said, lowering her voice. She cast a look to where the boy was rummaging through a pile of games and card decks. "We finally had enough money for our wedding in Hawaii when he, uh, found someone else."

"What about the kid?"

Why was he asking this stuff? It was as if he was channeling Carol.

She lowered her gaze and bit on her lip. Her words came out as a whisper. "He didn't want to be a father."

Stanley had no patience for men who committed to a woman and then bailed. Even worse to bail on his child.

"Sounds like a shit to me," he said.

Carol would have come up with something softer, more comforting, like *You poor girl. I'm so sorry that happened to you.* Stanley scratched the back of his neck, suddenly uncomfortable.

"What he did was shitty," Lexie said. "But it showed me that he wasn't the kind of man I wanted. Of course, before everything blew up I thought he was perfect. Pretty stupid."

"There's no such thing as perfect. There's only the one who's perfect for you." Gack. What was he now, Oprah?

"I wish I could find that person. I'm not sure I will. I'm beginning to think there aren't any good men out there."

What a bunch of baloney. "How hard are you looking?" Stanley asked.

Her only answer was a shrug.

The kid was back at the table now, game in hand. "I like this game," he informed Stanley. "Do you?"

"I did when I was your age. Haven't played it in a long time."

"I'll help you," Brock said.

And so, Stanley Mann, the guy who'd never had kids, found himself absorbed in saving King Kandy from the ravenous candy snake. It wasn't exactly sudoku, so why the heck was he grinning?

The kid wasn't grinning when he lost.

"Hey, now," Stanley chided. "No pouting."

This made the corners of Brock's mouth slide lower.

"Sometimes you lose. That's what makes you strong. And you don't always lose. Sometimes you win."

"That makes me happy," Brock said. "Can we play again?"

"Only if you promise not to pout if you lose."

The kid nodded eagerly.

He did win the second game. "I won!" he crowed.

"Yep. See? Sometimes you win, and sometimes you lose, but no matter what you always got to man up and be a good sport."

"Man up and be a good sport," Brock repeated with a nod.

"And now it's time for my little man to have a bath," Lexie said.

"But I want to play with Grandpa Stanley," Brock protested.

"A good man always minds his mom," Stanley said.

That was all it took. The boy raced for the stairs.

"You are so good with him," Lexie said.

Stanley shrugged. "Kids aren't my thing. That was my wife."

"They may not be your thing, but my boy sure likes you. Thank you for being so good to him. To both of us."

Okay, this was getting uncomfortable. "No problem. I better get going. Bonnie needs to go out."

She looked a little shocked by his abruptness. "Oh, sure. Of course."

"Thanks for dinner," he said and started for the door.

"You're welcome anytime," she said. Then added "Oh, wait." She hurried to the fridge and pulled out a plastic leftover container. "Take some of this home. Brock and I can never eat it all."

Well, why not? "Thanks."

It was nippy out, and it smelled like snow. If the weather did turn, maybe Lexie would need a ride to school in the morning. Or to her next physical-therapy appointment, since that friend of hers didn't drive in the snow.

The woman needed more than some old guy to drive her around, he thought as he walked across her lawn to his. She needed a young buck she could do things with, grow old with.

"What a good idea," Carol whispered in his ear.

"Hey, it was just a thought," he said.

And thoughts were not the same as doing things. No way was he going to interfere in Lexie's life and play matchmaker. That was chick stuff.

Cupid's a man.

Stanley frowned. He knew where tonight's encounter with his wife was going to go.

18

SURE ENOUGH, STANLEY WAS BARELY SETTLED IN his recliner, looking for a good cop show on TV, when the screen went wonky and flipped from a murder scene to a cutesy café all decked out for Christmas. This looked suspiciously like the kind of movies his wife loved to watch every holiday season. There was the requisite adorable waitress, serving a customer a piece of pie, and here through the door came the man who would wind up falling in love with her. Stanley knew how these TV movies went. He'd watched enough of them with Carol.

"Oh, no," he said and aimed the remote. Back to the murder scene. The detective was squatting next to the bloodied body. "It looks like—"

Before Stanley could learn what it looked like he was back to the café. "Love," said the adorable waitress's friend.

"Come on, Carol," he said, exasperated. "I got the message already."

The TV settled down, and the murder investigation began in earnest. Obviously, she'd gotten the message, too.

Okay, maybe not. Here she came again, in the middle of the night. This time she was perched on a little pink cloud, dressed in a short pink dress with lots of ruffles, and she held a bow and an arrow with a heart-shaped tip. Oh, boy. Just as he feared.

"Babe, you know I love you," he said. It was how he'd always prefaced a refusal to cooperate. "I always have, I always will."

"I know," she said and smiled at him.

That sweet smile. It could still make his heart do a backflip.

"We had a lot of happy years together, didn't we?"

"Yes, we did. Carol, I still miss you so much."

"I know, darling. But try to remember how happy we were, how blessed to have had a lifetime together."

It had been a good life.

"And now you have this lovely young woman who needs a father figure and a little boy who calls you Grandpa."

Stanley rubbed his chin. Only a few days ago he would have replied *The kid's a pest*, but he'd gotten used to having the boy around. And he had gotten a kick out of playing Candy Land with him. Playing a kids' board game, after all these years. Who'da thought it?

"I know you're coming to care about those two. Don't you think Lexie deserves to be as happy as we were?"

"Well, sure. But, come on, Carol, what do you expect me to do about it? I'm not in the matchmaking business.

224 A LITTLE CHRISTMAS SPIRIT

That's stuff women do. And Cupid's not a guy," he hurried to add. "He's a naked baby."

"Actually, in mythology he's a youth, the son of Mercury, the winged messenger of the gods, and Venus, the goddess of love."

"Whatever he is, I ain't him," Stanley said.

Uh-oh. Her eyes were starting to take on that creepy red glow again. And was she actually getting bigger?

He squeezed his own eyes shut. "Don't be doing that, Carol. Please."

"Stanley!"

He opened one eye and ventured a look. Yep, still scary-looking. He slammed his eyelid back down.

Her voice softened. "I'm not asking you to set up a date or anything. Just if you happen to see someone nice, mention Lexie. Now, how hard is that to do?"

"Just mention her, huh?"

"And see if he's interested. You don't even have to give out her phone number. In fact, you shouldn't because you never know."

"Oh, so I'm supposed to see somebody nice, hook him up with Lexie but not give him her phone number because he might not be nice."

She frowned. "Stanley, you are being difficult."

"No, I'm being smart. It's never a good idea to try and set people up. Remember that book-club friend of yours you tried to match up with my poor old buddy Mickey?"

"Well, how was I to know she had a drinking problem?"

"That's my point. You can't always know about people."

She sighed, and he ventured another look. Good, she was

back to the genial woman he knew and loved. No more fiery eyes, and she'd shrunk back down to size.

"All right, Manly Stanley. You know best."

"You bet I do," he said.

"And I know you want to see your new friend happy. She's benefiting so much from having you in her life. I'm proud of you, darling."

He'd always loved to hear her say that. It left him feeling all warm and gooey.

He smiled wistfully at her. "I wish I could hold you again."

"You are. In your heart." She blew him a kiss and was gone.

Yes, she would be in his heart for the rest of his days. But he sure missed being able to hold her in his arms.

Everyone needs someone to love.

It was the last thing he heard before he fell into a dreamless sleep.

And it was the first thing inside his head when he woke up in the morning. "Lexie's nice enough," he said to Bonnie as he dished up her dog food, "and I get what Carol's saying, but I don't know anybody the girl's age. What am I supposed to do, put an ad in the paper? She's young. She knows how to use the internet. She can find someone there."

But how did you really know about people you met on the those dating sites? Hard enough to find out about someone when you saw them in person. Hiding behind a computer screen, people could tell all kinds of lies about themselves.

"Not my problem," he explained to the dog.

Bonnie wagged her tail, a sure sign of agreement, and dug into her breakfast.

Yep, not his problem.

But then he found himself in the supermarket meat section, and there was Jayce Campbell, putting out packages of steak.

Nice-enough fella, and friendly. Always used to chat up Carol. The first time Stanley had come in the store after losing her, Jayce had asked about her. He hadn't gotten all sloppy sentimental on hearing she was gone; he'd shaken his head and said, "That sucks." Then he'd given Stanley a free steak and suggested he get a case of beer. "That's on me, too."

Stanley had never seen a ring on the guy's hand. He could almost feel Carol prodding him. The guy was okay—not bad-looking, either. Maybe Lexie would like him.

But Stanley was not in the matchmaking business.

"Hey, Mr. Mann," Jayce greeted him. "How's it goin'?"

"It's goin'," Stanley replied.

"Steak tonight?" Jayce asked.

"Yeah. Give me a good one."

"They're all good here. You know that," Jayce said with a grin as he handed over a nice rib eye.

"That'll work," Stanley said.

He could have sworn he felt a poke in the ribs.

Say something.

He'd imagined that.

Stanley!

Shit. What was he supposed to say? He didn't know how these millennials or Gen Xers or whatever this guy was thought. How was Stanley supposed to start a conversation about his love life?

He stalled. "Give me another one while you're at it."

"Sure," said Jayce and handed over a second package. "You having company or stocking up?"

"Stocking up." Okay, if there was a way to smoothly transition from talking about steak to women Stanley didn't know it. He took the blunt approach. "Got a woman in your life?" Maybe he should have been more general. Maybe the guy was into men.

"You know somebody?"

Stanley shrugged, keeping it casual. "Got a nice neighbor. She's new in town."

"Yeah? Is she quiche?"

Quiche. *Real Men Don't Eat Quiche.* Stanley remembered that expression. So, Jayce was asking…what?

"Is she hot?" Jayce clarified.

That term Stanley knew. "Yeah, she's pretty cute. She's looking to hook up. You interested?"

Jayce's eyes lit up like Stanley had just offered him a winning lotto ticket. "Sure. Why not? Got a number for her?"

Lexie wouldn't want him passing out her phone number like it was a party favor. "Tell you what. Give me yours, and I'll pass it on."

"Okay," Jayce said and did. "Tell her to call me if she's interested."

That had been simple enough. Stanley smiled as he made his way to the checkout stand. He'd done a favor for his neighbor and made Carol happy. All in a day's work.

Lexie was surprised when Mr. Mann stopped by her house Saturday morning. Lately he'd only been coming over to fetch Bonnie or drop off some grocery item she needed, so him popping over to visit felt about as natural as Scrooge dropping by with presents.

Brock had been right there the minute he heard their neighbor's voice. "I have a wiggly tooth," he informed Mr. Mann, then opened his mouth and demonstrated.

"You sure do," Mr. Mann agreed. "Want me to yank it out?"

Brock took a step back and shook his head violently. "Mommy says it will fall out all on its own. When it does I'll put it under my pillow for the tooth fairy."

"When I was your age and had a loose tooth, we tied a string around it, then hooked the other end to a doorknob and slammed the door," Mr. Mann said. "Came right out."

Brock's eyes got big, and he took another step back.

Okay, that was probably enough reminiscing about past tooth experiences. "Is there something we can do for you, Mr. Mann?"

"Stanley," he reminded her.

"Stanley," she said. That whole first name thing was going to take some getting used to. Her grandma had always told Lexie it was disrespectful to call her elders by their first names.

"Uh, no. I just, uh, happened to, uh, be talking to a guy at the grocery store and, uh, mentioned you."

"Mentioned me?" Where was he going with this?

"He works in the meat department. Nice guy, not married. I told him you were new in town." Stanley produced a slip of paper with a name and phone number on it. "He said to call him if you're interested."

So Stanley Mann was playing matchmaker. How sweet, Lexie thought, touched.

"That's awfully kind of you," she said and took it.

"Maybe you can meet for coffee or drinks or something."

"Maybe we can," she agreed. "Thanks."

He nodded, cleared his throat. "Well, uh, see you two later." Then he turned and went down the front-porch steps, looking like a man anxious to escape.

Lexie smiled as she shut the front door. A nice man. Wouldn't that be a change.

She did call later that day.

A sexy, low voice answered, making her body vibrate like a tuning fork, and she had an instant image of a cowboy on the cover of a romance novel. Was the rest of him as gorgeous as his voice?

"I'm Lexie Bell," she said. "My neighbor, Stanley Mann, told me about you."

Jayce Campbell gave a half chuckle. "He's a cool old dude. He said you're new in town."

"I am."

"That can be a pain in the ass. But hey, I can fill you in on everything you want to know."

"I'd like that."

"What are you doing tonight?"

"Tonight?" she repeated. Gosh, instant date.

"Sure. Why not? I'm in-between."

In between what? Well, women. Duh. All right, he was in-between and so was she, so why not?

"Okay," she said.

"I can pick you up."

The few first (and usually last) dates she'd had she'd chosen the place to meet and had arrived separately. She wasn't going to change that strategy, no matter who had recommended this man.

"I'll meet you," she said. "Where's a good place?"

"Smokey's. That place is lit."

"All right." Hopefully, Shannon could stay with Brock. "What time?"

"Seven?"

"Seven it is," she said. It would give her time to feed Brock before she left. "How will I recognize you?"

"I'm pretty tall. I'll be wearing jeans and a leather jacket. But don't worry, I'll spot you. I'll be looking for the best-looking woman in the place."

Flattery and he hadn't even seen her. She hoped he wouldn't be disappointed. She hoped *she* wouldn't be disappointed.

"All right. See you later," she said. And just like that she had a date.

She was grinning like she'd won a prize at the fair when she ended the call. Until she looked down and saw the stupid boot on her foot. Yeah, that was attractive. She should have told him she'd be the one in a walking boot.

Oh, well. There wasn't much she could do about the boot. She wouldn't be in it forever, and any man with a brain would understand that.

She called Shannon. "Any chance you can come over and hang out with Brockie for a couple of hours tonight? I have—wait for it—a date."

"A date? You met somebody? You used that dating app and didn't tell me?"

"I didn't. Actually, it's someone my next-door neighbor knows."

"The old guy set you up?" Shannon sounded disbelieving.

"He said he's nice. And he sounds nice."

"Here's hoping," Shannon said, although she sounded dubious.

That didn't stop Lexie from being excited. She fed Brock his dinner, then put on leggings and a long red tulip-edged sweater. It had a cute faux-fur trim and a scooped neckline. Sexy but not desperate. Perfect. She'd like to have worn some stylish boots with her outfit, but that wasn't an option so she settled for a black ballerina flat. The shoe didn't quite tie the sexy bow around her outfit, but oh, well.

Brock was playing with the vintage candles on the coffee table when she came downstairs. "You look pretty, Mommy," he told her.

"Thank you, sweetie." At least she passed a first grader's inspection.

"I wish I could go meet your new friend," Brock said.

"I'm going to see if he's someone you'll like," Lexie said. No way was she bringing around any man she hadn't checked out thoroughly. It would be a long time before Brock got to meet her new friend.

"This guy is going to fall crazy in love with you," Shannon predicted before Lexie left.

"Thanks for the vote of confidence." With her track record, Lexie would take all the votes she could get.

It was drizzling when Lexie's Uber pulled up in the graveled parking lot of Smokey's. It looked like a log cabin on steroids, with a big front porch. That was where the resemblance ended because the windows sported all manner of neon signs advertising different brands of beer. And dangling from the roofline was a neon cowgirl in a short skirt, holding a big glass, one booted foot kicking back and forth.

The minute Lexie got out of the car she heard country rock blaring out at her, and as she got closer to the door she could also hear loud conversation mixed with laughter. This was obviously the place to come for fun in Fairwood.

The inside was rough-hewn timber with pictures of mountain scenes and cowboys riding broncos hung on the walls, along with old Marlboro posters of cowboys smoking cigarettes. She could smell barbecue and grease.

Several couples already had taken over tables in the dining area, and the bar section was packed with singles—guys in jeans and T-shirts or casual shirts with the sleeves rolled up. Some of the women milling about wore jeans so tight Lexie wondered if they could even sit down. Others were in short, tight skirts and shimmering holiday-festive tops. Killer heels, stylish boots—totally on fleek, nothing like the ugly blue Frankenstein boot on Lexie's right foot. She suddenly didn't feel quite so sexy.

Speaking of sexy, here came a built-to-order guy in jeans, a gray T-shirt and a leather jacket—a real drool-maker with a perfect square chin, brown hair and eyes, and a mouth that she just knew would be capable of all kinds of amazing things. This couldn't be Jayce Campbell. She couldn't be that lucky.

He came up to her, smiled and asked, "Are you Lexie?"

Lucky Lexie. "I am," she said and wished she could hide her big, booted foot.

The Frankenstein boot didn't seem to bother Jayce. He

looked her up and down and the smile went from friendly to bedroom ready. "Yaas."

Her thoughts about him exactly. *Wow.*

One of her grandma's favorite sayings popped into her head. *If something looks too good to be true, it probably is.*

No, no, Lexie wasn't going to go there. It was important to give people a chance. Between Granny's pearls of wisdom and her own past disappointment, Lexie was already prone to giving up on finding her Mr. Forever. She was not going to do that with this guy even before the drinks arrived, for crying out loud.

The host led them across a peanut shell–covered floor—peanuts on the floor, what was with that?—and seated them at a booth where a red candle bowl tried to cast some light on the scarred wooden tabletop.

He took off his jacket, slouched against the wall and put a leg up along the bench, making himself at home. He idly pointed in the direction of her foot. "What happened to your foot?"

"Chip fracture," she said.

"Yow," he said and made a face. "How long are you stuck in that thing?"

"I hope to be out of it by Christmas."

"No dancing for you tonight, I guess," he said and she felt that she'd disappointed him.

"You like to dance?" she asked.

"Hey, good foreplay," he said with a wink.

No points in the suave department for Jayce Campbell. Lexie didn't smile back, but he failed to notice. He was focusing on their waitress, checking her out from boobs to butt.

She set down water for both of them and a red plastic bowl filled with peanuts in the shell, obviously the source of the mess on the floor. "Can I get you guys started with something to drink?"

"Hale's pale ale for me," he said and looked to Lexie. "What do you want?"

Someone with a little more class. Maybe she *should* give Shannon's dating app a try.

"White wine?" she asked the waitress hopefully. This didn't look like a white-wine kind of place.

"You got it," the woman said and left them.

Lexie took a peanut from the bowl and shelled it, searching for a conversation topic that might give them a fresh start on the right foot. "I like your sleeve," she said, nodding at the herd of longhorn steers stampeding up his arm.

She put the shell back in the plastic bowl. He took it out and tossed it on the floor. "Meat's my thing. So, you met very many people since you moved here?"

"A few."

"It's gotta be hard being new in town. Not that I ever had to move. I've lived here all my life. Went to Fairwood High. Lettered in baseball. My batting average was over three hundred."

Even though Lexie wasn't into baseball she assumed that was a big deal. "Did you play in college, too?"

"Didn't go. Too expensive. Just as well. I'm not a college kind of guy."

Lexie had been a college kind of girl. She'd loved taking classes, enjoyed all the social aspects. She'd especially enjoyed taking English lit and history classes.

"I wanted to get out and start earning money. Wound up working at the store, and that's fine with me."

Okay. Earning money was good.

"What do you do when you're not working?" she asked.

"Same as anybody else, I guess. I work on my car. I'm fixing up a Dodge Charger I found in some old guy's field a couple years ago. That thing is going to be dope when I'm finished." He gave her a grin. "Maybe I'll take you for a ride when I get it done."

She wasn't into cars any more than she was into baseball, but she knew he thought he was offering her a big treat, so she smiled politely and said, "Thanks."

"When I'm not doing that I like to game, like to watch TV."

"What do you watch?" She had a suspicion the Hallmark channel didn't make his top list.

"Cop stuff. *Game of Thrones*. Anything with some action. How about you?"

"I like mysteries, rom-coms. PBS always has something good on." Everybody liked PBS.

"Boring," he sneered.

Okay, it was now official. This date was going to end up in Nowhere Land.

Their drinks came, and they ordered barbecued ribs and steak fries. Ribs. Something in common. Oh, boy, what a stretch.

"So, nobody in your life right now?" he asked.

She shook her head.

"Maybe we can fix that."

No, *they* couldn't.

He talked some more about himself—his job, his favorite

sports team, the Christmas cookies his mom made every year. Then he actually got around to asking Lexie about herself. Did she bake? No hidden agenda there.

"I like to bake."

He flashed her that sexy grin again. Except now the sexy shine had worn off.

"Well, whaddya know? I like to eat," he said.

Oh, boy. How soon could she leave?

They finished their meal, and the waitress offered dessert.

"I'll pass," Lexie said.

"Guess we're done here," Jayce said to the waitress.

The bill came, and Lexie offered to pay half.

"Nah, it's on me," he said and whipped out his plastic.

Okay, he wasn't stingy. That was a good thing.

But it wasn't enough.

Lexie quickly took out her phone to request an Uber.

"Hey, I can drive you home," he offered once he realized what she was doing.

"No, that's okay. But thanks."

By the time the bill was paid her ride was five minutes away. It couldn't get there soon enough.

As they walked out the door, she started to make her escape, but he said, "I'll walk you to the car. Where is it?"

"Looks like it's over there."

At the dark end of the parking lot. Ugh. Was he going to want to kiss her? Of course he was, and the last thing she wanted was to waste time smearing lips with this tool. Funny how, when she'd first seen him, that had seemed like a great idea. Now, uh, no. And what if he got pushy? She mentally prepared to knee him in the groin.

"Next time I'll pick you up," he said as they started off the porch.

Not a chance. She quickened her pace, and clumped off the last step. "Thanks again for dinner."

"Whoa, what's your hurry?" He edged her against the wall and moved in close to her and slid a hand around her middle.

It might have been a turn-on if he hadn't already turned her off permanently. "The driver's waiting," she said crisply.

"He'll wait," Jayce said, edging closer. "How about a little taste to tide me over until next time?" His mouth went for her lips and his hand went for a boob.

Okay, enough of this. She dodged his mouth and gave him a shove. "No. I'm done here."

He stumbled back, half-laughing. "Oh, I get it. Next time we party. You can come to my place or I can come to yours. I'm easy."

But she wasn't. "No next time," she informed him.

He frowned. "I thought you wanted to hook up."

"What?"

"That's what the old man said. Sounded like you were thirsty, looking for some action."

"I'm not that thirsty," she said firmly.

He looked at her in total disgust. "Well, sooorry. Guess I got it wrong."

"Somebody sure got it wrong." And that somebody was going to get an earful.

19

SHANNON HAD JUST GOTTEN BROCK INTO BED when Lexie walked back in the house. "Hey, Cinderella, midnight's a long ways away," she greeted Lexie. "Was Prince Charming that big of a frog?"

"Afraid so. Nothing in common at all, and on top of that he was ready for a parking-lot sex party."

"Wow. Locked and loaded, huh?"

Lexie shook her head. "Stanley Mann apparently told him I was looking to *hook up*."

"So your neighbor is some kind of dirty old man pimp?"

"I don't think so, but he sure isn't a very good judge of character."

"Oh, I don't know. He's latched on to you, and I'd say that makes him a pretty good judge of character."

"Aww, thanks. Since you're here, how about some pop-

corn and Hallmark?" Lexie suggested. There was no point
in having the whole evening be a waste.

"Sounds good to me," Shannon said. "Let's find a Christmas movie. Even if we haven't met the perfect man in real
life, at least we can pretend they exist."

Lexie made popcorn and brought out the eggnog Stanley had picked up for her at the store, and they settled in
to watch a movie. She found herself actually feeling jealous as the perfect romance played out before her. The hero
wasn't full of himself, and the couple's first meet was sweet
and involved no mention of *good foreplay.*

It's fiction, she reminded herself. Real life was always
messier. And boy, was hers a mess. What *had* Stanley Mann
been thinking when he set her up with Mr. Meat Market?

She spotted her neighbor taking Bonnie for a walk the
next afternoon and called him over for a front-porch visit.
"Mr. Mann," she began.

"Stanley," he corrected.

She ignored the correction. "I met your friend from the
meat market." Her tone of voice was a dead giveaway that
her neighbor's good deed was not going to go unpunished.

He looked at her warily. "Yeah?"

"Yeah."

"You two didn't hit it off?" he guessed.

"No, we did not. What did you tell him about me?"

He picked up his dog as if for protection. "Nothing. I
told him you were new here and that you were nice."

"What else?" she prompted.

"Nothing. Like I said, that you were new here and you
were looking to hook up."

"You really told him that?"

"Well, yeah." Bonnie was starting to lick his face, and he put her back down, patting her head. An avoidance tactic if ever Lexie had seen one.

"Well, that's what he was ready to do," she said with a frown.

Stanley straightened and mirrored the frown. "So what's the problem?"

"I don't have sex the second I meet someone," she informed him. Had she just said that to a man old enough to be her father, a man she barely knew? She could feel her cheeks heating up.

Stanley's bushy eyebrows shot up toward his receding hairline. "Is that what he thought?"

"That's the impression you gave him."

Now he was nonplussed. "I don't understand."

Okay, what they had here was a generation gap, and Lexie had fallen right through it. "Mr. Mann—"

"Stanley," he corrected. He was starting to sound grumpy now.

"I don't know what *hooking up* meant in your day but in mine it means *sex*."

His eyes doubled in size, and his cheeks flushed pink.

He dropped his gaze and mumbled, "Well, uh, all you kids do that. Right? Maybe that's how he got confused."

All you kids? Now she was offended.

"Not all of us," she informed him. "I'm an adult and I have standards. I have a son to think of. I'm not going to fall in bed with somebody I have nothing in common with." Hmm. That didn't quite come out right.

He took a step backward as if fearing she might slap

him. "I thought he was an okay guy. My wife liked him. Thought I was doing you a favor."

It was the thought that counted, she reminded herself. And Jayce probably wasn't such a bad man when it came right down to it. It wasn't his fault that Stanley Mann had accidentally painted her out to be the thirstiest girl in Fairwood, so there was no point scolding Stanley.

"I appreciate the thought," she said, opting for magnanimity. Still, the words came out as stiff and cold as an icicle.

"I'll have a talk with him," Stanley said, now looking ready to flay the meat man.

Lexie sighed and shook her head. "Never mind. It was just a miscommunication."

Stanley looked relieved. Then embarrassed all over again. He nodded. "Okay, well, uh, that's good," he said. Then he turned and fled down her steps and down the front walk.

Lexie felt bad as she watched him go. Poor Stanley had simply been trying to do a good deed, and she'd verbally smacked him. She could see that wall he'd had around him when they first met going right back up.

Stanley did go to the store first thing Monday, ready to punch Jayce's lights out, only to discover that the kid felt the same way toward him.

"Jeez, Mr. Mann. You set me up with an iceberg."

"I set you up with a nice girl," Stanley protested. What was wrong with this kid? Didn't he know a great woman when he saw one?

"I don't want a nice girl. I wanna have a good time."

Jayce was looking at Stanley like he was clueless. Maybe

he was. Or maybe this young fool didn't know a good thing when he saw it.

"You're just lucky I don't clobber you," Stanley said. "And I will if you ever come around her," he muttered as he wheeled his cart off. Without so much as a package of hamburger in it.

"That's why you don't mess around in people's lives," he grumbled that night, turning his back on Carol, who was hovering by the bed. She'd at least had the good sense to abandon the Cupid getup.

"You tried," she said. "It's not your fault you had a little miscommunication."

"Little?" He pulled the covers up over his ears.

He could still hear Carol, though. "I think it was sweet of you to try."

"Well, I'm done with that stuff."

"Everything we do in life doesn't turn out perfect, you know that."

He acknowledged her observation with a grunt.

"But other things do, so it all balances out."

He wasn't going to acknowledge the truth of that. It would only lead to her thinking up more things for him to do. He kept quiet.

"Good night, darling. Pleasant dreams," she whispered.

He didn't have to turn over to know she was gone. He felt her absence. Just as he'd felt it the moment he lost her.

He did have pleasant dreams, though. He dreamed they were in the Cascade Mountains, walking hand in hand on the bank of the Wenatchee River. He was carrying a wicker picnic basket in his other hand. The sun was out, the birds were singing, Carol was smiling at him.

"Life can be a beautiful thing," she said. "Every minute of it."

He set down the picnic basket and drew her to him. "I like this minute," he said and kissed her.

"Oh, yes," she said happily. She pointed to a flat, grassy spot. "Let's have our picnic right here."

Carol magically produced a blanket and laid it out, and they sat down to enjoy their feast. The picnic basket was full of everything Stanley liked: ham sandwiches, deviled eggs, home-baked cookies and a thermos of hard lemonade.

"Tomorrow let's go to that antique store I saw in Cle Elum and see what nostalgic goodies we can find," she said.

"You mean junk," he said, and she laughed at him.

"No, I mean treasures," she said.

"You're the only treasure I need," he told her.

"And you're mine. I love you, Stanley."

He awoke the next morning, smiling and content. Until reality rushed in and reminded him that he wasn't picnicking in the mountains, and his wife was dead. There were no more tomorrows left for them.

Meanwhile, today, here was his dog licking his face.

"You need to go out, don'tcha?" he said to her, and she gave him a yip and a tail wag.

He pulled on his bathrobe, went downstairs and let her out, then got his coffee going. Today he was going to stay in the house all day and do nothing. With nobody and for nobody. Especially the pest next door.

Once Bonnie was inside he filled her dish with food, and she fell on it as if it were her last meal. When she was finished she came and sat next to him as he ate his morning cereal, leaning against his leg. He reached down and

A LITTLE CHRISTMAS SPIRIT

scratched behind her ears. She thanked him by licking his hand.

Somebody still appreciated him. He didn't need to go looking for more *somebody*s to add to his life and more things to keep him running in all directions. He had plenty to do.

He finished his breakfast, brushed his teeth, changed a light bulb in the living-room lamp, took out the garbage. Worked a sudoku puzzle. Yep, he had plenty to do.

Later that afternoon he took Bonnie for a walk, and they just happened to pass Lexie Bell's house. He knew she was home from school because both her living-room and kitchen lights were on. She hadn't needed him to pick her up. If it had snowed would she have called him? What was she doing in there? Baking? What did he care if she was?

Back in the house, he gave Bonnie a treat and fixed a treat for himself, a mug of instant hot chocolate and some packaged chocolate chip cookies. "So what if they're not home-baked? They're cookies, right?" he said to Bonnie.

She didn't appear to have an opinion one way or another. She merely looked at him, hoping for another dog treat.

"I think these cookies and what I'm giving you have something in common," he told her. "They're both as hard as hockey pucks."

There was more to life than cookies. And homemade lasagna. And cheese bread that *killed*.

And enjoying them with someone. For a moment he could almost see Carol at the stove, an apron tied over her sweatshirt and jeans, pulling a pot pie from the oven. They'd eat at the kitchen table, talking about how their day had gone, then move into the living room to watch

TV. Sometimes they'd stay at the table and play a game of gin rummy.

He never ate dinner at the table anymore.

He was about to read a little before watching the evening news when his phone rang. It was Lexie Bell. He wasn't going to answer it. He'd had enough drama. Let her call someone else with her latest...whatever.

After several rings the phone quieted, and Stanley opened his book.

He'd barely started reading when the phone began to ring again. Nope, not answering.

But this time he did abandon his book to check his voice mail when whoever was calling gave up on him answering.

A little boy's voice said, "Grandpa Stanley, my Winter Holiday program is tomorrow night at seven o'clock. You are coming, right? I'm gonna be a snowflake."

Oh, boy. He looked down at Bonnie, who was studying him, awaiting his decision.

"He can be a snowflake without me," Stanley said. And that was that.

Until Carol rang in on the matter. She came for a visit around midnight, dressed like Mrs. Claus, with a white wig complete with a bun on her head and old-fashioned wire-rimmed glasses. She wore a high-collared blouse that looked like it belonged in a museum and a red skirt and red-and-white-striped apron complete with ruffles.

He recognized the getup immediately. It was one she used to wear on the last day of school before winter break. She always sent the kids home with candy canes and a Christmas card, each one with a special greeting written especially for the child.

"I'd forgotten about that outfit," he said to her.

"It's still in the red bin in the guest-room closet," she said. "Maybe you can find someone who will appreciate it. Another teacher, perhaps."

He knew exactly where she was going with this but refused to follow. "Maybe," he said, not committing to anything.

"You are going to go to the school program, aren't you?"

"I've gone to more than my fair share of those over the years," he reminded her. It was one of the obligations of being married to a teacher.

"Yes, but someone has invited you specifically to this one. You don't want to disappoint Brock."

"The kid won't know if I'm there or not," Stanley said.

"Children always know."

Stanley pulled his pillow over his head.

Of course, a small thing like a pillow didn't stop her. Her voice came through loud and clear. "Go, darling. Make the effort. You'll be glad you did."

He would not. He didn't say it, though. Instead, he clamped his lips tightly shut. The last thing he wanted was to argue with her.

"Pleasant dreams," she whispered and left.

He did dream, but it wasn't pleasant. He found himself floating over the grade-school auditorium. Adults were milling around, kids racing here and there, wearing elf hats and reindeer antlers.

Everyone was laughing and whooping it up except for one little boy, sitting in a dark corner of the stage. He was wearing white pants and a white sweatshirt topped with some kind of giant plastic blue-trimmed snowflake that had a hole for his face. The face wasn't smiling. In fact it was crying.

"Grandpa Stanley didn't come," the kid wailed.

Stanley woke up with his bushy eyebrows pulled together and his mouth drawn down at the corners. School programs. Bah, humbug.

But the next night found him walking into the school gym along with about a million parents and their noisy offspring. There were rows and rows of metal chairs and, beyond them at the far end of the gym, a stage had been set up. On it was a backdrop of wooden trees painted to look snow-covered. They didn't look very well constructed to Stanley. Whoever had been in charge of props could have used some help.

A boy dressed in a suit with a little red bow tie went racing past him and managed to tromp on his foot in the process, making the corn on his middle toe very unhappy. A small band consisting of some of the older kids was stationed in front of the stage, and they were playing an off-key rendition of "Deck the Halls." Stanley was no musician, but he knew bad when he heard it. His ears joined the protest along with his throbbing toe. *Why are we here?*

Good question. All this happy exuberance—it was the emotional equivalent of having to get dressed up in a suit and wear a necktie. Uncomfortable and suffocating. Where was the exit?

Don't you dare.

He knew that voice. He decided he didn't dare. If he ducked out he'd hear about it come bedtime. He found a seat on the end of one of the rows of metal chairs a ways back from the front, sat down and braced himself for the torture that lay ahead.

He'd barely gotten seated when a middle-aged woman wearing a black parka over red pants and enough perfume to burn every hair in Stanley's nose laid a bejeweled hand on his shoulder and pointed to the seats next to him.

"Are those taken?" she asked. She had a sonic-boom voice that bounced down to Stanley and slapped him in the ears.

She wouldn't believe him if he said *Yes, by the Invisible Man and his wife*. He had no choice but to say "No."

"Wonderful," she enthused. "Come on, Gerald," she said to the man behind her, a tank wrapped in jeans and a fur-lined parka with a head the size of a giant pumpkin.

Stanley himself wasn't exactly svelte, but this man made him look downright emaciated.

Before Stanley could stand up to give her room the woman started sidestepping her way to her chair. In the process she managed to tread on Stanley's other foot, making him wince. He was still trying to get up and out of the way when the tank barreled through, and he got the foot with the corn. Stanley's eyes crossed, and he sucked in air.

"Sorry," the man mumbled as he sat down, his shoulder butting right up against Stanley's.

"No problem," Stanley said, making the extreme effort to be polite and hoping Carol was still around and watching. This was too cozy for comfort. He gave his chair a little scoot sideways to buy them both some breathing room. It didn't help all that much. He gave it another scoot. Scooting wasn't really helping. The best solution would be to move.

The woman struck up a conversation before he could,

leaning across her husband and saying, "We came to see our granddaughter. She's one of the Sugar Plum Fairies. She's taking ballet lessons."

Stanley nodded.

"Who are you here to see?" the woman asked.

Stanley could have said *the neighbor kid*, but instead, to his surprise, out popped, "My grandson." Well, he was Grandpa Stanley, wasn't he?

"These programs are such fun, and the children are so sweet."

Stanley thought of the urchin who'd tromped on his foot and said nothing. The rows were filling up now, and the place was buzzing with excitement as if they were all at the 5th Avenue Theatre in Seattle, waiting for the curtain to go up on a musical.

"Kind of hot in here, isn't it?" said the man next to Stanley and proceeded to struggle out of his coat. He only got Stanley in the ribs once.

Okay, time to move. Stanley saw a seat on the end in the row in front to his left. A pretty, slender woman was in the seat next to it. She probably wouldn't elbow him in the ribs or tread on his foot.

He had just stood up when a good-looking man seated himself next to the woman and kissed her. Okay, so much for that seat.

Stanley looked farther afield. Good grief. The place was now a sea of parents and grandparents. Only a couple of seats available, all smack-dab in the middle of a row. How many feet would he trample getting to one? He gave up the idea, covered his aborted move with a stretch and sat back down.

And just in time. Here was the principal of the school, taking the mike, tapping on it and asking, "Is this on?"

The thing let out a squeal, and people yelped and covered their ears. Yes, it was on.

Take two worked better, and she was able to welcome everyone to their holiday celebration. "The children have worked very hard, and I know you'll all love the show they put on."

Stanley had to admit, the show was creative. A little girl and boy dressed in winter garb came on stage, both dragging sleds and announcing to the crowd that they were lost.

"How will we ever find our way to Grandma's house?" asked the girl.

"Maybe the reindeer will guide us," said the boy.

Cue the reindeer. A couple dozen little ones, all wearing antlers, filed on stage. And there, herding them, was Lexie Bell. So this was her class.

They sang—surprise, surprise—"Rudolph the Red-Nosed Reindeer," complete with hand motions. Cell phones were pulled out, cameras flashed. The kids finished their song and departed to enthusiastic applause.

But the two stars of the show were still lost, so then it was time for the Sugar Plum Fairies to guide them to Grandma's. Six little girls in frilly skirts leaped and twirled, one losing her balance and nearly taking out the rest.

"Oh, no!" gasped the grandma seated near Stanley, and he figured her granddaughter must have been the off-kilter fairy. There wouldn't be any more bragging from Grandma.

Cell phones were busy capturing the dance. The poor stumble fairy would probably be all over the internet by morning.

More students got involved. A choir sang "Winter Wonderland," and a student recited a poem about Christmas
being a time for good cheer. "To lonely ones and sad ones,
and those we hold most dear," she finished and curtsied.

Oh, brother.

Finally, the snowflakes made their appearance, singing
"Let It Snow." To Stanley's surprise there was one solo at
the end, and the kid who stepped up to sing the last *Let
it snow* turned out to be Brock. He threw his arms wide,
half-singing, half-shouting, and it came out loud and clear.

"That's my grandkid," he said to the Sugar Plum Fairy
grandparents as they all applauded. Stretching the truth a
little? Yeah, but so what?

"Isn't he cute," the woman said half-heartedly.

Actually, he was.

The two lost kids found their way to Grandma's, and the
program ended with all the children singing "We Wish
You a Merry Christmas," as the band slaughtered the song.

Then the performance was over, and kids were racing everywhere, looking for their parents. And Brock was racing
toward Stanley. He felt an odd sensation of pride, which was
stupid since he was no relation to this boy. Still, it warmed
him when Brock plowed into him and hugged him.

"You came, Grandpa!"

"Wouldn't miss it," Stanley lied.

Lexie joined them. "Thank you for coming out. It meant
so much to Brock."

It looked like he was out of the doghouse. Funny saying, that, considering the fact that you never saw a dog in
a doghouse anymore. Only men who messed up.

"Did I do good?" Brock asked Stanley eagerly.

"Yeah, you did."

The kid was looking up at him with adoring eyes. Lexie Bell was looking at him gratefully. He felt like he'd just bowled a perfect game. Stupid, really.

He cleared his throat. "Do you need a ride home?" he asked her.

"No, we're fine. My friend Shannon will run us home. I have to stay and visit with the parents, anyway. You won't want to wait that long."

Yeah, he had to get home. He wasn't disappointed. It was no big deal.

He nodded. "Okay, then."

"I'm making chicken and noodles for dinner tomorrow," she said before he could walk off. "If you'd like to join us, that is."

Yep, all was forgiven.

"Sure. Uh, I'll bring ice cream."

And so he had a dinner invitation for the following night. His calendar was filling up.

"Something going two nights in a row. Aren't you turning into the social butterfly, Manly Stanley?" Carol teased that night.

She'd lost the Mrs. Santa outfit and was back in that red sweater again. Carol always could fill out a sweater.

He smiled at her. "You look awful cute tonight, babe."

"And you looked cute in that sports jacket."

"Nobody else was wearing one. I thought parents dressed up for stuff like that."

"Not anymore. Nobody dresses up for anything. A shame, really," she said with a sigh. "I'm glad you did, though. And I'm proud of you for going. You made the night special, for both of them."

"Yeah, I guess I did that," Stanley said. "You know, Carol, I think I'll give your Mrs. Claus outfit to Lexie. I bet she'd like it."

Surprisingly, Carol didn't say anything.

He looked around. She was gone.

He sighed and smiled and let himself drift into sleep.

The next day he drove to the grocery store and bought some peppermint ice cream. "I'm going to the neighbor's for dinner. Gotta bring something," he told the checker.

"Uh-huh," he replied in a voice that said *Big deal*.

Considering how much trouble Stanley had been in only a few days ago, it was.

He was still feeling pretty darned good when he went to Lexie's house for dinner. The lights he'd strung for her were on and gave the place a festive air. Next year she should hang some along her porch, too, and the rest of her roof. He could help her with that.

She greeted him wearing jeans and the boot. But on her other foot was a big, floppy slipper made to look like a unicorn.

"Interesting," he said, pointing to it as he stepped through the door.

"It's fun to have something fanciful to wear," she said.

Was that what you called it.

The house smelled like...cookies? "Something smells good," he said as she took his coat.

"Oh, I have a candle burning," she told him. "Cinnamon."

That was disappointing. He'd been hoping for cookies.

But he'd brought cookie deprivation on himself. He was the one who'd opened his big mouth and said he'd bring the ice cream.

Brock was on hand to take it from him and put it away for later.

"We have cookies to go with our ice cream," Lexie informed him.

No cookie deprivation after all. Here was good news, indeed. But he felt like he needed to earn that treat. And really clear the air about that little misunderstanding.

"I, uh, talked to Campbell. He won't be bothering you again."

Her cheeks turned pink.

"I'm sorry about—"

She cut him off. "Let's forget it. Okay?"

Fine with him. "Okay."

The dining table was already set, and in the middle of it sat something he hadn't seen the last time he was over—a circle of gold-tipped pinecones of varying shapes and sizes hugging a fat, red candle. As he got closer he could tell the candle was the source of the cinnamon he'd smelled.

"That's nice," he said.

"I made it."

Impressive. "Yeah?"

"I like to make things," she said.

Obviously. Food, pretty decorations. Lexie Bell was a nice young woman. She deserved to find some nice man and be happy. Not that Stanley would be assisting with that search. Ever again.

He enjoyed the dinner, especially the cookies, little round ones dusted with powdered sugar.

"My wife used to make these," he said. The memory made him wistful but, surprisingly, not horribly sad.

"My grandma made them. So does my mom. We call them snowball cookies," Lexie said.

"I hope it snows again," Brock said. "I want to make another snowman."

"We might get some more," Stanley said. The kid would probably need help with that snowman.

"I want to make snowballs, too," Brock said and popped half a cookie in his mouth.

"Yeah? How come?" Stanley asked.

"So I can have a snowball fight," Brock crowed.

"Be careful what you wish for, kid. Getting hit in the face with a snowball hurts."

"Who would throw a snowball in someone's face?" Lexie said, shocked.

"Your brother," Stanley said, remembering.

Brock frowned at that. "I don't want a brother."

"At the rate we're going you won't have to worry," Lexie muttered, then blushed.

"Brothers are okay," Stanley said.

"They are?"

"Sure. You always have somebody to play with right there with you in the house," Stanley told him.

"Then, I do want a brother. Maybe I'll ask Santa for a brother."

Stupid custom, thought Stanley.

"I think Santa specializes in toys," Lexie told her son.

"I like toys, too. When are we going to see Santa, Mommy?"

"Soon," Lexie said.

"Will you take us to see Santa, Grandpa Stanley?" Brock asked.

Stanley gave a snort. "There's no such thing."

Silence fell over the room, the kind of silence you heard right before a big storm broke.

Uh-oh. What had he just said?

The one thing you should never, never say to a kid, that was what. What had he been thinking? The truth was, he hadn't. He'd been feeling at home and so comfortable he'd let his guard down.

Lexie looked at him in shock. Brock blinked. Then blinked again. Then the storm broke.

20

THE KID BURST INTO NOISY TEARS AND PUSHED away from the table so hard it knocked over his half-melted ice cream, sending a pink puddle spreading across the tabletop. Then he bolted.

"Uh, I'll get that," Stanley said, reaching for a napkin.

"Don't bother," Lexie said stiffly. "I'll take care of it later. After…"

After she first cleaned up the mess Stanley had made. He scratched the back of his head, suddenly at a loss for how to explain what he'd just done.

"Mr. Mann, how could you?" she scolded, looking at him like he'd just committed a murder.

Maybe, in a way, he had.

"I guess I shouldn't have said anything." There was a bright remark.

"I guess not," she snapped. "Children have to grow up so quickly these days. Brock's going to have enough hard truths to hear later. He shouldn't have to…" Her lower lip began to wobble.

Great. Now she was going to cry, too.

"It's just as well," Stanley said. "After all, it's true."

Not the right thing to say. "Maybe you should go home now. I'll probably be busy with Brock for quite a while," she said with a Frosty the Snowman accent.

An arctic chill invaded the room. Warm welcome had turned into winter cold shoulder. Like Stanley had meant to make her kid cry, for crying out loud.

The ice cream was dripping onto the carpet now, but Lexie didn't notice. She turned her back on him and rushed up the stairs after her son. The party was over.

Just as well. He'd had enough drama with these two. He grabbed his coat and marched out the door.

Lexie raced up the stairs after her son, steaming as she went. Where did Stanley Mann get off, telling her child there was no such thing as Santa! How could he have been so thoughtless and mean?

She found her son sprawled across his bed, his face buried in his pillow, sobbing his heart out. She wanted to cry, too. He was just a little boy. To take the joy of Santa away from him had been wrong. Sick and wrong.

Brock was a human earthquake, his little body heaving and rolling with sobs. What could she say to her son to take away the sting of harsh reality? She laid a hand on his back, and he rolled over and looked at her, tears racing down his cheeks, his face red from crying.

"There has to be a Santa," he wailed and threw himself into her arms.

Her poor little boy. He so hadn't been ready for this.

She kissed the top of his head and stroked his hair and searched her mind for the right words.

"Grandpa Stanley doesn't have it quite right," she said. "There really was a real Santa once."

Brock pulled away enough to look up at her half doubtful, half hopeful. "There was?"

"His name was Nicholas. He was a bishop."

Brock's brows pulled together, and he looked at her in confusion. "What's a bishop?"

"Like a minister," she improvised. "He was a very kind man, and he loved to help people who didn't have any money. He especially liked to help children and would leave little gifts for them."

"Like Santa?" Brock asked, hope returning.

"Like Santa. People called him Saint Nicholas. You could say he was the first Santa."

Now came the smile. Brock sat back on his knees and began to bounce excitedly, turning the bed into a trampoline. "There is a Santa!"

Her son was so anxious to be a believer. She should let him.

But then, if he learned the truth yet again, maybe from some older child on the playground or one of her cousin's children, he'd be doubly disillusioned. "We did get our idea of Santa from him, but Santa is pretend, sweetie. He's a fun friend mommies invent so their little boys can have a special present under the tree. He's a game you and I play so I can find extra ways to do nice things for you."

"But I saw Santa last year. I asked him for Legos."

"And he told me," Lexie said. Okay, stretching the truth a little, but a woman had to do what a woman had to do. "He was pretending, too, all so you could have a happy Christmas Day."

Brock frowned, processing this.

She pulled him close and put an arm around him. "Santa is something fun mommies and daddies have been doing for a long time. Grandma and Grandpa played the Santa game with me, and their mommy and daddy played the Santa game with them. Someday, when you're grown up and have children you'll play the Santa game with them, and they'll have fun finding that special present under the tree just like you do."

Her son didn't say anything, just sat there, still processing this huge turn of events.

"It is fun to pretend, isn't it?" she prompted.

He nodded, slowly. "Will I still get my Christmas stocking?"

The treats for it were already hidden in her closet. "Of course."

"And the extra present under the tree?"

It was ordered and supposed to ship soon. "Yes. So you see, the only difference is when you go see Santa, you'll know it's a game."

"Can we still go see Santa?"

"Of course we can."

He smiled. Finally. "Good. Because I want to tell him I want a Junior Handyman tool set."

"I'm sure you'll get it," she said. "Now, how about a bath and a bedtime story?"

He nodded, slid off the bed and started for the bathroom, his earlier misery forgotten.

Lexie was finding it harder to let go of her emotions. Seeing her son so upset had been distressing. Thank you, Stanley Mann.

She should never have baked him cookies or invited him to dinner, should never have invited him to Brock's school program. If she'd known what it would lead to she'd never have accepted so much as one kind gesture from him.

But later, after her son was in bed and she was sponging up the mess on the carpet, she was able to admit that her neighbor wasn't a monster. Under that gruff exterior beat a kind heart. He wasn't the Grinch, out to ruin Christmas. He was simply a grumpy, lonely old man who needed love.

Which he was more than welcome to look for somewhere else. He wasn't all bad, but he was bad enough, and they really didn't need him in their lives, spreading negativity over everything.

She shouldn't have rushed so quickly to attach herself and her son to him. She certainly didn't do that with men her own age. Maybe with Stanley she'd figured since he was older he was harmless. Ha!

There had been plenty of red flags—his standoffishness, his sour attitude and rare smiles. She'd been so excited to befriend her neighbor, so desperate for a male figure in her son's life, she'd ignored those red flags.

Well, she was done with that. From now on she was going to ignore Stanley Mann.

Enough was enough. Lexie Bell the pest could live her life, and Stanley would live his. He'd known all along it would be a dumb idea to get involved with those two, and he'd been right. Well, he'd had enough of them. And he'd had enough of cookies and fudge and cheese bread. And stringing lights and decorating trees. And Christmas.

Oh, no. What was that he heard? Voices. He went to the living-room window and twitched the curtain.

Carolers were coming down the street. He turned off all the lights and retreated to his recliner. They continued to come closer, approaching like a freight train. "Fa-la-la-la-la."

Oh, cut it out.

Soon he could tell they were on the sidewalk right in front of his house. He could hear them out there, gustily singing that it was the season to be jolly. Bonnie heard them, too, and began to bark.

"Stop that," he commanded. "Don't encourage them."

This was no season of joy. He was now more miserable than ever.

Santa. Ugh. Santa was a crock, and Christmas was nothing but a stupid holiday full of commercialism and fat guys who pretended they could bring you what you wanted. Well, he wanted his old life back, and neither Santa nor anybody else was going to make that happen. He went in search of ice cream.

The ice cream didn't make him feel any better. Neither did his encounter with Carol that night. Bad enough that the kid was upset and that Lexie Bell wanted to strangle him with a string of Christmas lights, but Carol had to weigh in as well.

"Stanley, what on earth were you thinking?" she scolded. Tonight she was dressed like an old-time schoolmarm. She held a ruler and was slapping it on the palm of her hand. He half expected her to whack him with it.

"I don't know." But he did. He'd been remembering his own disappointment on learning there was no Santa. Santa was a crock. "Parents shouldn't lie to their kids," he muttered.

"It's pretending, Stanley. It's no different than a child having an imaginary friend."

"I never had an imaginary friend," he argued.

"Don't be obtuse. You shouldn't have said what you said, and you know it."

"It just slipped out. Okay?" he said defensively.

"You need to make it up to that girl."

"Carol," he said sternly. "I'm done. She as much as kicked me out. What do you want me to do?"

"I want you to think of something. That's what I want you to do."

"I'm tired of thinking. I'm just plain tired."

"Well, then, I'll leave you to get some rest," she said in a huff.

And with that she was gone without leaving behind so much as a hint of peppermint.

After she left he tossed and turned, and once he finally made it into what should have been a restful sleep, he found himself far from resting. He was having Christmas dinner with Ebenezer Scrooge. The only other dinner guest was the Grinch. The scarred, old wooden table they sat at had nothing but a soup tureen, cracked bowls, and three spoons. No tablecloth, no pinecone centerpiece, no candles.

"You're one of us now," said Ebenezer. He pointed to the tureen. "Have some gruel."

"Gruel for Christmas dinner?" Stanley protested.

"You expected me to roll out the red carpet?" sneered Scrooge, and the Grinch laughed.

The room was cold, and the fireplace in the corner only a blackened mouth.

"Can't you light a fire?" Stanley begged. "It's cold in here."

"Coal costs money. Why should I spend money on the likes of you?" his host demanded.

"You're supposed to be a changed man," Stanley protested. "A man who keeps Christmas well."

"Don't believe everything you read," said Scrooge.

Stanley looked to the Grinch for confirmation.

He merely shrugged. "People never really change, you know."

"They can," Stanley insisted. "You two are a couple of downers. I'm not like you, and I don't like you. I'm leaving."

That made them both laugh. The Grinch laughed so hard he fell off his chair.

Stanley pushed away from the table and marched across the room, which, he suddenly realized, looked mysteriously like a dungeon. The door was thick and heavy with a barred window that looked out on nothing but darkness. He grabbed the metal handle and pulled, but it refused to budge.

"We're locked in," Scrooge informed him. "Locked in by our own bad attitudes."

Stanley gave another tug. The door still wouldn't budge. He ran to the one window in the room. It was barred.

He grabbed the bars and rattled them, crying, "I want out! Let me out!"

He was still crying "Let me out!" when he woke up.

21

ON FRIDAY THE LAST OF THE AFTERNOON LIGHT shone on a truck with a U-Haul trailer attached pulling into the driveway of the house across the street from Lexie's. It was followed by a car.

"Look, Mommy!" Brock cried. "Kids!"

Lexie joined him at the living-room window and looked out. Sure enough, two little girls had jumped out of the truck and were running across the yard to the front door where a tall, lean man with brown hair and glasses stood, opening it. A woman got out of the car and followed them. The girls looked somewhere around Brock's age, and the adults looked to be in maybe their late thirties or early forties.

New neighbors! Maybe they were actually nice. One could hope.

"Can I go over and play?" Brock asked.

"May I go over and play?"

"May I?"

"Let's give them a chance to unpack first," Lexie said.

Brock's pout showed what he thought of that idea.

"I tell you what, though. We can make some cupcakes to welcome them to the neighborhood and take them over later. How does that sound?"

"Yes!" he hooted and raced for the kitchen.

Yes! Lexie thought. *Oh, please let these people be normal.*

After the requisite handwashing, she put her son to work helping with the baking. The thought occurred that, nice as it was to have him enjoying helping her in the kitchen, it would be equally nice if he had a father with whom he could share these kinds of bonding moments. Or a grandpa.

The image of her son and Stanley Mann standing by the snowman they'd made popped into her mind. She erased it with the memory of Stanley Mann making her son cry when he killed Santa. There would be time for male bonding later. With someone else.

Brock was getting very good at cracking eggs into a bowl (and then fishing out the eggshells) and enjoyed using the mixer under her close supervision. She'd gotten giant marshmallows and chocolate chips to make snowmen to top the cupcakes and Hershey's Kisses for their hats. The project kept Brock occupied for a good couple of hours. After dinner they had to decorate a little box to put the cupcakes in, and that took more time. But then Brock's patience was at an end, and he was begging to go meet the neighbors.

Lexie hoped they'd given the newcomers sufficient time to at least catch their breath. She also hoped they'd appreciate getting a treat and a welcome to the neighborhood. She knew she would have appreciated such a gesture when she'd moved in.

They bundled up and crossed the street to the house that had stood empty for so long, Brock carrying his box decorated with red construction paper and cut-out white snowflakes as carefully as if he were a Wise Man bearing a gift for the Christ Child. The day was clear and the ground dry, which made walking so much nicer. Like her house, this one had a long front porch. There was something about a front porch that was so welcoming. Maybe the neighbors, themselves, would be as well.

As they approached the front door she could hear children laughing inside. Laughter was always a good sign. It meant the people were happy.

There was never any laughter coming from Stanley Mann's house.

She shoved away the thought. That was his own fault.

Lexie rang the doorbell and heard high-pitched voices accompanied by a stampede of feet.

"I'll get it!"

"No, I will! Daddy, Arielle's shoving!"

The two little girls they'd seen earlier opened the door, each fighting for the best hold on the doorknob. They both had ponytails and big eyes and looked like Disney princesses in the making. Each stared curiously at Lexie.

"Who are you?" asked the smaller of the two girls.

Brock said, "I'm Brock. We brought snowman cupcakes." He held out the box.

The taller one was quick to take it. "Thank you."

They'd been taught manners. That was a good sign.

The woman Lexie had seen earlier appeared at the door. She was slender, and her hair was perfect. There was no wedding band or glinting diamond on her left hand, but from the suspicious way she eyed Lexie it was clear that she wasn't going to be inviting Lexie in for a chat.

So a girlfriend, and an insecure one at that. Lexie's pleasant vision of neighboring back and forth vanished with a poof.

She made the effort to be neighborly, anyway. "I'm Lexie Bell, and this is my son Brock. We live across the street," she added, pointing to her place, "and thought it would be nice to welcome you to the neighborhood."

"I'm Isobel," said the littler girl.

"I'm Arielle," said her sister. She handed the box over to the woman. "You want to see our rooms?" she asked Brock.

"Let's get your room squared away before you start having company," the woman said to her in a tone of voice that brooked no argument. She gave Lexie a smile that almost moved the meter up to polite. "Thanks for these. The kids will enjoy them."

"Our pleasure. Welcome to the neighborhood," Lexie said.

"Thanks," said the woman and shut the door.

Of course there was no *Looking forward to getting to know you.* No *We'll have to have coffee sometime.* No nothing. Lexie found herself feeling cranky as they walked back across the street.

"Can I go over… May I go over and play tomorrow?" Brock asked.

"We'll see," Lexie answered and sighed inwardly. Apparently they were doomed to have sucky neighbors.

Still, she found herself looking out her window at the house across the street a lot after they got home. Not spying. She just happened to look that way once in a while.

She could see lights on inside, people moving about. Around ten the woman got in the car and left. So together but not living together yet. But obviously serious since she was helping her boyfriend move.

Oh, well, so what if he'd been nice-looking, if he had kids. There were other nice-looking men out there who liked kids.

Somewhere.

Meanwhile, she'd live her life, and the neighbors would live theirs. They'd wave occasionally. Maybe the kids would play together. But that would be it.

Except the next afternoon there was the man, standing on her front porch. He smiled at her. It wasn't a sexy smile like Jayce the Meat Man's, but it was a friendly one, set in a nice face with kind, gray eyes, a face that said *You'll like me once you get to know me.*

"Hi, I'm Truman Phillips," he said. His voice was warm, and it, too, promised she'd like him.

"I'm Lexie Bell," she said.

"The Cupcake Queen. Those were spectacular."

Not simply *good* but *spectacular.* Why did he have to have a girlfriend?

"It wasn't much," Lexie said modestly.

"It was great, and the girls and I appreciated the gesture. And the sugar. We drove straight here yesterday—seventeen hours—and the girls had been up since the crack of dawn. It was a long day, and I was bushed before we even started unloading. The place is chaos."

"Maybe you and your girlfriend could use some help," Lexie offered. "I'm pretty good at putting away dishes." Where was the girlfriend today? Lexie had seen no sign of her car.

Not that she'd been spying. It was just a casual observation she'd made.

"No girlfriend," he said. "It's just my daughters and me. My old college pal, Margo, lives up here, though. She helped us get our stuff unloaded. You must have met her when you dropped off the cupcakes."

"I did."

No girlfriend. Oh, happy day! Truman Phillips was easy to look at, and he had two nice little girls. How was he single? *Why* was he single? What happened to the mom? It was hardly something you could ask a new neighbor, but she was dying to know his story.

"Well, if you could use some help," she offered again.

He looked as if she'd offered him an all-expenses-paid vacation to the Caribbean. "Really?"

"Sure." The sound of voices had brought Brock downstairs from his room. "Brockie, would you like to go to Mr. Phillips's house and help them?"

He immediately began jumping up and down. "Yes!"

"It looks like you've got some helpers," she said to Truman.

"Great. We could use it. Margo had things going on this weekend, and I wasn't looking forward to unpacking the kitchen stuff alone. We only got as far as setting up the beds last night."

"Moving is exhausting," Lexie said as she took Brock's coat from the hall closet. "But it's also an adventure."

"That it is, and the girls and I were ready for one."

"You sure your husband won't mind?" Truman asked as they crossed the street.

"It's just Brock and me."

He nodded, taking that in.

The moment they were in the house Arielle had Brock by the hand and was towing him up the stairs, her sister following with a squeal.

"They're excited!" Truman explained.

"Of course they are. How old are they?"

"Arielle is ten going on sixteen, and Isobel is seven."

"They're sweet."

"They are," he agreed as he led the way to the kitchen. "They have their moments, but they're good kids. When you've got good kids it makes everything bearable."

Had Truman Phillips's life been unbearable with his ex? Lexie was dying to know.

He gestured to her foot. "Are you sure you're okay to do this?"

"Oh, yes," she assured him. "It's only a chip fracture, and I'm hoping to lose the boot and get into a brace by Christmas."

"I bet you're ready for that. I broke a leg once. Was stuck in a cast for an eternity and a half. I hope you don't have the kind of job where you have to be on your feet a lot."

"I do. I'm a teacher."

He looked impressed. "There's a noble occupation. Where do you teach?"

"Fairwood Elementary."

"Any chance either of my girls will have you?"

"I'm afraid not. I teach kindergarten."

"Is your son in your class?" Truman wanted to know.

"He's in first grade."

"So just one grade behind Isobel." Childish laughter drifted down to where they sat. "Looks like the kids are getting along well," Truman said. "It'll be nice for the girls to know someone when they start school. It's hard starting halfway through the year."

"It is unusual to see kids moving in partway through the school year," Lexie said, avoiding a direct question. Was that still being too nosy? Not compared to asking what happened with his ex, which was what she really wanted to do.

"It just worked out that way. I bought the bookstore in town. It took a while to get all the proverbial ducks in a row."

A man who loved books. It was all Lexie could do not to sigh like a girl who'd just gotten a chance to meet her favorite rock star.

"I've been in there a few times and loved the friendly vibe."

"Hopefully, we can keep that going."

"What made you decide to buy a bookstore?" she asked.

"Books are what I do. I owned a store in Los Angeles and it was great, but I really wanted the girls to grow up in a small town. My friend told me about Great Escape and got me in touch with the owner. I came up and checked it out. Checked out the school and was impressed. Everything fell together."

"It sounds like it," Lexie said. Upstairs she could hear little feet running and more squeals. Brock was probably in heaven. Play buddies, at last. Maybe things were falling together for her and Brock as well.

"You like it here? Are the neighbors nice?" Truman asked.

What to say to that? "It's a quiet neighborhood." She'd tell him about Mr. Mann when the time was right.

He nodded. "Well, at least we have a kid across the street for the girls to play with."

And a woman for you to play with.

Don't be in a rush, she cautioned herself.

But after organizing spices and pots and pans together, and after he'd sprung for pizza delivery, it only seemed right to invite him for dinner the following night as she was getting ready to leave. Not rushing. Just being neighborly.

"That'd be great. What can I bring?"

It was easy to see where his girls got their good manners.

"Nothing but your appetite."

"I can do that."

He called for the girls, and they ran to the head of the stairs, Brock with them. They all looked overheated, their faces red, hair damp. All three were smiling.

"Time for us to go home, Brockie," Lexie said.

"I don't want to go," he protested.

"Can he stay and help us?" asked little Isobel.

"No, but we'll see you all tomorrow. You're coming over to our house for dinner," Lexie said to her.

"Yay!" hooted Brock.

"Can we have spaghetti?" Isobel asked.

"Isobel," her father chided.

"It's okay. We like spaghetti," Lexie said. Except she had no makings for sauce and no hamburger in the house. She'd have to make a run to the grocery store.

She'd get an Uber.

22

I THINK MY FAMILY ALL NEED BOOKS FOR CHRIST-mas, Shannon replied when Lexie texted her about her new neighbor.

Your book binge won't be able to compete with my cheese bread, Lexie texted back.

Or your cuteness. Should I hate you? ☺

LOL. Maybe.

But she wouldn't once the monster box of Godiva chocolates Lexie had bought her got delivered.

Call me after. I need deets!

Maybe there wouldn't be that many deets to share. Maybe Truman Phillips wasn't looking to jump into something. And even if he was, he might not want to with her. Maybe he was simply happy at the thought of not having to deal with making dinner for his kids.

Or maybe there really was such a thing as Santa, and he'd delivered a great man just in time for Christmas. One could always hope.

Lexie made it to the grocery store on her own just fine without any help from a certain neighbor—thank you, Uber—and was able to serve the requested spaghetti along with her killer cheese bread and a salad. Truman had come bearing eggnog ice cream, which paired quite well with Christmas cookies, and everything was consumed with much chatter and giggles. It was a happy time, and she could tell by the appreciative look in Truman's eyes as he watched her that he was interested in her. Sooo…maybe he was looking to jump into something. Or at least walk into something.

After dinner, Brock and the girls played Candy Land, which gave the adults time to visit. Truman, Lexie learned, was a big fan of PBS and every British mystery he could get his hands on. Naturally, owning a bookstore, he loved to read.

"So far my girls are big readers, too," he said, looking fondly to where the kids sat at the table playing.

"It sounds like you're doing everything right as a parent," Lexie said.

"I'm trying."

He looked wistful, and she couldn't help asking, "What happened with their mom?"

His lips crumpled up like he was trying to swallow something distasteful.

Lexie immediately regretted her nosiness. "I'm sorry. I shouldn't have asked."

"Don't be. She had some problems. She'd always been kind of a, uh, partyer, which, I confess, I thought was exciting when I first met her. But somewhere along the way the partying got wilder, and then completely out of hand. Drugs. She's in rehab. Again."

"Oh, I'm really sorry," Lexie said.

He looked so sad. She wished she could think of something else to say but found herself at a loss.

"This stuff happens. I'm just grateful it didn't happen when she was pregnant with either of the girls." He shook his head. "When we first got together she loved being with a *smart man*," he said, using air quotes. "And, of course, I loved how vivacious she was. I guess we're your typical case of opposites attract. Nobody tells you that opposites also can drive each other crazy. We were like puzzle pieces that seemed like they should fit together but didn't. Anyway, I couldn't stand to see what she was doing to herself, and I sure couldn't let the girls be around that."

"Of course not. Do they miss their mother?"

"Sometimes. We've been separated for four years now, so they were little when we were still together. They know Mommy has some troubles and include her in their bedtime prayers."

"Children are so forgiving," Lexie said.

She could easily picture the two little girls kneeling by their beds, hands clasped just like Brock did, asking God to bless Mommy—a Hallmark movie, a Debbie Macomber novel and a Thomas Kinkade painting all rolled into one.

"So far so good. I make it a point to never bad-mouth their mother. It's hard not to sometimes, but I want the girls to understand that everyone has faults."

Like Stanley Mann. Lexie felt a sudden poke to her conscience.

"And if you were to cut everyone out of your life who wasn't perfect, you'd wind up with nobody in it."

Another poke. Ouch!

"Not that she gets to be around them when she's messed up like this," he hurried to say. "We're taking it one day at a time. If all goes well with rehab, we're talking about her coming up to visit this summer. We'll see."

"You are a good man," Lexie said, impressed.

"I try the best I can. It's hard to keep all the balls in the air sometimes. Margo's always been supportive. She's got someone in her life now, but she's determined to make time to watch out for us."

Which explained her not-so-welcoming attitude when Lexie showed up at his door.

"So that's me. What about you?"

Fair was fair. She'd stuck her nose into his love fail. It was only right that she share hers. She looked over to make sure Brock wasn't listening. Of course he wasn't. He was having too much fun with his new friends.

She summed up the sad story in one sentence. "He cheated when we were engaged, and we broke up."

"Maybe it's a good thing you realized what you were about to get into before you actually got married," Truman said.

She nodded. "It is. It hurt, though."

"Does he see Brock?"

She shook her head. "He gave up parental rights."

Truman shook his head in disgust. "You really did have a lucky escape."

"I guess I did," Lexie said. "Anyway, I got a great little boy out of the deal, so I'm not complaining. And I love my job and my house. And I like this town. We only moved in a few months ago, so I'm still getting to know people."

"I think I'm going to like it here," Truman said. "I sure have a nice neighbor," he added, making her blush.

Happy holidays! she texted later to Shannon.

OMG! For me, too. Chocolates just arrived. You are the best.

No, you are. Shannon had been a lifesaver for her.

Now bring me a perfect man. ☺ And tell me about yours? How was din-din?

He loves my cheese bread.

And you, I bet.

Maybe.

Who knew? One thing she knew for sure. Truman Phillips was one neighbor she was really going to enjoy.

About that other neighbor. Truman's words hovered over her like a pesky ghost.

★ ★ ★

Stanley had seen the new neighbor when he was out walking Bonnie. He'd also seen Lexie over there on Saturday, taking the man goodies. He supposed she'd never bring him anything again.

On Sunday he watched from his dining-room window as the man and his girls trooped across the street to her place, probably for dinner. Stanley supposed, now that she'd found someone her own age who also had kids, that there'd be a lot of that. She had no need of him anymore.

Even if she needed him, she didn't want him. After his goof he wouldn't be getting invited over for dinner. Or needed to run errands. He certainly wouldn't be invited to any more school programs.

What did he care? He was fine on his own.

He was lying. He already missed being part of Lexie and Brock's life. Spending time with them had become a habit, and now that she'd broken the habit he found himself feeling...empty. Even Carol didn't seem to be speaking to him.

"What do you think I ought to do?" he asked Bonnie.

She gave a yap and wagged her tail. *Give me a dog treat.*

Life was simple when you were a dog, he reflected as he tossed her a treat. You ate, you barked, you pooped, you chased a squirrel or two, and then you slept. You didn't think about people you missed or people you'd managed to irritate and alienate. You simply wagged your way through the day.

It was so much more complicated for human beings. Maybe humans thought too much. Maybe, like dogs, they needed to simply go by instinct.

Stanley's instincts told him that if he ever wanted the

human equivalent of a dog treat he was going to have to apologize to Lexie for upsetting her kid. He still didn't think he'd done anything all that wrong, but sometimes you had to apologize even when you felt you shouldn't have to.

He went in search of his phone, Bonnie trotting after him.

"You gonna make sure I do this?" he said to her. He sure needed someone to give him courage.

He could feel his heart rate speeding up as he made the call. What should he say? How should he begin? That ringing felt like a countdown. Before a bomb was due to go off.

The ringing stopped, and his call went to her voice mail. Then came the tone that signaled it was time for him to talk. His brain chose that moment to take a nap.

"Uh," he said. There was a great beginning. Good grief. He tried again. "Uh. Lexie." *I miss your cookies. I miss hanging out with you and Brock. I don't mind driving you places. I'm sorry about the Santa thing. It's for the best, though.* No, not that. That was stupid. Start with…not about missing cookies. That would put him right on the same level as Bonnie. May as well bark. And it wasn't about the cookies. It was about what they'd meant, that someone cared.

He was still choosing his next words when the beep that said *You're done, fool,* went off. He clicked off his portable phone with a scowl and went in search of peppermint ice cream.

His last words before nodding off that night were, "Sorry, Carol, I just can't get it right."

For a minute there, he thought he felt a gentle touch on his cheek. But he knew he'd only imagined it. Carol was still silent, and his life was empty once more.

★ ★ ★

Lexie's doctor gave her permission to ditch the walking boot, and she came home with a lightweight brace, which meant she could start wearing cute shoes again. And driving!

"Just in time for Christmas," she told Shannon, who'd driven her. "And a nice present for you, too. Now you don't have to take me everywhere."

"I didn't mind," Shannon assured her. "And you'd do the same for me. Only I might not spend as much on chocolate for you," she joked.

"With all those rides you've given me I owe you chocolate for life," Lexie said.

"I like the sound of that."

"Want to stay for dinner?"

Shannon shook her head. "I can't. I'm meeting another potential Mr. Perfect."

"Oh?" Lexie prompted.

"He seems promising, but then they always do until you spend some time with 'em. I think my New Year's resolution is going to be to quit trying so hard, let things happen naturally. And enjoy my life just as it is."

"That sounds like a good plan."

"Unless, of course, tonight's man du jour turns out to be great. Then, forget the resolution," Shannon finished with a grin.

"You never know. You can find love anywhere." Maybe even across the street.

It was way too early to tell, but a girl could hope.

Free to drive, Lexie decided it was time to make good on her promise to take Brock to see Santa. She fed him a quick meal of mac and cheese and chicken fingers, then got him dolled up in his slacks and red sweater, and off they went to the nearby mall where Santa was making an appearance.

"Come up with me," Brock said when it was his turn to sit with Santa.

"Well, who have we here?" the man greeted him and added the requisite "Ho, ho, ho!"

"I'm Brock, and this is my mom," Brock said. "I know we're just pretending, but I still like you."

The man shot an amused look at Lexie. "Well, now, that's good to hear. I like you, too, young man. I think I need to bring you something extra special for Christmas. What do you think?"

"I want a Junior Handyman tool set. I thought you should let Mommy know in case she forgot."

"I bet she remembered," said Mall Santa.

"I bet she did, too," Brock agreed.

Mall Santa smiled up at Lexie. "And what would you like for Christmas, young lady?"

My mother to be with me, a good man. Neither were things she could ask for in front of her son.

The first wasn't going to happen: she was resigned to that. But the good man? She pictured Truman's smile and felt as warmed as if she'd consumed a hot buttered rum. Maybe the New Year was going to be a happy one.

Meanwhile, she had her pretty new house, a good friend in Shannon, and her adorable boy. She had much to be grateful for.

"You know, Santa, I think I'm good," she said.

"Well, then, let's take a picture together," Mall Santa suggested. "Ho, ho, ho! Merry Christmas."

Yes, it is looking merry, she thought when Truman came by that evening with a book for her. "A thank-you for dinner," he explained as he handed it over.

It was wrapped in red ribbon, but she could easily see the title: *Living Your Best Life Yet.*

"Not that you aren't," he hurried to add, "but I thought you might like this. It's by a woman named Muriel Sterling. She's pretty popular with a lot of my women readers. She actually lives here in Washington, in a town called Icicle Falls. Her family owns a chocolate company."

"Ooh, I like her already," Lexie said. "Thank you. I love self-improvement books." And she was more than ready to live her best life yet.

"Good. Well, I guess I'd better get back over to the house. I promised the girls I'd send out for pizza again." He didn't move.

"Do you normally eat this late?"

"For a while. Have to keep the bookstore open, and until I find an employee, that job falls on me. I gave them cheese and crackers and some apple slices at the store, so they're not starving."

"An apple a day, that's what my grandma used to say." Who cared? What a dumb remark.

"So did mine," he said, smiling. "I'm a big believer." Still he stood there. "I guess you and Brock have already eaten."

Never turn down an opportunity to be with a great guy. "We have, but there's always room for pizza."

His smile grew. "Yeah?"

"I could come over and help you finish unpacking," she offered.

"That would be great," he said.

Yes, it would. She called up the stairs, and her son came racing down them. "How would you like to go over to Mr. Phillips's house for pizza?" Lexie asked him.

"Yes!" he whooped and yanked the closet door open.

"I guess that settles it," she said and reached for her coat.

Winter darkness had fallen, and the Christmas lights Stanley had strung for her sparkled like jewels. His lights were on, too. His house looked deceptively festive. What was he doing in there, all by himself?

Who cared?

And what would her grandma say about her attitude? She already knew what Truman would say, and she suddenly felt a little small.

Once inside his house, though, she quickly became absorbed with the children and helping organize more of the chaos scattered around the Phillips's house and forgot about Stanley Mann. Laughter and pizza. Merry Christmas from Truman's home to hers.

While the children raced around, the two adults talked about the holidays, both past and present. Truman's plans included spending some time with his old friend on Christmas Eve and doing an online chat with his family back home on Christmas morning.

"Then I guess the girls and I will tuck in for the day," he finished.

"You're more than welcome to come over to my house in the afternoon," Lexie said. "As it turns out, it's just going to be Brock and me."

"No family coming to visit?"

She sighed, then told him about her mother.

"That's too bad," he said.

"Hopefully, by next year it will be different. I still wish I could get her to come up this year. I think it would do her good. But there's not much I can do if she doesn't want to."

"It sounds like she needs more time," Truman said. "When you've gone through something bad, it can take a while to see anything good in life."

Like Stanley Mann? Why, oh, why, did he keep coming to mind? She pushed him firmly out and kept him out for the rest of the evening. She had other things to think about besides him.

Once the house was pretty much squared away, she decided she really didn't have an excuse to hang around any longer. They'd been at the kitchen table relaxing with glasses of soda pop, but now the glasses were empty.

"I should go," she said, and got up and set hers on the kitchen counter.

He set his down, too, and they stood there, looking at each other. The heat growing between them was enough to start a whole troop of little elves running around in her tummy.

"It's probably too soon to kiss you," he murmured and moved closer.

"Probably," she agreed. *Darn.*

"But we have spent a lot of hours together," he pointed out.

And unpacking a lot more than dishes. They'd already shared so much of their personal lives.

"But we still don't know each other very well." And they had children. They needed to be cautious and responsible.

She didn't make a move to leave.

He inched a little closer. "What else do you want to know?"

"What are you like when you're not being so…" *Perfect*. "Nice. Do you lose your temper?"

"When I'm tired. Sometimes I yell. Mostly, though, I give myself a time-out. Send the girls to their rooms, chill and reassess. I swear if I hit my finger with a hammer. But I've never hit a woman, never spanked my girls."

She bit her lip. "Ever cheated?"

His eyes popped wide. "No. Good God, no."

"Sorry. I had to ask."

"Understandable. How about you? Do you have a fatal flaw I should know about?" he asked. "I can't imagine you do."

She thought of how long it had taken to forgive the man who had once wanted to be her husband and then dumped her, and of how upset she'd been with Stanley.

"I hate to confess it, but I think I have a hard time forgiving and letting go."

"That's understandable, too" he said. "But if there's one thing I've learned, it's that you can't move on to what's better until you let go of what was bad."

"How true. You know, you are a very wise man."

He also looked good in his jeans and shirt with its sleeves rolled up. They showed off his strong arms. And those lips sure knew how to smile. What else were they good at?

She closed the last few inches between them. "I think moving on to what's better sounds like an excellent idea."

He raised an eyebrow, half smiled. "Yeah?"

"Oh, yeah."

He took off his glasses and set them on the counter.

"Should we pretend it's already New Year's Eve and about to strike midnight?"

"I think we should."

He slipped his arms around her waist. She slid her hands up his chest, and they pretended.

Truman was a fabulous pretender.

Later that night, as she snuggled in her bed, it wasn't sugar plums Lexie dreamed about.

Monday was the last day of school before Christmas, and Lexie had a party with her students. Before they arrived she sprayed a cinnamon-scented air freshener around the room and sprinkled cookie crumbs on their desks. When they came in she informed them that the Gingerbread Boy had been to school.

"Is he still here?" asked one of the children, looking eagerly around.

"No, but I think some of his friends might be. Shall we look for them?"

The search was mounted, with the children exploring every corner of the classroom. Alas, the Gingerbread Boy's friends were nowhere to be found in class. Which meant coats had to be donned, and the children had to be taken outside to search the playground. While they conducted their search, the two room mothers came in and set up for a party, decorating and distributing Lexie's baked, wrapped gingerbread boys. When the children returned they found a giant cardboard Gingerbread Boy waving at them, and edible ones at each desk. Then there were stories to read, songs to sing and a game to play. The children left for their holiday break happily wound up and buzzing.

Her own son was buzzing at the end of the school day, also, full of details about his class holiday party. "We played pin the hat on Santa," he told her.

"And did you get the hat on the Santa's head?"

Brock shook his head. "I pinned it on his shoulder. Teacher said it looked good there. Emily thinks Santa is real."

Oh, dear. She hoped Brock hadn't passed on what he'd learned from their neighbor.

"Did you tell her he wasn't?" Lexie asked nervously.

Brock shook his head. "I didn't want to make her cry."

Like *someone* had made him cry. Lexie's brows dipped into an irritated V.

"I don't think she's big enough to know yet," Brock continued. "Not like me." He was silent a moment, then asked, "Can Grandpa Stanley come over and play Candy Land?"

"You want to see Grandpa Stanley?" Lexie asked, surprised.

"I miss him."

Faults and all. Her son was more forgiving than she was. What did that say about her?

More important, what did that say to her?

Stanley Mann had a crusty exterior, but inside he had a soft heart. That had been evidenced in the things he'd done for her and her son. She contrasted that to herself, all sweet and kind on the outside, but when it came to forgiving a grumpy old man who'd made a misstep, she had a heart as hard as a lump of coal.

This had to be a lonely time for the man. She could fix that. It was the season of peace on earth, goodwill toward men. Even curmudgeons.

The next day, with Brock riding shotgun, she drove

to the supermarket—it felt so good to be able to drive herself!—and picked up buttermilk, red food coloring, and cake flour. She'd make red velvet cupcakes and take some to Stanley and maybe even invite him over for dinner.

On her way back she happened to drive by the bookstore. What a coincidence! Ha.

"This is the bookstore Mr. Phillips bought. I bet he and the girls are in there working. Should we go in and say hi?" she said to Brock.

As expected, her son said an emphatic *yes*, so they parked the car halfway down the block and made their way to the store. Walking with that light brace felt so good.

Once they got to the store she saw the sign on the door. *Closed, but not for long. Please join us for our grand reopening February 1.* Darn.

Oh, well, she had cupcakes to bake.

"I guess they're not open yet," she said to Brock.

He had his face pressed to the window. "But I see Mr. Phillips."

She joined him at the window. Indeed, Truman was there with the former owner. They both were seated in armchairs, and each had an iPad and the woman had a notebook and pencil. They were obviously working. The girls were over in the children's book section, reading.

"Come on, Brockie, let's go. They're not open," Lexie said.

Too late. He was already knocking on the window.

"Brockie, don't bother them. They're busy." Casually dropping by to purchase a book was one thing, but ignoring a Closed sign and hovering at the window probably looked more like stalking.

But Truman was on his way to the door.

"We came to see you," Brock told him once he'd opened it.

"Well, come on in."

"You're closed," Lexie protested. "And you're obviously busy. I thought you were open for business."

"We will be. And June and I were just going over a few things," he said. "We could probably use a break."

He ushered Lexie in and introduced her to the former owner, June Yates.

"Oh, yes, you've been in before," June said with a smile. "Nice to see you."

The girls came over, each with a book in hand. "Hi, Brock," said Isobel. "I'm reading this." She held up a Dr. Seuss book. "We have a whole bunch. Want to come see?"

He nodded eagerly and ran for the books.

"I shouldn't be bothering you," Lexie said to Truman.

"It's no bother. Sorry we're not open for business. I'm going to do a little remodeling."

"Feel free to show her," said June.

"I'll give you the two-minute tour," he said to Lexie.

It wasn't a large store, but he had good ideas for making better use of the space. "These—" he said, pointing to two rows of shelves "—we're going to put on rollers and make them movable. That way we can push them aside and make extra room for seating when we have author events."

"That's a great idea."

They moved to the children's book section. "Going to have different bookcases here, too. They'll be circular and rotate. Then, right there we'll make a space for story time. I'm hoping to find someone who'd like to come in on a

Saturday afternoon once a month and read to the kids. Know anyone who might be interested in that?" he asked, raising both eyebrows.

Reading to children? Gee, twist her arm. "I think I might know someone," she said with a smile.

Brock held up a book to her. *Splat the Cat.* "Can we get this?"

She turned to Truman. "I know you're not officially open, yet but can you ring up a sale?"

"I'll do better than that. How about I give that to you for Christmas, Brock?" he asked.

Brock hugged the book to him. "Yes! Thank you."

"How will you make any money if you keep giving away your books?" Lexie protested.

"I'm sure you'll be a loyal customer," he said.

He had that right.

They stayed a few more minutes, then Lexie herded her son toward the door, saying to Truman, "We need to let you get back to work."

He walked them to the door. "I'm looking forward to Christmas," he said to her.

"Me, too," she told him.

As she was about to follow her son out, he caught her hand and drew her close enough so he could whisper in her ear. "And maybe celebrating New Year's Eve."

His breath tickled, and those little elves all began to dance around in her tummy again.

"That sounds like an excellent idea," she said.

Brock grabbed her other hand and pulled. "Come on, Mommy. I want to go home and read my new book."

"See you later," Truman said.

Oh, yes.

"I like our new friends," Brock said as they drove home.

"Me, too," Lexie said. This was going to be such a good Christmas.

Back at the house, Brock dived into his book, reading aloud to Lexie as she put together the cupcakes. By the time they were out of the oven and cooled, he'd had enough of Splat and was ready to help frost and decorate. Of course, many sprinkles were needed on the top of each one.

"Can I take some to Grandpa Stanley?" Brock asked as they decorated.

"This time I'm going to make the delivery," she told him. "I need to talk to him."

Once on his front porch she found she wasn't quite sure what to say. She thought back to that voice mail he'd left. He hadn't known, either.

Maybe the best approach was to simply say *Let's start again. Why don't you come over for dinner on Christmas Day?*

She rang the doorbell. A moment later she could hear his dog barking on the other side of the door. Stanley was taking his time opening it. Maybe he was hiding in there.

Meanwhile, her phone was going off. It was Aunt Rose's ringtone. Her aunt rarely called. Curious, Lexie pulled the phone out of her coat pocket and took the call. At the rate Stanley was going she'd have plenty of time to talk.

"Hello," she said as she rang the doorbell again.

"Lexie, dear, I'm at the emergency room with your mother. You need to get down here right away."

23

STANLEY STILL REMEMBERED HOW IT ALL HAP-pened.

As usual, he'd balked at the idea of having a party. This time Carol wanted to have one to celebrate Halloween. He especially hated Halloween parties. Dressing in silly costumes that made you look like a dork, playing those goofy games she and her sister always came up with.

"Why don't we go out instead," he'd suggested. "Have dinner, take in a scary movie."

"We can do that anytime. Halloween only comes once a year."

There was something to be grateful for.

"Come on, Stanley, don't be a party pooper."

"I'm not a party pooper," he insisted. He hated it when she called him that. Just because he didn't want to play stupid games with a houseful of people didn't make him a party pooper.

"Yes, you are," she insisted.

"Can't we just have one couple over and watch movies?" he suggested.

"We did that last year. And the year before."

"And it was fun, right?"

"It was. But I miss having a party. I want to play dark tag again."

Oh, Lord, chasing each other around in a pitch-dark room. They'd played that game plenty when they were young, but they weren't young anymore. People in their sixties should have a little more decorum, if you asked him. Not that Carol was asking.

"Somebody's bound to run into something and get hurt or wreck the furniture. Remember the last time we played that? Jimmy ran into the curio cabinet and broke the glass. And it wasn't cheap to repair."

"We'll move it."

Yes, moving furniture around, that would be fun. "Don't you think we're a little too old for some of these games?"

She frowned at him. "Darn it, Stanley, we're not that old yet."

"I am," he said.

"Is this the same man who once told me age is just a number?"

"The number's gotten bigger since you turned fifty," he argued.

"We're not dead yet."

He sighed. This was a losing battle. May as well give up and give in.

She smiled, knowing what that sigh signified. "It will be fun," she promised.

"Fun," he repeated, unconvinced.

Carol didn't ask much of him, and she did everything he liked with him: fly-fishing, snowshoeing, bowling. (She hadn't ever mastered the game and opted out of joining a league with him, but she'd still hit the alley once in a while on a Saturday night.) Car shows, of course. So if she wanted to have a party once in a while and play some crazy games, the least he could do was be a good sport and go along with it.

Anyway, she was right. He did always manage to have a good time once things got going. Especially if he and some of the guys could slip away for a game of Ping-Pong. You were never too old for that.

Carol loved decorating, and soon ceramic figures of ghosts and witches and pumpkins started appearing all over the house, and she set out a miniature patch of honeycomb pumpkins on the dining table as a centerpiece. She also drafted him to help her carve pumpkins for the front porch the week before the party.

That he could get into. He'd loved carving pumpkins as a kid, and he enjoyed creating a couple of downright creepy faces, one traditional with triangle eyes and nose and a crooked mouth; the other he made to look like the famous painting she'd showed him once called *The Scream*.

"That is truly terrifying," she said, looking at it.

"Maybe it will scare everyone away," he joked.

"Ha-ha," she said, unamused.

They set their creations up that very night, lining the steps to the front porch, then lit the candles and stepped back to check out how they looked.

"They look great. I think we are now ready for Halloween," she said, smiling.

"Yep," he agreed and slipped an arm around her.

Christmas was her favorite holiday, but Halloween came in a strong second. Carol not only enjoyed finding an excuse to entertain a mob, she also loved handing out candy to the kids who came trick-or-treating.

"Don't you look pretty!" she'd say to all the little princesses. To the Darth Vaders and ghosts and monsters she'd say, "You look so scary!" And she'd always beg the little witches not to turn her into a toad, which would make them giggle. "You won't do that if I give you candy, will you?" she'd ask. Of course, they'd promise not to because Carol was always generous with the candy. And she guarded the candy bowl like a dragon, getting after Stanley every time he raided it.

At least he'd get plenty of treats at the party. It would be his reward for having to walk around dressed like a giant salami.

They'd finished dinner and were loading the dishwasher together the Friday night before the big bash when she said, "I think I'll go pick up the last of the food I need for the party."

"Just wait until tomorrow," he advised. "You've got all day."

"I want to bake some more cookies and make a pumpkin roll."

"That doesn't take all day to do," he pointed out.

"But I don't want to be pooped by the time everyone gets here."

"You already look pooped. Stay home and relax. You can send me to get the stuff tomorrow."

She refused to take him up on the offer. Even after all the years they'd been together he still managed to come home with a brand she didn't like or the wrong size of something.

"Okay, then, I'll go with you. I don't like you driving at night."

"I'm a better driver than you are," she said.

Stanley's night vision wasn't as good as it once was, but he could handle driving to the grocery store.

"I won't be that long," she assured him. "And I'd rather do it by myself. You get antsy after a while."

Only because it took her a million years to decide between ice cream flavors, and she had to inspect every apple in the produce section. They invariably ran into someone she knew, and that meant standing around talking, blocking the aisle. She'd take forever.

"Come on, babe, stay home. I found a movie for us to watch."

"I'll be back in plenty of time to watch a movie," she assured him.

But she wasn't. She didn't come back at all.

Instead two policemen showed up on his doorstep, looking for Carol's next of kin, politely asking if they could come in.

No! Stanley already knew they were there with bad news. *Don't give it to the old guy on the doorstep.*

His heart shut down; his brain shut down. He could hardly breathe. He stood back and let them in, managed to lead them into the living room.

"I'm afraid there's been an accident," said one of the cops.

"An accident," he repeated. "Is she alive?"

"I'm sorry, sir. She died while paramedics were attempting to revive her."

Stanley's mind kept rejecting the image. Not Carol. She was too full of life. She couldn't be dead. Not so suddenly, with no warning.

"What do I do now?" he asked.

Of course, they thought he was talking about procedure. He was talking about the rest of his life.

Amy was almost as much of a wreck as Stanley, so it fell to her husband, Jimmy, and Carol's best friend, Lois, to make the calls canceling the party. Other family members stepped in and helped with funeral arrangements. Stanley filled out forms, barely seeing what he was writing. Her wrote her obituary for the paper. How did you sum up a person's life in only one paragraph? Especially a person like Carol, who was so kind and thoughtful, who made life special for everyone who knew her?

Women started showing up with casseroles; cards flowed in. He couldn't bring himself to read any of the cards, and the food got dumped in the garbage.

The church was packed for her memorial service. So many of her former students came to pay their respects and sing her praises. The woman who'd never had a child of her own had touched hundreds of lives.

Afterward family and close friends came to the house to help consume the latest offering of casseroles, along with cakes and pies, telling him how sorry they were, how great Carol was. They clustered in groups and chatted like they were at a cocktail party. Carol would have loved seeing the house full of people. But Carol wasn't there, and Stanley just wanted them to all go away.

"Life goes on," said one of the neighbors, and it was all Stanley could do not to punch him.

"You'll see her again one day," Georgia Wallis, one of the church ladies, assured him, giving him a hug.

Easy for Georgia to dish out the platitudes. Her husband was still hale and hearty. She had no idea how it felt to lose the love of your life. And he didn't want to see Carol one day. He wanted to see her now.

But, like his insensitive neighbor had said, life did go on. Stanley just didn't want to be a part of it. He sold the mangled Mustang for scrap, made her sister and mom take away her clothes and lotions, and he hid her jewelry box under the bed. Then he turned into a robot, going through the motions of everyday life.

He found it impossible to feel thankful on Thanksgiving, and he didn't open a single Christmas card that came. He didn't put up a tree, and he didn't put up lights. Too many reminders of his life with Carol.

Memories flooded him, anyway: buying their first tree, Carol baking cookies, her delighted expression when he gave her the ornament he'd made for her, sitting next to her on the sofa watching Christmas movies.

Christmas morning he looked at the spot where they had always put the tree and cried.

★ ★ ★

He didn't cry anymore, and he was seeing Carol again—a lot sooner than Georgia had predicted. Funny how, even as a ghost, she managed to bring out the best in him.

Or had been until he blew it with the Santa thing. Just when he was beginning to almost enjoy life. He just wasn't equipped to live without Carol.

24

STANLEY CAME TO THE DOOR, LEERY OF WHAT HE'D find. He looked out the side window and saw Lexie standing on the porch, yakking on her phone. Good grief, you couldn't even go to somebody's house without...

Never mind the device. She was here, and she had a paper plate with cupcakes on it. The block of cement that had been sitting in his chest since that ill-fated dinner crumbled. It looked like he was forgiven. He'd still say he was sorry, though.

He opened the door just as the plate fell from her hand, sending cupcakes tumbling in all directions.

She looked at him bleakly. "My mom," she said. Then the poor kid broke into tears and hurled herself against him.

It had been a long time since Stanley had held a crying

woman, but his arms remembered what to do, and they quickly responded to the need and wrapped around her.

"It's okay," he said, patting her back, even though it obviously wasn't. "Tell me what's going on."

"She's in the emergency room. She's had a heart attack." Lexie pulled away. "I have to get to her." She turned and started back to her house at a run.

Stanley followed, not quite so fast. *He* was going to have a heart attack trying to catch up with Lexie. She wasn't wearing that big, clunky boot anymore, just a brace. The girl could really move now.

She slowed when she got to her front porch, hesitated at the front door. Whirled around, panic on her face. "What am I going to tell Brock?"

"Tell him she's sick."

"What if she…"

Stanley had been down this road. He understood the shock and fear that rode on your shoulders with every step.

"You don't know what if. Take this one minute at a time."

Lexie nodded, bit her lip, opened the door.

Brock came bounding up. "Grandpa Stanley! Did you come to play with me?"

"No, I came to help you and your mom. You're going to be taking a trip." To Lexie he said, "Go pack what you need. I'll see how soon I can get a flight out for you two."

She looked at him gratefully. "Thank you. So much."

"What are neighbors for?" he replied.

"Are we going someplace?" the boy asked.

"We have to go see Grandma," Lexie said. Her lower lip

trembled, but she managed to fake calm and added, "She's not feeling well. Come on, let's get some clothes packed."

They went upstairs, and Stanley returned to his house and went to work on the phone. He was able to book a flight and pay for it in record time. He pulled on his coat, told Bonnie to behave while he was gone, then grabbed his car keys and backed his SUV out of the garage.

By the time he got to Lexie's house she was packed and ready to go.

He handed over her flight information. "The car's waiting. Come on."

She bit her lip and nodded, hustled her son out the door.

As soon as she had Brock and herself buckled in, Stanley took off, resisting the urge to speed. The last thing they needed was to get stopped by a cop. Or, worse, get in an accident.

He hoped Lexie's mom would be okay. Why did things like this always seem to happen during the holidays?

"I can't thank you enough for this," Lexie said, tears making her voice waver. "We're always imposing on you."

"It's not imposing if I offer."

"Especially after..."

He knew where she was going and cut her off. "I was wrong."

"You're a rock," she said.

It was what Carol used to tell him. Steady Stanley, always there when you needed him. No one had needed him for a long time. Except now someone did, maybe would continue to need him for some time. He sure wasn't going to let her down.

"Oh, God," Lexie whimpered. "First my dad. Now... I

don't want her to—" She bit the words off, looked to the back seat where her son sat, hugging his little backpack.

"It's gonna be okay," Stanley assured her.

Yeah, as if he knew? But it was no use her spending the whole flight down in a panic.

"This is not how I pictured Christmas," she said miserably.

He sighed. "Stuff happens."

She bit her lip, nodded.

"Does Grandma have a cold?" Brock asked.

Tears were leaking out of the corner of Lexie's eye. "No, honey, she's sicker than that."

"Are we going to make her chicken soup?" he asked.

"Maybe," Lexie said and wiped her cheek.

Poor kids, Stanley thought.

At the airport he unloaded her carry-on for her, wishing he could do more. Of course, there wasn't more you could do when somebody was going through something like this.

"I'll keep an eye on the house," he told her.

"Thanks," she said. "I do have something coming." She lowered her voice and leaned in. "It's Brock's present from Santa. Even though he knows the truth, he's still looking forward to that extra gift under the tree. Could you keep an eye out for it?"

"Sure," Stanley promised.

"Although we probably won't get back in time," she said, and her lower lip began to wobble.

"I'll bring it in," he promised. Then added, "You can do this."

She dashed away the last of her tears, nodded. "Thank you for everything. I'll pay you back for the tickets."

"No need. Think of it as a Christmas present."

She shook her head. "No, that's too much."

Considering the Santa mess it was a small-enough penance. "I don't think so. I hope your mom does okay."

"Me, too," she said. Then she surprised him by leaning over and kissing him on the cheek. "Thank you again. For everything. Come on, Brockie, we have to hurry," she said to her son and pulled him through the entrance.

"Bye, Grandpa," the kid said as he followed her. "We have to go help Grandma get better."

"You will," Stanley said and hoped he was right.

And then they were gone. Stanley stood there a moment, trying to process everything that had just happened. He wasn't sure he could.

He got back in his SUV and drove home. Bonnie was waiting to greet him, tail wagging.

He picked her up, and she immediately got busy trying to lick his face. "You're a good dog," he told her. "Let's find you a dog treat, and then we're going to put up our Christmas tree."

He could have sworn he smelled peppermint when he went into the garage to bring in the big artificial tree they'd bought that last Christmas before Carol died. He couldn't help smiling.

"I know, babe. Better late than never."

Once he had the tree and the bin with the ornaments set out in the living room, he put on her favorite radio station that played Christmas music all day long. A chorus began to sing "We Need a Little Christmas."

Yes, they did.

The flight to LAX was torture. Lexie longed to lay her head on the drop-down tray and wail, but mommies didn't get to enjoy that luxury. She tried to keep the tears dammed and pay attention when her son was talking to her, but it was a challenge.

Brock was oblivious to his mother's consternation, enjoying the view out the window and the novelty of airplane food. She kept him busy with coloring and let him play some games on his tablet. He only began to get squirmy toward the end of the flight.

"When will we see Grandma?" he asked.

"Soon," she said and hoped it would be soon enough.

It was dark by the time the plane landed. She called her uncle as soon as passengers were allowed to turn on their cell phones.

"I've got Jen with me. We'll pick you up in the loading zone," he told her.

If she'd been coming in under normal circumstances she'd have been delighted to see her cousin. Like her, Jen was a teacher.

"How's Mom?" she asked her uncle.

"She's going to be okay," said Uncle Fred. "They ran an EKG and took an X-ray. Did a blood test. Looks like it wasn't a heart attack after all."

Lexie sagged in relief. No heart attack. Her mom was all right.

But if not a heart attack, why was she in the hospital? "Then, what was it?" Lexie asked.

"Some kind of panic attack."

Panic attack. That was what Lexie had just had. Honestly, she was going to let her mother have it.

People ahead of her were taking down their carry-ons, starting to move up the aisle. "We're getting off now," she said to her uncle and ended the call.

"Was that Grandma?" Brock asked.

"No, that was Uncle Fred. He's going to take us to Grandma." *Who is fine. Thank God!*

Her uncle and cousin were waiting in Uncle Fred's Lexus when Lexie and Brock emerged from inside the terminal. At the sight of her he hopped out and took her luggage. "It's good to see you, Lexie. Sorry we got you down here for nothing, but when it happened your aunt was terrified."

Poor Aunt Rose. Lexie could only imagine.

"I'm glad everything's okay," her cousin said, hugging her. "Angie and I are taking you to Back on the Beach tomorrow for chill time."

After the stress of the last few hours, she'd need it.

"So don't commit matricide," Jen teased.

Lexie giggled. She felt practically giddy with relief. "How did you know that's what I was thinking?"

"Because that's what I'd be thinking," said her cousin.

Once at the hospital, Uncle Fred and Jen took Brock to find a treat in the hospital cafeteria, which was open late, and Lexie went in search of her mother and aunt. She found Mom waiting to be discharged, sitting up in a hospital bed in her emergency-room cubicle, still wearing the latest style in hospital-gown ugly, Aunt Rose seated in a chair nearby.

There was only a two year difference between the sisters, and Mom was the youngest, but no one looking at them would think that. Aunt Rose was fit with tanned, youthful skin, thanks to fills from her dermatologist. Her hair was stylishly cut and highlighted. Mom's hair, on the other hand, was now a drab dirty-blond streaked with gray. She looked gaunt, and the lines around her mouth had turned into crevices. She'd aged overnight. Still, Lexie couldn't imagine a better sight.

"Oh, Lexie, darling," she greeted her daughter. "You shouldn't have come all this way."

Lexie hurried to the bedside and kissed her. "Are you serious? Not come when I think you're having a heart attack?"

Both her mother and aunt looked embarrassed at this.

"I'm sorry to have worried you," Aunt Rose said, "but it looked serious, and I knew you'd want to know what was going on."

"Of course I would," Lexie said. "What happened?"

"We were at my house, just looking through some old pictures, and suddenly your mother couldn't breathe. And she had pain in her chest."

"I feel so foolish," Mom added. "I had no idea a panic attack could mimic a heart attack. I don't even know why I panicked. One minute I was looking at pictures of all of us at the beach, and the next your aunt was calling 9-1-1."

Pictures of all of us. There was a big clue. Her father had to have been in them. Poor Mom.

"The important thing is that you're okay," Lexie said. She took her mother's hand and gave it a squeeze. She could feel the tears rising.

"Where's Brock?" Mom asked.

"He's here. Uncle Fred and Jen took him to the cafeteria to get something to eat."

"Oh, dear. I've turned your life upside down," Mom fretted.

"No, you haven't," Lexie lied.

But the next day when it was just her and her cousins at the popular Santa Monica beachfront restaurant, she did some serious venting. "I don't know how to help her," she finished and took another bite of her grilled fish taco. It didn't taste so good anymore.

Lexie's cousin Angie pointed a perfectly manicured finger at her. "You're definitely going to have to have a come-to-Jesus meeting. Your mom's got to get a grip."

Lexie pushed away her plate. "How do you get a grip on losing the most important person in your life?"

Neither cousin had an answer for that.

Once back at the house, she found her mom and Brock at the kitchen table, working a puzzle together. The sun was shining in through the window, creating a nimbus around them. Her mom wasn't exactly exuberant, but she didn't look totally miserable, either. Lexie came to a decision.

Later that night, after Brock was sound asleep in Lexie's old bed, she made peppermint tea and then settled them on the living-room couch. "I've booked a flight home for tomorrow," she said.

Disappointment was plain on her mother's face. "So soon?"

"Yes, so soon. Tomorrow is Christmas Eve, and I want to be back at the house for Christmas. All Brock's presents are

310 A LITTLE CHRISTMAS SPIRIT

there. Plus I have red velvet cupcakes on the counter going stale and a turkey in the fridge that needs to be cooked."

Mom sighed and set her mug of tea on the coffee table. "Of course."

Lexie laid a hand on her mother's. "And you're coming with us."

"Oh, darling, I'm not up to it."

"I think you are," Lexie said, determined to be firm. "And besides, we should be together. You scared the crap out of me, Mom," she added softly.

"I didn't mean to scare you," Mom said, sounding defensive.

"I know, but you did. And, frankly, I've been worried about you."

"I'm fine," Mom insisted.

Right. Lexie had just witnessed an example of how fine her mother was.

"No, you're not. And I'm sorry you're having such a hard time. I've had a hard time, too, but I have a son who needs me to be there for him, and I need you there for me. I need my mom back."

Her mother's lower lip began to wobble, and she put a hand to her chest.

Lexie scooted next to her and wrapped an arm around her shoulder. "Take a deep breath, Mom. It's okay."

"It's not," her mother said, her voice tripping over a sob.

That was all it took. The dam broke, and Lexie started crying also. They sat there together for a long time, holding each other and sharing a fresh helping of grief. At last Lexie went in search of tissues so they could mop their wet faces and blow their noses.

"We both have to keep living," she said after her second nose blow. "Daddy would want us to, you know that."

"I...can't," her mother said softly.

"You have to try, at least for Christmas. Can you do that? Please? For us?"

Mom bit her lip.

"And to honor Daddy?"

A fresh tear slipped down her mother's cheek.

"Our flight leaves at six." It meant they'd get in late but Lexie didn't care. At least she'd found a flight out and getting home late was preferable to not getting home at all.

Mom sighed, nodded. "I'm tired. I think I'll go to bed."

Lexie felt tired, too. And drained. She went to bed shortly after her mother. Curled up next to her little boy in the bed that had once been hers, she let out a deep sigh and shot up a quick prayer of thanks that Mom would be with them for Christmas.

Her mother didn't initiate any conversation on the way to the airport, but she managed a smile or two for Brock and put an arm around him as they waited in the airport terminal to board their plane.

It's a beginning, Lexie thought.

Their plane landed at Sea-Tac at nine that night, and it took another forty-five minutes for their Uber ride to get them home. By the time they arrived, Brock was cranky and yawning, and her mother looked ready to drop. Lexie felt overwhelmed with relief and happiness at the sight of their house. Home sweet home.

As they went up the front walk she realized she'd never even told Truman that she'd had to fly back to California. If she hadn't booked that return flight, he'd have come over the next day with the girls and wondered what kind of flake invited him for dinner and then wasn't around to serve it. Living so close, she'd never even thought about exchanging phone numbers, so she couldn't have texted him.

Truman and his girls. Would Mom be up for being sociable with strangers? Lexie hoped so.

The front porch was bare of packages. Stanley must have intercepted Brock's present and taken it to his house. She'd call him once she had her son and her mother settled in.

Inside, she sent Brock straight to bed, skipping the nightly bath routine, then gave her mother a quick tour of the house.

"It's very nice, darling," Mom said. "You've done a lovely job decorating."

"I'm glad you're sharing our first Christmas in it," Lexie told her.

"I am, too," Mom said, and Lexie hoped she really meant it.

Whether she was glad or not, she needed it. There was nothing in the old house but sadness. Her mother hadn't even bothered to put up a tree.

Not that Christmas was about trees. Or presents. But it was about hope. Maybe Mom could find enough to take her into a better New Year.

She settled her mother in the guest bedroom, then called Stanley. She'd seen a light on in his house so hoped it was okay to call him after ten at night.

He picked up on the second ring. "How's your mom?" he asked, and the concern in that gruff, old voice warmed Lexie's heart.

"She's fine. It turned out she had a panic attack, not a heart attack."

"Good," he said.

"I'm sorry to call you so late."

"I was up."

Great. She'd run right over. Then, once that final present was under the tree she, too, could go to bed.

"I didn't see anything on the front porch and figured you must have taken in Brock's present," she said. "Would you mind if I came over and got it now?"

There was moment of silence and that uneasy feeling of uh-oh tippy-toed up behind Lexie and said *Gotcha!*

Oh, no. Please don't say what I think you're going to.

25

"IT DIDN'T COME," STANLEY TOLD LEXIE. "I WAS watching," he added, in case she thought he hadn't been vigilant.

There was a long silence on the other end of the call, and he could envision the tears collecting in her eyes.

"But I, uh, have something. I'll bring it over."

He ended the call before she could tell him to forget it. His old Lionel train set was a leftover from his childhood that he'd never gotten rid of. From the late fifties, it was still in mint condition. Some of those old sets went for as much as ten thousand dollars. He figured his would fetch at least five, probably more.

But he'd never wanted to sell it. At first the thing had been a bit of nostalgia he couldn't bring himself to part with. Then he'd kept it, thinking he'd give it to his son one day. The son never arrived, and the train set eventually was forgotten.

Until after the Santa fiasco. Then, when the present for Brock never arrived, the idea of giving the train set to him had popped into Stanley's mind like a gift from... Santa.

Carol had probably planted the thought there. At least, he hoped she had. Maybe, if he put it to good use, she'd visit him again. He had a feeling those visits were coming to a close, but he longed to see her one last time.

He'd found the train set, checked to make sure everything was still working and cleaned it up, and now it was ready to go. Kids these days were into video games and drones and fancy games with lots of bells and whistles, so maybe this was a dumb idea. But maybe Brock was still young enough to think a train set was cool. After all, the boy liked to play Candy Land.

Stanley threw on his coat, picked up the giant cardboard box that contained all the smaller boxes with the engine and boxcars and passenger cars and the extra tracks and headed next door.

Lexie must have seen him coming, because by the time he got to her front porch she already had the door open.

"I'm sorry what you ordered didn't come, but maybe this will work," he said and moved past her into the living room.

The tree had a few presents around it, but she hadn't turned on the tree lights. In fact, the whole living room was a little dark, with only one light on.

She sighed. "*Guaranteed delivery before Christmas.* That's what they promised."

"Things don't always go the way you plan," he said. And

he should know. He set the box down on the floor by the tree and knelt in front of it. "I need some light to work by."

She turned on some more lights, then came and knelt next to him, watching as he opened the box. "Oh, my gosh," she said as he took out the vintage engine. "How cute is that!"

"It was mine when I was a kid."

"It's an antique, then."

Just like him.

"We couldn't take it. It's probably valuable."

"Yeah, it is," Stanley agreed.

"There's probably someone in your family…"

He thought of Carol's prissy nieces and their spoiled little girls and shook his head. "No, there's not. They're into other stuff. It's not a fancy video game."

"No, it's not." She grinned. "It has…heart."

"Yeah, it does," he agreed and knew he'd found the right home for his childhood treasure.

Together, they laid out the tracks so the train would circle the tree and coupled the cars. She turned on the tree lights, and he plugged in the transformer and set the little Lionel chugging its way around.

"It's so cute. It looks like something out of an old movie," Lexie said, and Stanley saw that she was smiling. She turned the smile on him, and it felt like sunshine on his shoulder on a winter's day. "I can't thank you enough."

"This should square us," he said hopefully.

"It more than squares us," she said and stood up.

He stood, too. Time to go.

"It's been a long couple of days. I need to unwind," she said. "Would you like some eggnog?"

The warmth spread from his shoulder and wrapped around his heart. "Yeah." And if she'd had a long couple of days he knew exactly what she needed. "I have just the thing to go with it. I'll be right back," he said and grabbed his coat.

He speed-walked back across the lawns. He was tempted to run, but the temperatures had dropped, and the grass was frosty. The last thing he wanted was to slip.

Although if he fell and broke something, then it would be her turn to drive him around, he thought with a chuckle.

Once inside the house, he went to the cupboard where he kept the booze and grabbed a bottle of rum. Bonnie was sure he had to be looking for something for her and stood on her hind legs, dancing in anticipation.

"Okay, something for you, too," he told her and gave her a treat. "I won't be long," he promised, then hurried back out the front door.

Lexie grinned when he stepped back inside and held up the bottle. "Yes, that is exactly what I need," she said.

He followed her to the kitchen where she had two glasses of eggnog poured and added the rum.

She picked up her glass, and he picked up his. Then, before he could drink, she clinked them together. "To the New Year," she said.

"To the New Year," he echoed.

They wandered back into the living room, and she turned off all the lights except the colored ones on the tree, and they sat and watched the train circle it.

"You saved me, Stanley," she said. "If it wasn't for you, there'd have been no present from Santa under the tree."

"Yeah, but now the kid knows there's no Santa."

"He does, but we decided it's still fun to pretend, and I'd promised him there'd be an extra present for him. If I hadn't come through he'd have been crushed."

"My dad told me there was no such thing as Santa," Stanley volunteered.

"Were you disappointed?"

"You bet. It was a shock to hear it was all a big lie."

"That was what you thought, that your parents were lying?"

"Well, they were, weren't they?" he retorted.

"I prefer to think of it as pretending," she said.

He shrugged. "It wasn't a good time. The old man was out of work, money was tight. I guess the whole thing sort of stuck in my craw."

"Funny how those childhood experiences can do that," she said. "I had a great childhood. I sure hope I can give Brock one."

"Looks like you already are," Stanley told her. "You're a good mom."

"You really think so?"

"Sure. You kind of remind me of my mom. She was the best." Okay, they were getting kind of touchy-feely here. He downed the last of his eggnog and stood. "I better let you get to bed. Your boy will probably be up early."

She stood, too, and walked with him to the door. Before opening it she asked, "Stanley, do you have plans for tomorrow?"

He could have had plans. Now he almost wished he'd taken his sister-in-law up on her Christmas-dinner invitation.

"Not really," he said.

"Would you like to join us over here? I'm going to cook a turkey, and I've got the last of those cupcakes. The new neighbors are coming over."

"Sounds like a crowd," he said. She probably didn't need one more piehole to feed.

"It'll be a nice crowd. And I think my mom would like having someone her age to talk to. I know Brock would love to have you here. So would I."

Someone genuinely wanted his company. He smiled. "Okay."

"Great! Come on over around two."

Back home he let Bonnie out to do her thing, and while she was in the back yard, he set her present—a new chew toy—under the tree.

"We'll have Christmas morning together before I have to leave," he told her as they went up the stairs to bed.

It was a quiet bedtime. Carol still hadn't made an appearance. That night he slept dreamlessly, but he awoke feeling...not bad. Not bad at all. In fact, he decided, he was rather looking forward to the day, turkey dinner and all.

The traveling and later bedtime had worn Brock out, but by six he was bouncing on Lexie's bed, waving his stocking around. "Mommy, it's Christmas!"

"Yes, it is," she said.

Her son was happy, her mother was with them, and the candy cane in the Christmas stocking was that they had company coming to join them. A true gathering of the neighbors, just like she'd envisioned when she first bought the house. She could hardly wait. She could especially hardly wait to see Truman. It was going to be a great day.

"Look what I got," Brock said and dumped the contents of his stocking on the bed.

Out fell mini candy bars (bought on sale after Halloween at fifty percent off and hidden away). Also a tiny metal car, a set of Christmas-themed finger puppets, gummy worms and a small travel game—all ordered online. Thank God those had come in time.

"That's quite a haul," she said.

There was something else, a folded piece of paper. It wasn't folded as neatly as she originally had done it, which meant Brock had looked at it.

He nodded happily. Then sobered. "Mommy, are you sure there's no Santa?"

She tousled his hair. "There can be if you want there to be."

The nod became very enthusiastic. "I do. Look what I got." He handed over the paper.

She already knew what the little note said since she'd been the one who'd written it.

She unfolded the paper and said, "Let's read it together."

"'*Dear,*'" she began.

"'*Brock,*'" he read. "'*You are a good boy, and your M-m-m…*'"

"'*Mother,*'" she supplied.

"'*Mother l-l-lo…*'"

"'*Loves.*'"

"'*Loves you,*'" he said and beamed. "I know these words! '*Merry Christmas. Santa.*'"

"Well, what do you know," Lexie said.

His brow furrowed. "Did Santa really write me?"

"Let's not worry about who wrote that," she suggested. "Let's concentrate on what it says. *You are a good boy, and your mother loves you.* Now, your special gift from Santa is still coming but there's something else waiting for you. Should we go downstairs and see what's under the tree?"

His head nearly nodded right off his neck, and he bounced off the bed.

"Wait a minute," Lexie called. "Why don't you go knock on Grandma's door and tell her it's time to get up?"

"Okay!" He started for the door.

"First, come put everything back in your stocking."

This produced a slightly impatient frown, but he obeyed.

While he was busy restuffing his stocking, Lexie donned her brace. Then, as he ran off to wake Grandma, she raced down the stairs, turned on the tree lights and started the train going. She grabbed her phone so she could capture that most magical moment in childhood, when he first saw the tree with its presents and promise of fun.

"Grandma's coming," Brock hollered. This was followed by the thunder of little-boy feet coming down the stairs.

Lexie had her phone set to Video and caught the intake of breath and the wide eyes followed by the squeal and the excited rush to the tree. *God bless you, Stanley Mann*, she thought as her son fell in front of the track and watched in wonder as the little train chugged its way around the presents.

Stanley, himself, had turned out to be a gift. Under those crusty layers of gruffness the man was solid gold. Like the valuable train set he'd given her son, he was a keeper.

Lexie had coffee ready by the time her mother came

322 A LITTLE CHRISTMAS SPIRIT

down half an hour later, a bathrobe over her pajamas. She'd gotten as far as combing her hair and, knowing Mom, had also brushed her teeth. Her smile, however, was a pale shadow of what it had been when Lexie's father was alive. But she was there with them. That was what mattered.

The pile of presents under the tree was small. A game for Brock, a book Grandma had sent back when she hadn't planned on coming up, some socks decorated with dinosaurs, and from Lexie's cousins, who'd been dubbed aunties, Legos and a Harry Potter wizard training wand that came complete with lights and sounds.

Lexie loved the bracelet Mom had sent: rose gold with a heart bearing an *L*. And she knew she'd forever treasure the tree ornament made of Popsicle sticks, painted red and shaped into a sleigh, that Brock had made for her at school.

She baked coffee cake for breakfast and got the turkey in the oven, and by early afternoon the house was filled with an aroma that said *Let's eat*.

Her mother helped her in the kitchen, made punch and assisted Brock in setting the table for their holiday feast. As they worked, Lexie kept up a line of cheerful chatter, but it was as if Mom was wearing armor and the arrows of cheer bounced off.

Still, she was there. It was a beginning, and you had to begin somewhere.

Truman and his girls arrived a little before two, the girls wearing red-and-green Christmas dresses and Truman in jeans and a tan Nordic-looking sweater with a border of reindeer running across his chest. He sure looked like what Lexie wanted for Christmas, and her heart gave a squeeze as if those little elves had moved from her tummy to trampoline on it.

He came bearing gifts, a box of candy as well as gift cards to the bookstore for both Lexie and Brock.

"We picked out the candy," said Isobel, the younger sister.

"It was a good pick. We like chocolates," Lexie said to her. "You didn't have to do that," she told Truman as Brock led the girls into the living room to see his train, but she was pleased nonetheless.

"My mother always told me you should never show up to dinner empty-handed," he said.

"It sounds like you have a very smart mother."

"I do. I should have listened to her more often."

She imagined he was talking about his ex but didn't say anything, figuring that was a conversation they didn't need to keep going. Christmas wasn't the time to talk about past mistakes. It was about new beginnings waiting right around the corner.

"Speaking of mothers," Lexie said, "come on in and meet mine. She wound up coming to spend Christmas with us after all."

Introductions were made, and the grown-ups settled on the couch while the kids sat by the tree, following the progress of Brock's new train, which hadn't stopped running from the moment he first saw it.

Truman was polite to Mom, asking questions about where she lived, then following up with more questions when he learned she lived in Southern California. When that conversation dried up, he asked what she thought of Lexie's new house.

"It's very lovely, but the weather's so gloomy up here," Mom said.

"I hear it rains a lot in the Pacific Northwest," Truman said. "But, looking at how green it is here, I think I can live with that."

"It's gorgeous in the summer," Lexie put in. "You'd like it here then, Mom."

Her mother said nothing, refusing to be drawn into admitting that was a possibility. Honestly, it was as if Mom was determined to do all she could to toss the merry out of Christmas.

The doorbell rang, and Brock popped up. "It's Grandpa Stanley!"

Her mother didn't look all that thrilled at her grandson having a replacement grandpa, and now Lexie wondered if it had been such a good idea to invite Stanley for dinner after all.

Brock opened the door, and in stepped Stanley Mann, looking festive in slacks and a shirt under a red pullover sweater. He'd accessorized with a red bow tie. And something even more amazing—a big smile.

"Merry Christmas, Grandpa!" Brock hollered as if their neighbor had suddenly gone deaf. "I got a train for Christmas."

"You did?" Stanley said.

Brock took him by the hand and towed him into the living room. "Come and see."

"That's a nice one," Stanley said and winked at Lexie as she approached. "Something sure smells good," he said to her.

"Turkey and all the fixings," she replied. "Stanley, I want you to meet our new neighbors."

The girls said a polite hello, and the men shook hands. Then it was time to introduce Stanley to Mom.

"Good to meet you," he said to her. "You've raised a great daughter."

So polite and…sociable. Had Stanley been taken over by aliens?

Mom murmured her thanks but didn't do anything to keep the conversation going. That didn't appear to bother Stanley. He settled on the couch and observed the kids, chatted with Truman about trains and how nobody was interested in them anymore.

"Only old farts like me," he finished.

"Brock looks like a convert," Truman observed.

"That one is courtesy of Stanley," Lexie explained, and her mother looked over at him in surprise. "He pretty much saved the day."

Stanley waved away her praise, but the corners of his lips sneaked up.

"I had a Transformers train set when I was little," Truman reminisced. "I loved that thing. Wish I still had it. I think it would be worth something now." He nodded in the direction of the vintage Lionel set slowly making its way around the tree. "That one looks pretty valuable."

Stanley shrugged. "It's worth a few pennies." Lexie brought the video up on her phone of Brock's reaction to it and showed him. "And that's priceless," he said, watching it.

Yep, he'd been taken over by aliens.

Dinner was a boisterous and happy affair with the children at their own little table, in high spirits and giggling. Even Mom almost smiled a couple of times. Until after dessert. The children wolfed down their stale red velvet cupcakes, then pulled out Candy Land and set up camp in the living room while the adults lingered over coffee.

That was when Stanley casually said to Mom, "I hear you lost your husband."

Lexie's good spirits plummeted, and she braced herself.

Mom set down her coffee mug, stared at it. Said nothing. Lexie and Truman exchanged looks. *What do you do in a moment like this?*

Stanley appeared oblivious. "Hard," he said. "I lost my wife three years ago." He shook his head. "I still miss her."

"I'd rather not talk about my husband," Mom said stiffly.

"I can understand that," Stanley said. "What's worse is people butting into your life, wanting you to smile and come to big holiday gatherings and pretend like nothing happened."

Gift or not, Lexie was going to wring his neck.

Mom looked at him in surprise, then nodded. Then frowned at Lexie as if it was all her fault that Mom had scared her half to death only three days earlier.

"Exactly," she said.

"Yep, tough to move on," Stanley said. He punctuated this bit of wisdom with a slurp of coffee. "But, you know, life is like living off your savings account. Each day you take another withdrawal, and pretty soon there's nothing left. You gotta spend those days wisely, make the most of them, you know?"

Mom nodded thoughtfully. "That's an interesting point."

"I never thought of it that way," said Truman. "That was really profound."

Lexie said nothing. She was too surprised, both by Stanley's advice and her mother's reaction to it.

Stanley merely shrugged. "It's something my wife once told me."

"I wish I could have met her," Lexie said.

"You'd have liked her. You remind me of her, always happy and positive. We need more of that in this world. Kind of balances out all the grumps," Stanley concluded with another wink.

"Yes, we do," agreed Truman, and the way he looked at Lexie promised a very happy New Year.

Back home that evening, Stanley turned on the lights on his Christmas tree. He put on a CD of Christmas songs, settled in his recliner with Bonnie and let the music wash over him. It had been a good day.

And to top it off, Carol paid him a visit later that night, perching on the end of the bed. She was dressed in a glowing white gown, and she looked like an angel, and his heart gave a squeeze at the sight of her.

"I thought you were mad at me, babe," he said.

She smiled at him, showing off her dimples. "You know I could never stay mad at you, Manly Stanley." She floated a little closer, and he caught a whiff of peppermint. "It looks like you had a nice day today."

"I did," he admitted and reached out to pet Bonnie, who was sleeping through the entire conversation.

"I'm glad to see you spending your life so wisely, darling."

"I'm trying," he said. Not defensively. He was, indeed, trying, and it felt good.

"It's going to be a wonderful year for you," she predicted. "Merry Christmas, Stanley, and have a happy life."

"That sounds like good-bye," he said and felt panic stirring in him.

"I can't stay here forever. You know that."

"Just a little longer," he begged.

"You don't need me now. You're going to be fine on your own. I'll see you much later. I love you."

Then she was gone, just like that. But, thinking of her last words to him, he decided it was okay. It was time to let her go, time to move on.

Stanley settled his head back against his pillow and closed his eyes.

The next morning he woke up to see a thick, white carpet of snow on the lawn. Plenty for making a snowman.

"Come on, girl," he said to Bonnie. "Let's get going. We've got a life to live."

And like Tiny Tim would have said, *God Bless Us, Everyone.*

One Year Later

THE TOWN OF FAIRWOOD RECEIVED A LIGHT DUST-ing of snow on the first Saturday in December. It was enough to paint the trees white and provide a lovely back-drop as wedding guests drove up to the little church, but not so much that people would be afraid to drive. Even Shan-non, who was one of Lexie's bridesmaids, had no trouble getting there.

The sanctuary was done up with poinsettias and greens and red and white candles and smelled like pine. The pews were filled with friends of the bride and groom from both Fairwood and California.

Lexie stood at the back of the church, wearing a faux fur–trimmed wedding gown. She also wore a pink–pearl necklace that had once belonged to Carol Mann. In one hand she held her bouquet, made up of red and white roses.

The other hand rested on Stanley's arm. Out of the corner of her eye, she could see him running a nervous finger under the collar of his tux shirt.

When she'd asked him to walk her down the aisle he'd protested. There had to be someone else, someone more qualified.

There was, but as far as Lexie was concerned Stanley was the man she wanted for the job. Neighbor, friend, confidant, still sometimes cranky, he had come to mean the world to her.

She watched as her son, the ring bearer, followed Truman's daughters down the aisle. He was trying very hard not to step on the red and white-silk rose petals the girls had scattered, tiptoeing or leaping over them as he went and drawing some chuckles from the onlookers.

She could see her mother sitting in the front with her aunt and uncle. Mom still hadn't moved up from California, but she'd visited during the summer and had accompanied Lexie and Truman and the kids on their trip to Icicle Falls to meet Muriel Sterling and check out the Sweet Dreams Chocolate Company. She was back for the wedding and would be watching over the children while Lexie and Truman honeymooned in Hawaii, then staying clear through Christmas.

Up at the altar, Truman stood looking at Lexie with all the adoration a woman could ever want. Her heart squeezed in response.

Funny how once upon a wish Lexie had been so determined to have a fancy destination wedding. It turned out she didn't need it after all. She'd reached her destination when she moved to Fairwood, and there was no better place to start her new life with her wonderful man.

She smiled at Stanley, and he smiled back and patted her hand as if to reassure her.

She didn't need reassuring. She knew that she'd made the right decision. Her grandma would have approved.

The wedding consultant signaled that it was time for the bride to begin her walk down the aisle.

"You ready to do this?" Stanley asked her.

"Oh, yes," she said.

Stanley sat at the reception table with Lexie's mother and her aunt and uncle.

"They make a charming couple, don't they, Meredith?" Lexie's aunt said to Lexie's mom.

"Yes, they do," said Meredith. "I'm glad she finally found someone." She turned to Stanley. "It was sweet of you to walk her down the aisle."

He felt embarrassed with Lexie's uncle right there at the same table. "Probably should have been her uncle," Stanley said.

"Fred wasn't offended. We all know how much you've done for her and how much you mean to her."

"You've been a gift," said her mom.

Now that she'd gained back some weight and the color had returned to her face, Meredith Bell wasn't a bad-looking woman. Stanley knew Lexie had hopes that something would happen between the two of them, but it wasn't going to. Carol had been the only woman for him.

That didn't mean he couldn't make room in his life for friends, though.

332 A LITTLE CHRISTMAS SPIRIT

And an adopted daughter and grandchild or two. Or three.

"She means a lot to me, too," he said.

Okay, getting too mushy here. He dug into his salmon.

It was hard not to feel mushy when it came time for toasts, but he kept his simple and to the point. Actually, he was amazed he even remembered the few words he wanted to say with so many people looking at him.

He cleared his throat. "To Lexie, the daughter I never knew I wanted, and to Truman, the only man who deserves her."

He knew he got it right when he saw Lexie dabbing the corner of her eye with her napkin.

Much later that night he came back home and settled in his recliner with Bonnie and a bowl of peppermint ice cream to listen to Christmas music and read.

We wish you a Merry Christmas, sang a choir.

No need to wish it. He fully intended to have one.

★ ★ ★ ★ ★

Acknowledgments

I am indebted to many people for this book. First, a hearty thank-you to kindergarten teacher Patty Duncan, who shared with me some of the fun things she does for her children. Patty, I'd love to be a child again and be able to attend your class! Thank you to my wonderful editor, April Osborn, and my fabulous agent, Paige Wheeler. You ladies are the best! And, as always, a heartfelt thank-you to the team at Harlequin, who never cease to work hard on behalf of myself and the other authors lucky enough to have you in their corner. May Santa bring you lots of chocolate and cookies, and may the Grinch steal all the calories from them.

Discussion Questions

1. If you lived next door to Stanley Mann, would you bother befriending him?

2. How would you describe Stanley's marriage?

3. Was Carol's ghost always right in the advice she gave Stanley?

4. Have you lost a loved one? If so, how did you cope with the loss?

5. Did your parents take you to see Santa when you were a child? How and when did you learn that Santa isn't real?

6. Do you believe in ghosts? Would you be thrilled or terrified if you saw the ghost of someone you lost?